Dangerously Damaged

The Shadowed Souls Series Book Three

Abigail Cole

You can't spell Mental Health without Men.

Contents

Avery

Broken. I'm completely, utterly broken.

Slamming my palm onto the release button, I spill into the study and drop onto the rug where I watched my twin fight tooth and nail to save me. My tears pour onto the floor, my chest tearing open as I scream and rub the rough carpet with my fingertips. Blood rushing through my ears deafen me from the sounds scratching my throat raw as my anguish consumes me. She'd been right there while I watched through a screen, trapped beneath Dax's arms. Half frozen in fear and half bucking like a bull to get to her. If I'd been stronger, if I'd struggled harder – it could have been me in the trunk of a car right now instead.

A gentle hand curls around my shoulder, jolting me from my pain long enough for fury to force its way in. I glare into Dax's striking blue eyes, my nostrils flared, and jaw clenched as the tears continue to leak from my eyes. There'll be no stopping them and I don't want to. As he retracts his hand , through the sea swimming in my gaze I notice the claw marks I've left on his arm, blood seeps from the deep grooves and a perfect indent of my teeth in his flesh. *Good.*

A whirring sound outside distracts me, my heart jolting as I remember the others. I raise my hand as a beam of light passes by the window, temporarily blinding me and leaving spots in my vision as I dart for the door. My feet barely lift in time for me to make it down the staircase, only my tight grip on the bannister keeping me upright until I land on the bottom floor.

Dax is right behind me as we race across the living room and enter the kitchen to find Huxley slumped by the back door. His eyelids crack slightly before his head lolls to the side again, just like I'd seen him do on the camera feed upstairs. Ignoring the grip in my chest, I rush past him with the knowledge he can wait for assistance. Rounding the outside porch, not even seeing Axel's still body through a lens could have prepared for the real deal.

The moon's glow adds to his ghostly pale complexion, the line of blood trailing from his mouth glistening. Garrett is pushing all his weight onto the blood-soaked t-shirt at his lover's mid-section, his usual easy smile a distant memory. The whirring grows louder, filling the landscape with its urgency as the spotlight finds us on the porch. The air ambulance I called from the panic room begins its descent, my hair whipping across my face as I slide to my knees beside Axel. Pushing two fingers against his neck, I search for Axel's pulse frantically before finding its worryingly light flutter against his pasty skin.

Two paramedics jump from the helicopter before it's even touched the sand, racing over to us with a stretcher carried between them. Their heavy footfalls on the wooden deck has me scooting back, giving the professionals room to work. A woman of my height with a brown ponytail orders Garrett not to move while her partner checks Axel's airway with a torch before pulling an oxygen mask from his backpack. After firing a round of medical history questions at a barely responsive Garrett, the pair begin to prep Axel for moving. Pushing myself to my feet, I shift back on shaky knees and hide my sobs behind my hand.

My back collides with a solid warm body, Dax's arms wind around me for comfort. But I don't want it, not from him. None of this needed to happen if I had just offered myself up, no one needed to be kidnapped or hurt. And although the tiny rational part of my brain is shouting at me this isn't Dax's fault; I shove out of his embrace anyway. Unfortunately for him, he's here and I will self-combust if I turn my hatred on myself where it squarely belongs.

Garrett keeps his arms straight, despite their trembling as the paramedics shift Axel's limp body onto the stretcher. A groan escapes him with the movement which fills me with more hope than it should, his arm hanging uselessly over the edge as the stretcher is lifted into the air. Garrett releases his hold as Axel is carried away, his arms falling to his side. From this angle, I notice the dried flow of tears from his eyes to his stubbed jaw, the longing in his gaze breaking the last of my resilience. I'm desperate to run into his hold, kiss away his pain but it's not my place. I've caused this.

Shifting over to him, I gently push a hand against his bare back and force him forward a step. His body flinches and his hazel eyes blink several times once they've landed on me, as if he didn't realise the world still existed except for the man being carried to down the porch steps to his uncertain fate. "Go. We'll meet you there," I urge, pushing him another step forward. Garrett quickly assesses me, glancing up and down my body and nodding to Dax over my shoulder before lunging forward to catch up.

"I'm sorry, only family members can come with us." The woman's voice travels to me as the pair continue walking, clearly in a rush to get Axel the help he needs. Garrett keeps pace with them right up to the helicopter door, aiding them to lift the stretcher safely inside. The woman pulls herself up and shakes her head down at Garrett, readying to slide the door shut in his face as the propellers start to speed up once more.

"He's my boyfriend!" Garrett's shout is loud enough for us to hear over the growing noise, his hands fisted tightly by his sides. My eyebrows raise at the declaration at the same time my heart aches for him. After a shared glance with her partner, the paramedic nods and leans out to hoist Garrett up by the hand seconds before the helicopter takes off. The door is slammed shut and we stand wordlessly, silently praying for Axel as the helicopter lifts into the air.

Quiet settles upon us, only the gentle lapping of the sea against the shore sounding in the distance. If I don't look down at the blood stain on my left, I can almost imagine this is an ordinary night, just Dax and I gazing into the horizon in complete peace with one another. Except the emptiness in the pit of my soul is expanding, swallowing every trace of happiness I've ever felt, and the man beside me is partly responsible. My limbs are numb, my heart begrudgingly beating as I try to think of what to do now. A groan sounds from inside, jerking me from my misery.

"Shit, Huxley!" I push past Dax and re-enter the kitchen, gripping Huxley's face in my hands. His face is covered in red marks that are quickly bruising, his nose at a crooked angle and lip busted. Together, Dax and I gently lay him onto the lino flooring so Dax can check him over for serious injuries while I talk to him gently. His eyelids open slowly, the chocolate brown depths focusing on me as a small smile pulls at his lips.

"Y...you're safe," he croaks. Resting my forehead against his, I can't share his joy. If Nixon hadn't reclaimed me as his daughter, if I didn't even exist, everyone would have been safe. But their happiness has been shattered, their lives put at risk purely for knowing me. Dax confirms Huxley is only a little banged up so at least one part of me can breathe a little easier. Together, we lift his heavy weight to place him onto the sofa and I stroke his dirty blonde locks from his face.

"We need to move." Dax states while I focus on Huxley's hair and nod, not interested in conversing with him but understanding we need a plan. "I'll do Garrett and Axel's room, you do Huxley's. Grab what you can, meet back here in 10 minutes. Leave all phones behind." It's on the tip of my tongue to ask about Wyatt's room but the question immediately dies. I purposely haven't thought about Wyatt yet, needing to make sure everyone is safe before I allow the rage for his actions to take over. He will pay in turn though, for every drop of blood spilt and ounce of suffering he's caused. I'll make sure of that myself.

Telling him I'll be right back; I kiss Huxley on the forehead and race upstairs to his room first. Grabbing his black duffle bag from beneath his bed, I haphazardly stuff clothes from the drawers inside before moving into the bathroom. Throwing his toothbrush and insane amount of hair products inside, I zip the bag and leave it in the hallway as I dash up the next staircase to mine and Meg's room.

Pushing the door open and stepping inside, dread hits me like a freight train as I see the set of folded pyjamas on the pillow, patiently waiting for the owner that won't be returning tonight. My Meg, my twin. Where are they taking her? What are they going to do? Every worst-case scenario possible plays behind my eyes, the sounds of her screams filling my ears. I drop to my knees, violent shakes grip my body and refuse to let go. Allowing myself ten seconds to wallow, I begin counting down between whimpers. *Ten, nine*...be strong for her, she knows you won't rest until she's safe...*three, two, one.* On a long exhale, I open my eyes and grind my teeth with determination. I can't save her from here, I need to get up and get fucking moving.

In a similar fashion to Huxley's room, I grab my backpack and start shoving clothes in from the wardrobe, trying to select monotone items and avoiding designer labels at all costs. We don't need any extra attention whilst on the run from the mob. *Seriously what has my life come to?* My brain suddenly switches into survival mode, grabbing all the cash I can find from various handbags, jacket pockets and Meg's purse. Leaving our make-up and shoe collection behind, I grab Meg's hairbrush from the nightstand, a hand full of hair ties and empty the bathroom cupboard before moving to leave. One last glance back at the bed where she should be, I close the door and jog back to the second floor.

The door at the end of the hallway is ajar, darkness lying within. My curiosity peeks, pushing me forward as Dax crashes about in Garrett's room. Slowly, I push the door open to reveal Wyatt's room. I don't know what I expected to find, it's not like he'd have left a double-sided letter explaining himself, but I feel like there should be. He should have found a scrap of decency in his dead soul to explain his actions. Sibling rivalry is one thing, helping to kidnap and leaving your friend for dead it something else entirely. If I could understand- *no, Avery don't do that. Don't try to find the good in someone who is clearly too far gone. He made his choice and he will love to regret it.*

Reaching around the doorframe, I flick the light switch and glance around the illuminated room. A pile of splintered wood and sharp shards of glass sit in a heap in the corner of the room, his duvet crumpled like he's tossed and turned every night since arriving. Through the open bathroom door, I can see the empty frame where the mirror should be and several cracked tiles lining the wall. A buzzing sound makes me jump, the screen of Wyatt's cell phone briefly brightening on the chest of drawers. Trepidation licks my spine as I shuffle forward, expecting to stumble into a trip line and for a huge net to fall onto me. A plastic pill box sits beside his phone, which I lift to inspect. Two rounded, pink pills sit inside each of the sections, making me frown as I rattle them side to side. Judging from the letters on top, if Wyatt was sticking to them, he's missed yesterday and today's lot of whatever they are. His phone lights again with the same message which I snatch up to read several times in confusion.

Ray: *'Heard you're on your way back. Proud of you, son.'*

"Who's Ray?" Dax's voice breathes into my ear, making me jump and shriek in fright. The phone and pill box fall to the floor as I grab my chest, my heart hammering hard enough to go into cardiac arrest with the amount of stress it's had tonight. Dax apologises with his eyes, bending down the retrieve the items and giving the pills the same suspicious look.

"Ray Perelli, the mob boss has been hunting me." I manage to say eventually, focusing on my breathing. "I guess we know how they found us." The words sink in after I say them out loud, the extent of Wyatt's involvement becoming clear. Meg didn't sacrifice herself in my place, she was the intended target. They must have known about her since Wyatt arrived here and found out the truth himself. So much for this being a 'safe' house, the enemy was down the hall all along.

Fleeing the room, I grab the bags I'd dumped and run downstairs to find Huxley passed out again. Pulling the keys to the Nissan from the hidden drawer under the coffee table, I unlock Huxley's car with the key fob pointing out the window. The headlights flash as Dax reaches the bottom step, striding straight through the broken front door and pushing his bags into the trunk. After following and stuffing mine in, we silently return to drag Huxley's dead weight from the house and into the back seat.

Crawling over his body, Huxley mumbles and wiggles as I use the middle strap to secure him in place. Starting to climb back, his arm rounds my waist and crushes me into his body. A tiny frown pulls at my lips as he nuzzles my neck, my hair creating a fan of gold around us. Reaching to cup Huxley's bruised cheek in my hand, my eyebrows pull together as I inspect to curve to his nose that shouldn't be there.

"We're going to get you fixed up, good as new." My voice makes him smile widely, almost deliriously and I move back and shut him safely inside. The engine roars to life, the headlights on full beam as I move to the passenger seat. Slamming my door shut, my eyes trick me into seeing monsters lurking in the shadows, reaching out towards my window as we begin to creep through the thick forest on the barely visible dirt track. Goosebumps line my skin and I lock my door just in case, forcing myself to stare at the glove box instead until we're on the main road. The wheels hit the tarmac and a pent-up breath leaves me, although my elation at escaping the forest doesn't last long. We have no idea where Meg has been taken but I vow to find her, rescue her, and then kill for her.

Meg

My body lurches forward as I'm jolted awake, my stomach rolling with nausea. I shift onto my side, retching loudly, a burn igniting a path from my chest to throat, but nothing comes out. My head is pounding worse than any hangover I've ever suffered from, the constant bouncing beneath me not helping one bit. Opening my eyes a little, I hunt for a light to tell me where I am or how I got here. After blinking several times and reaching out to feel the space around me, I've come to the conclusion I'm in the trunk of a car. Or in more basic terms, a dark, confined metal box with no way out. Shit.

Full panic mode hits on cue, heat radiating through my thick sweatshirt like a furnace. I smash my fist upwards and scream with all my might, kicking my legs out as far as I can. My hair is plastered to my face, tremors are raking through my spine. I'm punished for every movement I make, my head seizing tightly and tears streaming from my eyes. The pain is unbearable but still doesn't come close to the turmoil I'm feeling within. Something is so very wrong.

I can't breathe, the air is thinning and the walls creeping closer to me. I'm going to suffocate on my own fear before I figure out where I am, or if there's a chance of escaping. Avery's voice rings through my mind, the soothing words she would say if she were here repeating like a mantra, I cling onto with all my might. "Do nothing but focus on steadying your heartbeat. The breathing will come naturally on its own."

Flattening onto my back, ignoring the frequent bumps beneath me, I close my eyes and press my hand flat over my heart. My heart is hammering as it tries to break free from my chest, but its strong and that's what I hold onto. I'm a survivor and I will find a way out of here, but first I need to relax. Keep my head. That's something I can control right now. The slowing tha-thump beneath my palm resumes its usual pace, my breathing evened out.

In a calmer state of mind, I shift my focus on finding something I can use. The floor beneath my body is a rough type of carpet, but itchier like a worn doormat. I skirt the edges of the material with my fingernails, digging them into the edges and trying to pry them up. Relying on my flexibility from some of the horrendous stretch-downs our lacrosse coach made us do after each big match, I manage to rotate myself ninety degrees until I'm aching and sweating once again. Shuffling out of my sweatshirt, I continue searching and gasp as a corner comes free in my hand.

Pushing myself up onto my elbows, I grip the carpet and yank it back, blindly feeling beneath for anything of use. My hand closes around a cold, metallic can, the thin tube on the side telling me its expanding foam for emergency puncture repairs. I can think of at least two ways to use this, so I push the carpet back into place and shove the can through the empty sleeve of my sweater, making sure only the tube is protruding from the opening.

On a loud screech, I'm thrown sideways and the blare of car horns sound all around me. Realising we've come to a stop, I start screaming and kicking, trying to catch anyone's attention. "Let me out of here!" I yell time and again, the sides of my fists aching from repeatedly throwing them against the lid of the trunk. My throat is raw like sandpaper, not enough saliva in my mouth to swallow, but still I continue. The headache that had dulled slightly comes back with a vengeance, a vice-like grip crushing my skull on the inside.

"Where'd you get your license, dickwad?! You nearly ran me off the ledge!" Wyatt's voice catches my attention, ceasing my movements. *That motherfucker!* I remember now, the way he fought and goaded me, pinned me down just before everything went black. I'd like to see him beat me in a fair fight, although it seems like Wyatt prefers cowardly ways out, rather than get his ass handed to him by a girl.

"I need to take a piss," a rough voice replies, slamming what I imagine is a meaty fist onto the trunk and making me flinch. "And she's awake, which makes her your problem now." If I ever saw Wyatt's face again, it would be too soon. However, I know I will be able to overpower and escape him since he felt the need to drug me, so I brace myself for a fight at the sound of the trunk's lock being released. The lid lifts quickly, the orange glow of a streetlamp burning my retinas. Three shadows loom over me, my hand tightening around the concealed can in my sweater.

"Where's the other one?" Wyatt says slowly, his voice laced with dread. My eyes adjust enough to tell he's standing in the middle, the huge frames either side of him large enough to stunt double for Dwayne Johnson.

"What do you mean? You gave us this one, we thought you had the blonde." My mind reels with their words. Does this mean Avery is safe? Wyatt's bunched shoulders sag on a horrified gasp, cursing under his breath.

"You expected me to capture *both* of them?! What the fuck were you three doing if not trying to find Avery?"

"Your boys kept us busy enough, that bald one was a savage." The brute on Wyatt's left running a hand over his head and signing dramatically, his shaded eyes fixed on me. "The boss isn't going to be happy about this, he wants both. You'd better go back and fetch the other." Wyatt flies into a rage, his fists clenched and square jaw tight as the three of them argue about who should drive back to the safe house. I bite my lip, praying

Avery has got as far away from California possible in the last few hours. judging by the fact it's still night and Wyatt's still in the cargo trousers he fought me in. Wyatt begins to walk away, the two thugs turning to suggest a game of rock, paper, scissors to decide for them and I see my opportunity.

Boosting myself up on weak legs, an assault of pins and needles spiking through me, I leap from the trunk and hit the ground on my knees heavily. Clutching my limp sweater in my fist, I force myself up and start to run without being able to properly see what's in front of me. My blurred vision clears up enough to notice the ground disappearing up ahead, my sneakers skidding to a halt before I tip over the edge of a steep cliff. Double shit.

My stomach rolls and plummets as if I were already falling, a smoker's choked laugh sounds further along the ridge. The biggest of the thugs is smirking at me, his fat dick hanging limply through his fly as he continues to pee whilst holding my eyesight. The potent smell of his urine suddenly fills my nostrils, making me gag. *Jesus fuck, what does that guy eat?!* Scuffling behind has me whirling around, Brutie and Brutelina grinning because they have me cornered. I glance over my shoulder, the drop not seeming as awful as the alternative, but I'm not done fighting yet.

Feeling for the cap through the material in my hand, I wait for the pair to take one more menacing step closer before lifting the lifeless sleeve and unleashing streams of white foam directly into their eyes. My heel almost slips on the rocky ledge as they make a grab for me, quickly darting to the side to avoid being thrown backwards by their sightless staggers. Spraying all the while, they fall to the ground like two sacks of shit and thrash around bellowing. A psychotic smile graces my lips, as I use the side of my sneaker to kick small stones and dust over them. The nozzle spurts a few last pathetic puffs of foam, the contents emptying faster than I've have liked.

Wyatt steps towards me cockily on the edge of my vision, his shoulders peeled back and long strides confident. Without looking his way, I spin the sleeve around me like a lasso and release an unexpected laugh as it connects with his head and knocks him back onto his ass. Not giving him time to recover, I run towards the beaming headlights of his sedan. The engine is still humming, my escape in reaching distance. Curling my fingers around the door handle, Wyatt collides with my side and slams me onto the rocky ground. All the air whooshes out of my lungs, crippling pain in my diaphragm keeping me immobile on the ground, even after Wyatt has stood up.

"She's a wild one. Maybe you can't handle her," Stinky Peete walks over with his fly still undone. I gasp for air and flinch involuntarily beneath them, completely helpless on a deserted road with four raving lunatics. Triple Shit.

"Nah, I've changed my mind. She's all mine." Wyatt bends down, lifting me easily against his chest and dumping me into the passenger seat. I jerk back into action, lunging for the keys in the ignition with the intent to throw them over the cliff's edge, but my movements are too sluggish. Wyatt catches me, climbing into the small space to pin me into the seat with an iron-tight grip on my upper arms. Using his body to hold me in place, he reaches over into the back seat to retrieve something while my face is smushed against his solid chest.

Returning his hand to my left shoulder and sitting back to straddle me once again, he strokes a path downwards, tickling my inner arm in a move that disturbs me more that if he'd tried to sever it. A glint of metal in the streetlight flashes as his hand closes around my wrist, swiftly locking a handcuff into place. Wyatt then leans to close the other cuff around the steering wheel. I struggle and buck beneath him, the metal cutting into my flesh as I fight to slip my hand through the gap.

Hopping up and slamming the car door shut, Wyatt rounds to the driver's side and commands for the others to head back for Avery before getting in. The three of them are standing shoulder to shoulder in front of the car, two sets of puffy eyes glaring at me as they all oddly nod in compliance. Apparently, Wyatt's official order actually means something to the group. Hanging my head in defeat, I hope to hell Avery is running as far away as she can right now.

Yanking on the cuff's chain to test its strength, Wyatt bends over to grin right in my face, his shadowed eyes regard me coldly. "All mine," he whispers, looking to my lips and hovering close as if he might kiss me. I remain completely still, not playing in his game. Chuckling, he begins to pull back and I can't resist anymore. Rearing my head back, I pull back as much salvia as I can muster onto my tongue and spit right into his smug face. A high-pitched cackle erupts from my lips, his revolted features glistening. Shouting in disgust, he lifts the hem of his t-shirt to wipe his face roughly. My eyes ashamedly fall to the hard outlines of his abs long enough not to notice his oncoming elbow seconds before the lights go out.

Avery

The sun is cresting over a mountain far in the distance as we roll into town, birds swirling overhead in hunt for their breakfast. The orange glow reflects on the hood of the similar coloured Nissan, my heavy eyelids open wide as anticipation sinks in. I glance down every alleyway along the long stretch of road, paranoid one of those gorilla goons will be lurking in wait for another chance to grab me. Each shop is dark inside, closed signs hanging in the doorways and not a single person to be seen.

"There," I lunge forward and point out a pale-yellow building with a doctor's surgery logo printed in the window. Dax turns into the alleyway alongside the building, parking around the back as I turn to check on Huxley. He's slept the entire journey with what I hope is from sleep deprivation and not a concussion, although he did rouse every time I gave him a rough shake. A part of me wanted to climb back there and curl up on his chest like a cat but I have too much on my mind to rest. I watched a mafia thug stuff my sister into the trunk of a car and drive off through the camera feed, I refuse to take comfort from anyone while she's trapped and alone.

We remain in the car for a long time, the tension between myself and Dax thick enough to choke on. We've barely said a word to each other unless it's been completely necessary. Occasionally, he turns towards me and opens his mouth as if needing to say something, but decides against it, slumping back in his seat and folding his arms with a huff. Although I have a feeling what he wants to say, and I don't want to hear it. A million apologies wouldn't be enough to forgive him and he knows it. The orange and pink sky gives way to a blue one with not a cloud in sight as more cars begin to drive past at the opposite end of the alley.

A man in a pristine lab coat appears, shuffling towards us with a doughnut stuffed into his mouth, holding a steaming travel mug and checking his watch every ten seconds. His thinning white hair gives way to a bald patch on top and thin glasses sit on the bridge of his nose. He's on the plump side, his coat buttons straining around his middle and short legs moving as fast as they can. Not noticing the fancy car facing him, he fumbles with his keys before finding the right one and pushing it into the rear door lock.

Dax throws his door open and flies from his seat so quickly, even I flinch as he rounds the car. Stepping a foot inside the surgery, the doctor wheels around as Dax calls out to him, making him spill his coffee onto his jacket and curse in fright. Sensing this situation will need a female touch, I step from the vehicle and approach the pair.

"Excuse me, we are so sorry to bombard you like this," I put on my sweetest voice and hold my hands up as I advance. "My friend was attacked last night and we're not from around here, we didn't know where else to take him." I point over to the back seat of the Nissan, Huxley sits upright and holds his head on cue. After another glance at his silver watch he nods and gestures for us to come inside quickly.

"Sit him down here," he asks as we help Huxley inside. He's almost walking on his own, but Dax and I have one of his arms around each of our shoulders as we edge him towards the medical bed. Electric blue leather is visible beneath a sheet of paper that crinkles when Huxley drops onto it, his shoulders slumped and hair falling over his half-mast eyes. After washing his hands and donning a pair of latex gloves, the doctor returns with a kind smile.

"I've got ten minutes before the surgery opens." He tells us while inspecting Huxley's face, although his tone isn't pushy. "My assistant is on holiday, so I have to man the phones and attend to patients. Bit of a one-man show at the moment," he muses in a light tone before he grips Huxley's nose and twists it back into place with surprising force. Huxley roars and hisses, torn between holding the newly set break and keeping his hands well away. After a few moments, he quietens down but his posture is still tense, anticipating another attack any moment. I shift forward to hold his hand, rubbing circles across the back with my thumb and earning myself a lopsided smile.

"That seems like the most I can do," the doctor says after inspecting all around Huxley's head. Pulling his gloves off and tossing them into the trash can in the corner, he retrieves a packet of painkillers and places them into Huxley's free hand. "If any other issues arise, feel free to pop back or try the emergency room." My ears prick up, knowing that's exactly where we should be heading next, but Dax beats me too it.

"Out of interest, where would the closest hospital be?" He asks coyly from the opposite side of the room. He's pulled his Afro back and fixed it with a hair tie., a blonde cloud hanging to the back of his head. He doesn't wear his hair back often; his square jaw is more prominent now. His icy blue gaze is firmly set on the doctor, clearly avoiding mine as I look at him properly for the first time all night. Leaning in the doorway with his arms crossed, Dax's tanned biceps push against his firm chest. Those arms that held me so gently in the throes of passion, cradled me safely as I gave him more of myself than I intended, and held me down while I fought and screamed to save Meg.

Dragging my eyes away, I focus on easing Huxley from the table as the doctor gives Dax directions to the hospital. It's another two-hour drive from here, my stomach growls on cue as I think of getting back into the car for that long. Huxley eases himself from the table and links his fingers with mine, holding my hand tightly. As much as I want to, I can't bring myself to pull away, I thank the doctor for his time and exit through the back door.

I want to feel isolated; I want to be alone and suffer the same way I can feel in my being that Meg is. But at the same time, I know the Shadowed Souls won't let me do that. They will sense my pain, take it upon themselves to console me no matter how much I push them away like the chivalrous bastards they are. And until I'm fully fed and have managed to get some sleep, I don't have the energy to resist them.

Dax moves around us to pop the trunk, shifting through Huxley's bag to grab him a clean set of clothes. He accepts them without a word, remaining quiet like he's been since waking and starts to strip. Discarding his bloodied t-shirt on top of the Nissan, Huxley bends to pull down his jeans and shorts without a care in the world. I quickly spin to step in the way of a gaping woman and her dachshund, frozen to the spot by the sight of Huxley's body at the end of the alleyway. Giving her a scowl, she visibly shakes herself and moves along, leaving me to peek over my shoulder. Huxley's not as toned as when I'd first met him due to not eating properly, but for some reason his ass is still a perfectly edible peach. I must be damn hungry because my mouth starts to water and I swallow thickly, dragging my eyes away as he steps into some tracksuit pants.

A black hoodie in placed into my hands, Dax's arm retracting before I can shove it back at him. Pulling the material over my head, I inhale his uniquely spicy scent and growl as my libido suddenly rouses from her sleep. *Traitor.* Forcefully shoving my head through the hole, I fix my hair and push the sleeves up to my elbows roughly. "I have my own hoodies, you know," I grumble and start to walk away.

The guys fall in behind me in silence, leaving the car hidden and strolling from the alley as casually as we can. Heads turn our way, the locals immediately noticing us as outsiders when we pass by, strolling for a café on the corner. My eyes flick between faces and vehicles, cataloguing everyone suspiciously to check we aren't being followed. A dark sedan appears further along the road, heading this way. I dive behind Dax, using his body to shield me from view as I peek through the gap in his arm. The vehicle passes without slowing, my heart is lodged in my throat and my mind is running away with panicked thoughts. Dax moves suddenly, leaving me exposed and walking into a small clothing store without glancing back.

Continuing without him, I link my arm through Huxley's and attempt to stroll down the sidewalk like an ordinary couple in search of breakfast. Well, ordinary if Huxley's job were to act as a human punching bag and I was a schizophrenic, scared of my own shadow but ready to squeeze the life out of my former stepbrother. *How did my life become this fucked?* The scent of warm pancakes and sweet honey sail to me on the breeze, dragging me onwards by my senses.

Reaching for the café's glass door, I luckily see Dax's reflection walk up behind me or I would have screamed as his hand slips beneath my hair. I want to wriggle away from the light brush of his fingers on my nape and run a thousand miles in the other direction, but the dangerous curiosity in me wants to see where he's going with this. He twists the golden strands in his hand, giving his full attention into coiling them onto the back of my head before placing a black cap over the top. The edge hangs low over my eyes, disguising me even from myself. His arm reaches over my shoulder to grip the handle for me, the familiar warmth causing my body to automatically lean into his before I give myself a mental slap. I grunt in thanks and walk into the sweet-smelling shop before I do something stupid like forgive him.

Selecting a booth hiding in the back corner, far away from the windows, I slump down and order three coffees from a passing waitress. Pressing the heels of my palms into my eyes,

I can't hold in a groan. My head is swimming with panic and fleeting thoughts, floating away before I can fully grasp what it was. I don't know where to start searching for Meg, and I don't have my cell to try to contact Nixon, even if I thought he might answer. The only thing I can do at the moment is sort myself out and get to the hospital to check on Axel. I pray Axel pulls through; nothing will be the same without his amber eyes and kind-hearted nature in the world.

The sound of a throat being cleared has me lifting my head to see a waitress placing our coffees down and flicking open a notepad to take our order. Her tightly curled blonde hair bobs with each movement of her head, her eyes torn between the two guys opposite me. Ignoring the fact I'm so tired, I feel physically sick, I pluck the menu from its wooden stand and point at the first item on the menu – 'The Big Boy Breakfast'. Dax and Huxley order the same without paying her much attention, although it doesn't stop the fluttering of eyelashes and cleavage squeeze she aims in their direction before slinking off.

No words are exchanged between the three of us, nothing needing to be said. We've all got someone we care deeply about with their life on the line, a part of our family in need and equally – we are all completely helpless. Huxley's foot hooks mine beneath the table, secretively soothing me as I glance into his chocolate eyes. I was worried about the affects this latest attack would have on him, considering he was still pulling through the previous one but by the look he's giving me, I can see he's going to be okay. The resolve in his expression, the determination in his gaze are from the man I knew before and lord knows, the one I need right now.

Our breakfasts arrive, huge plates heaped with everything fried and a side plate stacked with toast. Garrett would be in heaven; I think to myself and suddenly lose my appetite as tears begin to swim in my eyes. Pulling the cap lower so all I can see is my plate, I start to force food into my mouth and swallow it past the lump stuck in my throat. *Come on Avery, you need your strength. You need to buck the fuck up and save your family.*

Surprisingly, I manage to eat well over half and by the time I push my cap back up, Huxley has also made a sizeable dent in his. I offer him a genuine smirk, a wordless argument passing between us to push through together so we can be in best form for the others. Dax is slumped back against the aged red leather, inspecting his nails over his empty plate. I don't want to notice the stress lines beneath his eyes or the tic in his tensed jaw, telling myself he doesn't deserve to feel the same strain as us. Huxley got the shit beaten out of him for fuck's sake, and even though I was trapped by his muscles, I fought to help. My knight in shining armour has suddenly tarnished in my mind's eye.

Ripping the cap from my head and not bothering to fix my hair that is flying in all directions, I throw it down in the centre of table and slide out of the booth, stomping into the single bathroom and locking the door behind me. Leaning over the sink, I glare at my reflection with all the rage I feel for Wyatt, Dax, myself, even Nixon. My blue eyes are blazing, my skin turning red as my fury shows itself on the outside. So much for a calm existence, hiding away from the world and the pain it causes. I stupidly thought I'd already had my share of suffering, but no one can escape the endless spin cycle of shit we're all stuck in, waiting it out until we're rung dry, discarded, faded and wrinkled.

Well it ends now, no more hiding. No more feeling helpless. I've spent years building on my stamina, strength and resilience so no asshole would ever be able to make me feel weak again. I'm Avery fucking Hughes, a daughter, a twin and a survivor. Let them find me, take me to my sister and find out exactly who they've messed with.

Wyatt

My ears are bleeding from Meg's constant singing as she seems to know every single song the damn radio plays. Even after I switched from channel to channel, she's beatboxed, rapped, yodelled, belted Celine Dion, been headbanging and even managed to do the robot despite the limited use from one of her hands. She's not a bad singer, but the fact she is relaxed enough to enjoy herself as if this is a fricking road trip is sending me insane. Why isn't she crying and begging me to free her? I'm literally driving her to her execution, not a weekend at Summerfest. Her feet are even up on the dashboard, having kicked off her shoes and reclined her seat slightly.

"You know if I crashed right now, your knees would go straight through your eye sockets and crush your skull." I say during a brief reprieve of idle chitchat between radio hosts before the next song starts up.

"It's a good thing you're too vain to mess up that pretty face of yours then, isn't it?" she replies with a smile. Glancing past her into the side mirror, I notice an HGV truck thundering down the freeway in the next lane. Spinning the wheel, I swerve the car sideways and slam my foot on the brake harshly. She flies forward before her seatbelt locks her in place, her face inches from her kneecaps and a high-pitched scream leaves her lips. The truck veers into the lane I've vacated, the deafening sound of his horn blasting as the trucker also stops beside us.

Hollering and swearing down at me, I laugh wholeheartedly and give him the middle finger, pushing on the accelerator to leave him far behind. Multiple cars have had to brake suddenly and skid across the lanes, a mounting traffic jam starting to pile up in my rear-view mirror. Flicking on the indicator arrogantly, I causally take the next exit with a delightfully quiet companion. Following the winding ramp, I halt at an intersection and nod to a passing a cop car, the uniformed female in the passenger seat giving me a sly smile.

"Fucking lunatic," Meg mutters under her breath.

"You're the one that thinks I have a pretty face, so what does that make you?" I respond, rendering her peacefully speechless once again. I switch the radio off in case a song she can't resist comes on to boost her resolve and focus on searching for somewhere to rest for the night. I've been driving for almost twenty-four hours straight; the sun is dipping below the horizon in a cloudless lilac sky. The road narrows in preparation to wind through a refreshingly modern city up ahead, the LED signs above bars and restaurants switching on for our arrival.

Buildings stretch towards the sky all around us, the hum of civilisation seeping into me as hordes of people scurry from the revolving doors, eager to escape the stacks of paperwork and unrealistic demands of their bosses. A group of suits sprint over the crossing in front of my stationary vehicle, filtering into a strip club with their briefcases in hand, music pouring out into the street. Even before my life was upended, I never saw myself doing the mundane 9-5. I was a Hughes, only high expectations and a lavish lifestyle waiting in my future. Was. Now I'm stuck on fricking babysitter duty because three pinheads couldn't complete one simple task, expecting me to be the brains and brawn in operation 'Ray's Revenge'.

Driving through the vast city, I look longingly in the rearview mirror as I exit through the other end and continue onto a quieter road. As much as I miss the high life, I can hardly drag a captive into a busy hotel lobby and ask them to store her somewhere dark and soundproof. The streetlamps become few and far between with each passing mile, drawing us into the darkness of no man's land. Flicking my eyes across to the passenger seat, I find Meg curled onto her side sleeping softly.

My first instinct is to swerve sharply to wake her up, but for some reason I refrain. Maybe I'm slightly fascinated at the way she keeps surprising me, her ability to adapt to unusual situations a trait I've never been able to perfect. My hand brushes her outstretched arm which is hanging loosely against the handcuff on the steering wheel, the coolness of her skin has me reaching to switch the heating on. Because if I'm only delivering one of the girls Ray asked for, I should make sure she hasn't caught hypothermia on the journey. Yeah, surely that's the reason.

It's another hour until I find an almost derelict town, a serial killer-worthy motel sitting on the edge. Turning into the gravelled carpark, I switched off the engine and slump back in my seat. The block of concrete before me has been thoughtfully decorated with graffiti, no doubt from the understandably bored kids who live nearby. The same door is repeated fifteen times across each of the two levels, not a single light on behind any of the curtains. I'd think this place was abandoned if it weren't for the open door at the end, a grotesquely skinny woman milling about behind a counter.

Itching to straighten my legs, I step out of my door and stretch my arms high above my head. After bending my back side to side, I slam the door shut and retrieve an emergency bag Rachel had packed in the trunk for me. I'm buzzing with excitement to be on my way back to her, like a lovesick teenager or a boy craving a motherly hug. Shouldering the backpack, I press the button for the trunk to close itself and cross carpark with long strides.

"Hey, what about me?" Megs small shout barely reaches me, her fist bashing on the passenger window. I raise the key fob over my shoulder and lock the vehicle, the headlights flashing twice before going dark. The smile of my face widens as I step into the reception, if this small room with its peeling wallpaper and flickering bulb can be called that and pay for a room in cash. I don't care about the décor, as long as my room is dust and bug free, I'll just be happy for a quiet night to myself catching up on some dearly missed sleep. Staying under the same roof as Avery was hell, every waking and unconscious moment filled with her. Her laughter, her unbreakable spirit.

Unlocking the door, I step into the darkened room to see a shadow hunched in the corner. "Hey mom," I drop my bag on the plastic table and leave her to scratch at the walls. Reaching into the bag's front pocket and grabbing the backup vitamins Rachel packed for me, I glance between them and the figure in the corner before throwing them back into the bag.

It was easy enough to make the association between the small, pink pills and the hallucination of my birth mother since the last few times I took them, she disappeared instantly. And despite popular belief, I'm rational enough to know that wanting the illusion of her around is insane, but I find her presence oddly comforting. Or maybe I'm irrational enough to believe keeping her spirit with me will absolve me from killing her. Who the fuck knows anymore? I'm damned anyway.

Treating myself to a lukewarm shower, cranking the dial to as hot as it will go, I take my time blow drying my hair so it remains pushed back when I run my hand through its silky-smooth length. The double bed in the centre of the retro-wall-papered room is calling to me, but first I need to eat. Dumping the damp towel in a heap on the floor, I dress in fresh clothes and shove a wad of cash into my back pocket before heading out of the door.

There's a man standing by the sedan, Meg is desperately trying to enlist his help by miming through the glass. I stand against a pillar for a short while, watching the display with a smirk. When the game of one-handed charades becomes too pitiful even for me, I stroll across the space and save the hillbilly with the gormless expression on his face.

"Hey man, don't worry about her," I gesture to Meg with my thumb. "She's like my step-sister, sort of. You know what sibling rivalry is like." His glazed eyes slowly pass between us, an overpowering herbal scent radiating from him. *Oh, this is priceless, he's high as shit.*

"Here, take this for looking after her for me." I remove the money from my jeans pocket, pulling a few fifties out of the stack and handing it over easily. His tattered hoodie hangs low over some old-style army pants, the sneakers on his feet more like open toed sandals due to the gaping holes within them. "If you get someone to bring me dinner, anything fried and greasy, I'll double it for both of you. Number seven," I point back to the door, waiting for him to compute.

"Seven," he mumbles, his attention returning to the money in his hand as if he's shellshocked. Not waiting for him to leave, I unlock the car and open Meg's door, slipping inside to straddled her in the reclined seat.

"Are you going to behave or am I going to have to gag you?" I ask, her eyes lighting with the challenge in my tone. I'm sure she's seconds from spitting at me again so I clamp my hand over her mouth, muffling her protests. Using my free hand to twist the small key in the handcuff lock, I quickly grab both of her wrists as she tries to claw as me like I anticipated and pin them over her head.

"One day soon, I'm going to destroy you. You'll hurt more than you've ever known and beg me to take the pain away." Her top lip peels back in a snarl as she says the words, the feral twist to her pale blue eyes awakening a hunger in me to let her bring her dark words to reality.

"Mmmm, talk dirty to me," I mock biting down on my bottom lip, angering her further. She bucks and thrashes beneath me as I laugh, genuine amusement trickling through me until I drag her from the car. Shoving her into the motel room, I close the door with my back and continue to push her into the bathroom. She tries to squirm out of my grip, but I expect every move she throws my way, her wrists trapped in one of my hands and my opposite arm locked around her waist. Raising her arms above her head, I grab the loose cuff and loop it over the shower rail before quickly securing it back in place over her free wrist.

I slam the door shut between us, switching on the boxy TV and turning the volume as loud as it will go to block out most of her screams. Kicking off my sneakers and shedding my jeans, I lounge back against the headboard finally content. This time tomorrow, I'll be back in Chicago with Rachel and a purpose. In the incredibly short time I've spent at Ray's mansion, it's become more of a home to me than the house I grew up in ever was. Because even as a child, some small part of me knew I wasn't enough for my parents. There was always something missing, a void I couldn't fill. But when Rachel looks at me, her whole world is centred in my eyes.

I turn the TV off as a knock sounds at the door and I swear the hobo better not have touched my damn food. Casually swinging the door open, an actual delivery man stands nervously before me, his garishly green polo holding a matching logo to the one on his baseball cap and the pizza boxes in his hands. Despite having arrived on the moped parked next to my car, his eyes are equally as bloodshot, and his fingertips are stained yellow against the pizza boxes in his hands. A shadow to his left draws my attention to the original stoner and I give him a cheery thumbs up as he sways a little. Dishing out enough money for the pair to fund their disgusting habits for a month, I return to my position on the bed to flip open multiple boxes before noticing the shouting beyond the door has stopped.

"What is that? Is it garlic?" Meg asks, the yearning in her voice amusing.

"Oh yeah, a whole garlic flatbread alongside an extra-large pizza." I goad her. She goes silent for a moment, so I take a bite and moan exaggeratingly.

"Is it doughy?" She calls back, a smile pulls at my lips.

"So damn doughy, and cheesy too," I reply, not realising how much I've missed a bit of banter like this lately.

"Are there any dips?" I can't help but laugh, listing all the types of dips I've been supplied with. She must be starving too, the part of my conscience not wanting to take her to Chicago already on her death bed niggling me. Ray needs her for his revenge scheme, so I'd better ensure she makes it.

Opening the door separating us with a slice in my hand, I take in her sagged body, only the restraints holding her upright in a tight vest and leggings. Her eyes immediately land on the pizza, but she doesn't plead like I expected. Like I wanted. Unhurriedly taking a large bite, she licks her lips and swallows thickly. I continue eating, refusing to give her any until she's at my mercy, begging for the scraps I'm willing to give her.

The last bite of pizza goes into my mouth, only the curved crust remaining between my fingertips when she huffs and looks away. She's headstrong, I'll give her that, but stubborn as an ox too. Rolling my eyes, I walk over and hold the dry crust to her lips. Hesitating briefly, she gradually eases her mouth over the crust and bites off half, her lips brushing my fingers. Her eyes roll back and she groans loudly, my dick jerking at the sight. A memory from the Sinergy nightclub drifts to the forefront of my mind, Meg's lithe body pressed between me and the railing, her mouth feasting hungrily on mine.

The second she has swallowed, I shove the rest of the hardened dough into her mouth and stalk out of the room, once again shutting her out of sight. *Note to self – never do that again.* I must really be desperate if such a simple action has twisted me tighter than corkscrew. The pizza boxes across the bed no longer hold any appeal to me, my appetite shifting to something much leaner and brunette. Not to mention forbidden. Refocusing on the plans for tomorrow, I clear the bed and strip before slipping beneath the cover. Step one deliver Meg to Ray. Step two find Rachel. Step three get laid – not particularly in that order. But right now, I fist my dick in my hand and begin to pump furiously, giving my disobedient cock its one and only release for the girl behind the door.

Dax

Avery hasn't uttered a word since slipping back into the passenger seat of Huxley's Nissan, her expression closed off and unreadable. I shift uncomfortably, gripping the steering wheel with sweaty palms and the biggest impulse to poke the bear cub sitting beside me. It's when she's quiet like this I worry the most, needing to know what dark track her thoughts are leading her down. I'm well aware she hates me for my actions last night, but I won't apologise for them. In fact, I would do the exact same all over again, except I would have dragged Meg into the panic room too if I'd known how it was going to play out.

The moment Avery joined The Shadowed Souls, she had my vow to protect her always, but more than that, I needed to shield her. It was a necessity she's wasn't taken by those thugs, that she never felt any form of suffering again. But I've still failed on that front. She's more precious to me than she'll ever realise, her soul is calling to me to put it back together like a jigsaw and cherish until my dying breath. Call me selfish but being hated by Avery is better than not having her around at all. My heart squeezes every time I think of what could have happened, where she might have been taken.

Leaving the small town far behind and flying down the freeway in the fast lane, the wind blows through my open window and bounces my hair around wildly. Huxley's waves are also swaying in all directions in the back seat, in my rear view in the mirror is just his blonde locks creating their own tornado.

The sign up ahead shows we're approaching our turning so I slide over the empty lanes and veer off. Entering a thriving city of high-rise buildings and people in every crevasse, heavy traffic transports me back to civilization. Horns blare when the lead car fails to shoot through the green traffic light the second it changes, suited businesspeople in such a rush they play chicken dodging through the moving vehicles. My hands grip the wheel tightly as I'm forced to relax my speed, my chest aching to get to Axel.

Navigating through winding streets and confusing crossroads, finally a grey building looms in the distance, several storeys high with a giant H in the top corner. An ambulance rushes past, the urgency of its siren twisting my gut. I pull into a recently vacated space by the sidewalk and switch off the engine, unable to keep the tremors rolling through my arms to drive the rest of the way safely. The ambulance swerves alongside the sliding automatic doors, nurses rushing out to assist and all I can do is watch. Scared to enter the building and hear if Axel made it or not. Avery suddenly slams her fist on the dashboard and turns to glare at me, her face a mask of rage and solely directed at me. *Here we go.*

"We could have helped," she growls. "No fuck that, we *should* have been down there, fighting with the rest of them." Her beautiful features are taut, the weight of her accusation settling on my chest until it's hard to breathe.

"You would have got yourself kidnapped, harmed or probably both. Each of us knew what we signed up for." I keep my voice calm and even, another trick I learnt from my father. He constantly blamed me for situations that were out of my control, using his fists to sate the anger he couldn't contain. There was no use apologising, arguing or even crying. Remaining rational usually worked for him, but apparently not for Avery as her rage boils over and she throws a punch into my arm.

"I doubt they knew they were signing up for you to hide

me away like a coward." Pushing her door open without looking, a car swerves to avoid Avery as she exits. The taxi driver screams at her through his window, driving away while she flips him off. Darting after her, I grip her shoulders roughly and force her onto the sidewalk. Pushing her back against the edge of an apartment building, I lean into her body to speak into her ear.

"I'm not a coward. Every single one of the others would have done the exact same if they'd been on the stairs at that moment. Your safety is paramount." Her face shifts, her lips an inch from mine and our breaths mingle. For a second, I think she's going to press herself into me for a hug, but instead she shoves at my chest with more force that I expected.

"Not over Meg's! You barricaded me in that room whilst she was stolen away, by Wyatt no less! She was right there, beyond the door you refused to open and now she's gone, and I'll never forgive you." Her shoulder crashes into my arm as she barrels past, stomping towards the hospital without waiting. Huxley's hand rests on my shoulder and I lunge for him, burying my face into his neck and catching him by surprise. This is why I need Axel to pull through, I need the comfort of his hugs, the reassurance of his lingering touches. Not many men are comfortable to be affectionate the way Axel can, but now I can't live without it.

Huxley returns my hug, sighing deeply and dragging my sorry ass after the girl that has my emotions playing havoc. She's already at the receptionist's desk by the time we enter the hospital, the distinct smell of everything clinical and people on the brink of death filling the air. An escalator directly in front takes us to the second floor as Avery guides us through the maze of corridors. Every ceiling is lined with square polystyrene tiles, the brightness of the lights hurt my eyes until we arrive at a private ward.

Squirting hand sanitizer into our palms in turn, a nurse greets us by a set of heavy doors and escorts us to a room at the end of the hall. Garrett's floppy brown hair has flicked forward into his tormented eyes, too focused on the unconscious man in the bed to realise we've entered the room. The atmosphere in here is different to the rest of the hospital, the air filled with a perfumed scent and plush cushions laying behind Axel's shaved head. The nurses are unhurried, strolling behind trollies to do their rounds with leisurely strides.

"How is he?" Avery asks, moving to stand by Garrett's armchair. He jolts violently, shooting to his feet with his hands fisted, clearly expecting an intrusion. Avery doesn't budge, reaching up to stroke his cheek and push the hair back from his bruised face to reveal his softening hazel eyes. Garrett falls into her embrace, her legs nearly buckling beneath his weight, but I turn away, hating myself for the lick of jealously spreading through my chest.

Approaching Axel slowly, my lips tighten at the sight of multiple tubes leading into the crook of his arm. The heart-beat monitor beside the raised bed bleeps repeatedly, the pure strength of his heart sounding for everyone to hear. A pale blue blanket has been tucked tightly beneath his armpits, the top of his bare chest on show and littered with purple welts. He would look serene if it weren't for the small pinch between his eye-brows, as if he's trapped in a never-ending nightmare.

"He was in surgery first thing this morning, they brought him back about twenty minutes ago," Garrett explains behind me. "He hasn't come around from the anaesthetic yet." I reach forward to smooth the crease from between his eyes with my thumb, causing a protective growl to rattle from Garrett but I do it anyway. Axel doesn't belong to him alone, even if they share a more intimate bond. I don't have any other family than the four people in this room now Wyatt has scratched himself off the list. *Fucking Wyatt.*

My thoughts turn dark, needing to see him be punished for what he's done to Axel. There's no coming back, no excuse good enough when I saw him pull the knife from our brother through the laptop screen. It was in that moment, when my heart was crumbling into blackened dust. that I no longer had the energy to fight Avery. I suddenly felt what she must have been feeling as I pinned her into the chair and began hating myself more than she will ever be able to.

The nurse re-enters the room, ignoring everyone as she pushes herself between me and her patient to check his vitals. Her brown hair is tied into a low bun, a small white hat placed on top of her head as if she stepped right out of the 1940's. I move back to join the others, watching as she pulls down his blanket and reveals a blood soaked bandage covering Axel's abdomen. Tutting to herself, she presses a red button on the wall and a buzzer sounds further down the hall in response.

Another nurse in the same white and blue button-down dress soon enters, pushing a silver trolley holding multiple tubs filled with items such as dressings, swabs and wipes. The room is beginning to feel crowded, all of us hovering over the nurse's shoulders to get a peek at the angry stitched line below Axel's belly button. Pulling Garrett towards the door, he resists, his eyes tracking every moment of Axel's wound being cleaned and redressed.

"Come on Gare, let's give the nurses some space. I saw a canteen downstairs; we can grab you some food."

"I'm not hungry," he grunts, and I fall still for a second. I could have bet my life I'd never hear him say those three words, but then again, I didn't think he would openly accept Axel as his boyfriend either. So much has changed since we left Waversea to watch over Avery, and nothing will be the same when we return.

"He's in safe hands," I try to convince him, but Garrett's arms bunch and lip peels back in a snarl.

"I'm not leaving him."

"Look at me," I bite out, his bloodshot hazel eyes narrowing as they swing to me. "He's not going anywhere, and we have a lot to discuss," I say darkly, my jaw clenched and nose flaring. With one last glance back, he gives me a swift nod and moves to leave. Patting Huxley on the back, he then leans in to kiss Avery on the cheek on the way past, begging her to look after Axel in his absence. She softly strokes a bump on his forehead I hadn't noticed before, promising she won't let anything happen to any of us ever again. I catch her blue eyes for a spilt second before she looks away, but the truth to her statement was there.

Leaving the ward, Garrett cuts in front of me and leads the way towards a set of elevators I hadn't noticed before. A short woman gasps at the murderous look in Garrett's eyes as the doors separating us open, pushing her son behind her as we enter the steel box.. I notice a smear of Axel's blood poking out from the V necked t-shirt Garrett must have been given upon arriving at the hospital. He presses the button to the lower level impatiently while I shed my navy hoodie and shove it at him, straightening down my ruffled white t-shirt. The doors slide open a moment later, the general smell of old people washing over me once again. I seriously hate hospitals.

The canteen has a varied choice of stale sandwiches or lumpy yoghurt. I grab Garrett a BLT, order us a suspiciously murky coffee each and join him on a raised bench at the back with a row of tall stools. A wall of glass lines the bench, a small patch of green grass circling a water fountain and surrounded by the grey brick of wards on all other sides. Pushing his food away, Garrett leans on his chin on top of his fist.

"What are we going to do about him?" The him being clear. The one that backstabbed us all, the traitor who chose his side and left Axel for dead.

"We focus on Axel's recovery and rescuing Meg first; Wyatt's punishment will have to wait." I say evenly, breathing deeply to control my emotions.

"How can you be so fucking calm?!" Garrett slams his fist on the surface, the loudness of his voice halting everyone's movements around the canteen. A fork clashes loudly as its dropped, the silence hanging for a few seconds before people slowly return to their business, hushed whispers floating around behind us.

"I don't do violence." I lean over to speak directly into Garrett's ear. "However, don't be mistaken, I'm angry as shit. Wyatt's dead to me and I take solace in the fact you, Axel, Huxley and even Avery will not rest until he's got what he deserves. Bring a world of agony to his doorstep, rip away anything he still cares about and rain down hellfire until he begs for forgiveness. He will suffer, but I can't lose myself to do it." This allows a miniscule amount of tension to leave Garrett's shoulders, his head nodding slowly. I can practically see the visions taking place behind his eyes, the way he's going to make Wyatt suffer.

"I love him," Garrett's voice barely registers with my ears, a secret he could no longer hold inside but didn't want anyone to hear. Snatching his sandwich, he hops down from the stool and walks away before I have the chance to ask him if he was talking about Wyatt or Axel, but either way his heart is in for a rough ride. Emotion is a weakness in Garrett's mind, and loving someone gives them ammunition to hurt and abandon him. I'd like to think he knows by now I would always be here but considering the betrayal Wyatt has handed us, I can understand his unease.

None of us saw it coming. The switch in Wyatt was instantaneous since arriving home to care for Avery, the easy smile he always had at the ready wiped from existence. We were a team at college, and not just on the basketball court. A family unit who did everything together, it was us against the world. Maybe I should have tried harder when I saw Wyatt's pain, realized how fast he was slipping away. The others will be out for his blood but not me, I'd rather blame myself for his shortcomings. He could walk straight up to me right now, clasp my shoulder and say, 'hey sorry about that man, I don't know what came over me,' and I'd forgive him. Because that's what family does and ultimately, everyone is redeemable, right?

Meg

Soft snores filter under the door into the tiny bathroom, Wyatt having finally fallen asleep. It wasn't difficult to figure out what he was up to thanks to the paper-thin walls and series of grunts he was making, but it's good to know Wyatt isn't too far gone to be tempted like any other red-blooded male. Watching him eat that pizza was pure torture, the smell alone enough to kill my resolve, but damn was it worth it. Now I know I can affect him so easily, it gives me something to work with that makes me invincible – power over him. The weirdest part was when he began whispering 'goodnight' and 'see you tomorrow,' and I seriously hope he wasn't talking to his dick.

I twist to face the wall behind me, a set of four silver screws holding the shower railing I'm tied to firmly in place. I feel for any other poor sap that finds themselves trapped in a situation like this, through sex or force, because this place was built with the average sex fiend or serial killer in mind. But luckily for me, I'm always prepared.

So many things make sense now I know the truth, especially the way my mom made sure I was able to endure in any situation. I had thought she was being over-protective, always conscious of the troubled minds in the world through her therapy, but now it all makes sense. And secretly giving me the tools to survive has made me love her more. I've always taken for granted her constant presence, all the nights I went home in a bad mood and locked myself in my room, never allowing her to counsel me. Maybe if I'd been more open, she might have been too.

Stretching my back and rolling my neck, I limber up as much as possible in my tight confines of the shower cubicle. Well, cubicle might be a tad generous for the two-inch lip on the tiled floor and filthy once-white curtain against the opposite wall. Counting down from three in my mind, I high kick my leg up onto the wall so I'm doing a vertical split, silently cheering myself for my sporty outfit choice. Shifting my foot closer to my restrained hands, my fingers close over the laces of my sneaker and fully unthread them. Freeing the final cross, the tiny silver pick my mom insists I conceal in all my shoes becomes visible.

Grinning, I pull it free and drop the lace at the same time as my foot lands back onto the floor. Ordinary children may have attended camps or gone on vacations, but I spent more than a few summers learning survival hacks growing up. Mom insisted before I left for college, I could hold my breath underwater for an incredible length of time, build a fire from two pieces of flint, had the knowledge to reset bones or preform makeshift first aid, and the one I need now - how to pick locks. Pushing the tiny tool into the cuff's lock, my tongue sticks out as I listen intently for the miniscule clicks to release the lock piece by piece. My arms burn from being raised, the near end to my suffering causing my body to cramp in anticipation. With a final firm wiggle, the right cuff unlocks, and I gasp as my arms fall to my sides too quickly.

I hold my wrists to my chest for a moment, rubbing the raised sores that will surely blister. Not wanting to waste a second, I quickly grab my discarded shoelace and stuff it into my waistband, leaving the other cuff in place as I hop up onto the toilet seat. The rectangular window with obscured glass might be a tight squeeze, but it's the only option I have. Readying to pick the lock again, I'm surprised to find the handle lifts easily and hope that's not my good luck wasted on something I could have sorted myself.

My foot slips on the toilet seat, my shin connecting with the tank which clangs against the wall. Stilling, my skin pricks with goose bumps as I listen for the snores that continue beyond the door, a relieved sigh leaving me. Pushing the window wide open, I heave myself up onto the ledge and begin to shuffle through. There's a decent drop on the other side, nothing but a concrete pathway to break my fall. Bending my hands so they remain on the windowsill, I dangle myself further out until my hips make it through the tight gap. As slowly as my core can manage, I roll my body into a gradual flip before releasing the window and landing in a crouch on my feet.

Keeping my back to the building, adrenaline urges me onward until I approach the far corner. Peering round, my eyes land on the sedan. My only real chance to escape without leaving a way for Wyatt to follow. A group are huddled at the far end of the carpark, only their outlines and occasional flare up of multiple cigarettes visible under a cloud-heavy sky. Birdsong has already begun in most of the trees dotted randomly around the building, sunrise imminent.

Not having time to waste, I bend to pick up a chunky rock in my still cuffed hand before hiding it behind my back and casually strolling towards the car as if I'm not about to hot wire it. Fuck, my mom is the best. It's a good thing I didn't use all of the tricks she taught me to become a criminal mastermind. I haven't even made it to the car when the group spin to regard me, my eyes falling on the man I begged to help me last night. *Yeah, good job wank stain.* At his instruction, the men around him begin to walk towards me with a look in their eyes that doesn't scream concern. Sensing something isn't right, I ditch my carjacking idea, dropping the rock and bolt in the opposite direction.

Their heavy footfalls sound behind me instantly, my heart skipping a beat in panic. But then I remember, I'm the fastest on my lacrosse team and not pumping my body with drugs like the oxygen wasters chasing me, so I speed down the road with only one sneaker tied on properly. Darting down a back alley, I hoist myself onto a dumpster and use it to gain an advantage on the mesh fence behind, quickly climbing over and dropping down on the other side. Yells and shouts reach my ears, making me smile as I keep sprinting, needing another vehicle to 'borrow'.

Finding myself back on the town's main road, rows of shops lining each side, I curse and turn back towards masses of residential homes. Diverting from the streets, I take to hopping across back yards, vaulting over low metal fences. My eyes land on a plastic playhouse, the thought to hide out until the coast is clear crossing my mind. But I don't know this town or its people and maybe the community will help to flush out the outcast in their midst, a full scale manhunt. No, my best bet is to get as far from people as I can before finding somewhere to hide.

Jumping over the last fence, I end up back on the street as the sun crests over the horizon. A figure at the other end steps into the road the same time I do, letting out a battle cry that sounds more like a demented chicken as I ignore the stitch in my side to run once more. Damn, when did I become so unfit? The god-awful sound of moped engines rattle through the air seconds before a mass of them swerve around the corner I'm headed towards. Skidding to a stop, my shoe chooses right now to slip from my foot as I turn back and hobble down the road pointlessly. The mopeds are on me in seconds, forming a circle to trap me in a cage of metal shitcans. I glare from one asshole to the next, widening my stance and refusing to go down without a fight.

A weight collides with the back of me, not even facing me properly. Coward. I hit the floor just before more and more bodies pile on top, pinning me beneath their rancid body odours. My arms are forced behind my back, too many pairs of hands hauling me up and roaming my body. I squirm and kick as I'm forced over the back end of a black leather seat, some bastard actually sitting on me and reeving up his engine. Vibrations shudder through me as I'm driven back to the main street, the blurred lines beneath my face making me feel queasy. I kick and scream, not that it helps.

Less than five minutes later, I'm facing the brass number seven on the motel door with dozens of grubby hands roaming my body. There's a pause while the pussies surrounding me try to decide who should knock on the door, so I kick the toe of my sneaker against it, ready to face my own inevitable fate. Wyatt appears a second later, his hair wild as if he's been grabbing it. I can't help but smirk, seeing his unnerved expression making getting caught worth it. Almost.

"Err...A-are you that rich guy who needs to keep his sister in line?" A pathetic voice speaks up beside me, its owner as frail looking like the tone suggests.

"Story of my life," Wyatt mumbles loud enough for me to hear, reaching out to yank me into the room harshly. Crossing over to his bag, he shoves me down onto the bed and grabs a thick roll of cash from the central pocket. Returning to the doorway, Wyatt raises his hand above his head to throw the money far into the distance. The squad scramble to race in that direction, shoving and elbowing like a pack of hyenas scrounging over a scrap of meat. Wyatt slams the door closed, his emerald green eyes blazing with fury.

"Did you think you'd be able to escape me that easily?" Stalking towards me like a predator, I hold his gaze even when I have to tilt my head right up to do so.

"Yeah, I did to be honest." Slipping his hand around my neck and squeezing tightly, Wyatt pushes me back into the mattress and leans over my body. I could easily inflict some serious damage from this position, a few broken ribs, or a good old-fashioned punch to the balls but for some reason, I lie still. There's a twisted light to his eyes that says he's enjoying this, maybe even needs it. And stupidly, the thought that I could give him something he seems so sure he wants, doesn't disgust me the way it should.

His grip loosens, my lips parting as I watch the change of emotion in his face. His square jaw slackens, a confused furrow to his eyebrows as his hand trails south. Through the centre of my cleavage, over my toned abdomen. My pulse quickens, a strange fluttering taking root in my stomach. For one split second, nothing else exists, only me and him. The lingering scent of his cologne rolls through my senses, coiling with my rational thoughts until I can't remember what they were. His fingers graze my waistband and travel across to my side where my hand is lying uselessly.

A soft click sounds, my mind jarring back into action as the cool slice of metal at my wrist shifts. Looking down, I gasp seeing he has locked me to himself, a cruel smile twisting his lips.

"Try and escape me now, Sweetness."

Garrett

Pacing around the tiny waiting room I've been forced into while the doctor preforms his morning check-up, I can't stop replaying the other night in my head. Like a scratched DVD that plays the same scene, glitches and jumps back over and over. His blood coating my hands, the warmth leaving his body, the words lodged in my throat I wish I'd said. His life was literally slipping away and no amount of praying or crying could bring him back to me. I can't even consider if the air ambulance hadn't shown up when it did, I refuse to travel down that path knowing a part of me won't come back.

My fingers clasp into fists, my body shaking with the need to be back at his bedside. It's been two fucking days and not a single doctor can tell me why he's not woken up yet. Dax, Huxley and Avery have been staying at a motel on the edge of the city, returning during visiting hours like one of the nurses suggested I also did. Like I told her, either I'm allowed stay with Axel at all times or she'd better get a second bed ready in his room, 'cause I will jab a scalpel into my throat if that's what it takes. Not only was I permitted to remain, we now have security standing guard by the door, and I got a free evaluation from a psychologist so I can't complain. Nothing like a mental sweep of my childhood trauma to get the juices flowing and I know where to direct all of that unearthed murderous intentions. Wyatt fucking Hughes.

The same nurse who called security on me walks past the

glass door, rounding the safety of her desk before nodding for me to return. I fly into the hallway, making her jump as I jog back to Axel's. A part of me thinks she's kinda overreacting, although I had snatched a needle from her trolley and had it pointed at my jugular for extra effect. Nodding to today's guard with a cocky smile, I slip into the room and my heart finally settles at his sleeping form.

"Sorry that took so long," I talk to Axel, as I have been since we arrived. Pretending he can hear me is all that's keeping me calm, literally all I can do in this helpless situation. Reaching over to fluff his pillows, this private room and its small luxuries being the best thing I've ever spent my trust fund on, I kick off my shoes and jeans to slide beneath the cover beside him. Shuffling down, I rest my head on his shoulder and link my fingers in his.

"I was thinking after you're all healed, and I've painted my bedroom walls with Wyatt's blood, we should go away somewhere. You know, like a trip away. I've always wanted to visit Italy. We could hit Florence first to see Michelangelo's David, row on down the canals in Venice, rave it up in Vatican City with the Sistine Chapel, finish with the Pantheon and a villa in Rome. Just me, you and a never-ending supply of pizzas."

I've always had a secret passion for history and architecture, since I was a child who's only friends lived within the pages of books from my father's study. It never bothered me when my parents travelled the world, in fact I preferred it over lying in bed listening to their constant arguments. I'd learnt to look after myself from a young age, content in my own company and rarely scared of anything. Maybe it was because I only read non-fiction, no tales of monsters lurking under the bed or vampires in the closet filling my head.

If there was food in the fridge, I was happy – until there wasn't. My parents had decided to take a month-long cruise, leaving nine-year-old me with a wad of cash and a list of numbers for local takeaways, but I didn't call for any. I guess I'd given up on caring for myself, wondering how long it would take before someone else noticed I wasn't attending school, or I didn't turn up for basketball practice. Eleven days. That's how long. I barely remember being scraped off the floor by a police officer, the blue lights flashing beyond my eyelids, waking in a hospital bed with a tube through my nose leading to my stomach bringing me back from the brink. And that's the last time I gave a shit about being loved, until now.

I've decided to give Axel every part of me when he wakes up, including the monster hidden beneath my cocky façade. The one that's extremely close to the surface right now, teeth bared and claws at the ready to rip chunks out of Wyatt and this Perelli asshole and anyone else who dares to get too close to my family again. Then we'll see if Axel really wants me. Leaning upright, I pull across the TV suspended by a metal arm until its hovering over our knees. Unhooking the remote control from the side of the bed, I flick through channels until I find a Planet Earth documentary. When I run out of things to say, I read aloud the subtitles just so Axel can have the comfort of my voice should he need it. A bit of familiarity to latch onto and pull himself back to me.

"Hey, I've told you before – you can't be in the bed with him," a deep southern twang wakes me with a snort. A large woman with pale skin and a smirk on her lips jabs me in the side playfully, her blue and white dress straining to conceal her insanely huge breasts. Sitting upright, I stretch my arms high above my head and my back gives a satisfying crack before swinging my legs over the edge of the bed. The nurse, who attended to me when Axel was rushed into theatre insists I call her Mamma, scoops up my jeans and throws them at me. "Boy, you better put those chicken legs away before Dr Breeson comes back. One more strike and he'll have you removed from this here ward."

"Firstly, I'm paying his annual salary for Axel to stay here and secondly, I don't have chicken legs." I frown at my thighs, realising they've lost some muscle definition lately as I hop down from the bed and pull up my pants. Mamma laughs loudly, fixing the sheets around Axel's body to hide that I'd been in there. Rounding the other side of the bed, I take his palm in mine, careful not the touch the cannula strapped on the other side. My shirt is stuck to my torso, my body odour off the charts and my mouth feels like something curled up and died in there.

"Mamma, would you mind staying with him for 5 minutes while I have a quick shower?" Her eyes crinkle as she smiles, and she inclines her head. Placing a kiss onto Axel's forehead, I run my hand over the short brown hair that he's going to freak out about when he wakes up.

"He's lucky to have you," Mamma muses to herself, adjusting the IV drip. I step into the bathroom, glancing back at his peaceful expression as I slowly close the door.

"No, he's really not." I quickly strip from my clothes, twisting the shower dial to scalding knowing from the past two showers, the water will barely reach above cool. Stepping into the spray, I smother myself in the shower gel attached to the tiled wall and work up a lather on my chest. Once the bubbles have expanded enough, I rush to spread them over my body, the fissure in my heart starting to open again from the distance between us. Forgetting about the swollen bruises lining my ribs, I groan from with the contact of my own hand in my haste. Washing the suds away and flicking the shower off, I grab the world's smallest hand towel to dry myself.

A soft knock sounds at the door, my heart lurching that

something's happened to Axel or he's woken with the instant need to take a leak. Although I've been begging him to open him eyes, the thought of him not being the first person he sees rattles me. "It's me," a soft feminine voice sounds, one I recognise as Avery's. Holding the towel over my junk, not that she hasn't see it before, I push the door open wide. Mamma is nowhere to be seen, Huxley is positioned in the corner like usual and Dax is in the armchair. Avery's eyes widen, rolling across my exposed skin before visibly shaking herself.

"We brought you some clean clothes and toiletries." She hands her backpack to me over the threshold, careful not to come too close. I don't know who's benefit that is for, but it certainly isn't mine. I won't be making sexual advances on anyone anymore, especially not when Axel's unconscious in the adjacent room. If he wants to invite someone to join us sometimes, that's his call but there'll be no more fucking around for me. My eyes are set solely on the man I nearly lost, the one I'll never let come to harm ever again. I might not be much, but what I am he can have - wholly, completely, exclusively.

Emerging with a fresh set of clothes and sparkling white teeth, I feel marginally better. Placing Avery's bag down by Dax's feet, I pull out the ladies' razor I found in a hidden pocket. "Will you help me?" I ask of her, gesturing between the razor and Axel's head. "He'll hate waking up to that." Her eyes flick across the room and back to me, her eyes full of understanding. Grabbing a plastic cup from beside a water jug, Avery fills it while Dax and Huxley move to either side of the bed to help. As carefully as possible, they lift his head so I can slip the hand towel beneath and hold him there. Dipping the razor into the cup, I slowly shave from his nape to forehead in a reverse mohawk style.

Section by section, the four of us take turns to remove all traces of hair growth from our different angles. It's going to be a bit patchy at the back, but once he's awake and sitting upright, I'll take a strange sense of pleasure in fixing it for him.

Avery carefully does around his ears and passes the razor to me to finish his hairline across the front. Removing the towel with our help, Dax takes it and the hair-filled cup into the bathroom while we assess our work. Axel looks good as new, now I just need for his incredible amber eyes to open and I'll take the rest from there.

Huxley is the first to walk away, taking the armchair for himself for a change. His blonde hair shines in the sunlight gleaming through the window, his cheeks not as drawn and eyes not as bloodshot as before. Avery strolls over and settles herself into his lap, curling her legs into his chest and his arms circling her automatically. I raise my eyebrow as Dax returns, stopping in his tracks at the sight and turning back to join me.

"That looks cosy," I whisper. Dax is close enough for his Afro to tickle my shoulder through the basketball jersey they provided me with to match the shorts. I'd smiled upon seeing our black and yellow team name scrawled across the back, actually missing our 5am drills before a big game.

"Mmm," Dax growls in his chest. "They've been sharing a room again." There's a note of jealously in his tone, his posture rigid as he glances over to see Avery combing Huxley's hair through her fingers. "She blames me for Meg being taken."

"There's nothing any of us could have done. We had a spy in our midst, Meg would have been taken sooner or later – with or without Avery." I've put a lot of thought into this, since I've barely been able to sleep. I needed to understand what drove Wyatt to do what he did, why he'd put Axel's life in danger like that. The only conclusion I could come to was his loyalties now lie elsewhere.

The clicking of high heels echoes around the hallway beyond the door, loud enough to hear the steady approach. Glancing towards the door frame, my heckles rise and I grip onto Axel's hand protectively, instinctually knowing a threat is advancing on us. Dr Breeson steps into the room, followed by a woman dressed for a business meeting rather than a hospital visit. A navy jumpsuit clings to her curves, pink detailing around the bust to a matching sash tied tightly to cinch her waist. Her neck and ears are dripping with expensive jewellery, her dark hair pulled back into a chignon bun.

"Who are you?" Avery stands and confronts her, despite the foot in height distance even without the added six-inch heels. Ignoring the question, the woman's pale brown eyes drag over Axel lazily and come to rest on our joined hands. Her perfectly painted red lips lift in a sneer, the true reflection of her ugly personality coming to the surface. Lifting my shoulders and puffing my chest, refusing to be intimidated by this waste of oxygen, I answer Avery's question in a clear voice.

"Even though she doesn't deserve the title, this is Axel's mom."

Wyatt

Leaning back in the driver's seat, I settle in for another long haul. I'm not risking another overnight stop to give Houdini in the passenger seat a chance to get away again. I'm still baffled and slightly impressed she managed to slip out of the bathroom without waking me, but I had been trapped in the throes of a nightmare, so she got lucky. This once. I have one hand resting on the wheel with the one she's chained to propped on the arm rest between us. Every time her skin grazes mine, a bolt of pure energy zips all the way to my dick so I've learnt to be extra careful of my arm placement. Our morning toilet break and shower was great fun though, I don't think I've ever seen anyone turn a brighter shade of beetroot before.

Meg's chest rises on a loud sigh, my t-shirt swamping her frame and pooling over her crossed legs. She's drawing the figure of eight on her sun-kissed thigh over and over, my eyes unable to stop flicking across to watch the movement. I forced her to change with the excuse of ensuring she didn't have any more tricks hidden in her clothing, but even I'm not going to let someone spend their last few days living in their own grime and two-day-old clothing. I'd also made sure to take my vitamins before heading out this morning, needing a clear mind to stay alert. Shadowed figures creeping around on the edge of my vision won't help to soothe me whilst I'm on kidnapper duty, especially when my captive is as slippery as this one.

Raindrops patter across the windscreen, the overhead

clouds mimicking the heavy atmosphere within the car. If I keep my eyes fixed on the road, I can pretend I'm an average guy taking a girl home to meet his parents for the first time. Although in this scenario, the dad will be putting his carving skills to good use and the girl won't be walking back out again. Such is life when you're a pawn in a powerful man's game. Directly ahead, the sky is filled with streaks of rainfall which has the overly cautious drivers in the other lanes slowing already. *Pussy shits.*

"Answer me one question," Meg fills the silence as I refuse to let her have the radio today, despite dying of boredom myself. Disobedient prisoners don't get rewards. I grunt when she doesn't continue, her chestnut hair tickles my arm as she sets her baby blues on me.

"Just, why? Why are you a part of all this and why do you think I deserve the fate you're delivering me to?" I'm forced to slow behind a BMW's brake lights as the driver spots the torrential rain nearing up ahead, words fail me briefly so I grit my teeth instead. I can sense her watching me, waiting for an explanation to help her understand. But not everything can be summed up into a neat little box, not everything makes sense. I was floundering until Ray gave me a light, a purpose. That's all I have to hold onto.

"Because my whole life is a sham. I've been lied to since the day I was born. At least Ray treats me with enough respect to have given me the truth at last. For that, I'm in his debt." I indicate to undertake the BMW, a wide-eyed woman quivering behind the wheel at the sight of a bit of rain. Resuming the middle lane in front of her, I speed straight into the downpour. Rain ricochets off the car, the thundering around us finally giving me a reprieve from Meg's silent observant stare.

"Meh," she shrugs and shifts back to face forward.

"Did you seriously just say 'meh'? You asked for an answer and I gave it to you, which is more than anyone else has managed to get from my lips and you fucking '*meh*' me?!" I want to be furious but I can't say I expected anything else from her. It must have been so easy to live a simple life, never having to deal with detrimental issues of the soul.

"Well, I mean.... Does it really matter?" I nearly swerve the car, my fingers gripping tightly around the wheel. The rapid flailing of wipers across the windscreen has my stress levels rising, unable to shift the onslaught of rain like my heart is unable to rid the darkness that begins churning again for the first time in the past two days. I hadn't even realised it had dwelled until this moment as she continues on, unaware of the storm raging inside of me.

"Because in theory, you took the life *I* was owed. Biologically Nixon and Cathy are my parents and the lavish lifestyle you've led was mine, but do you see me being a mop about it? You should be thankful and move on." I snort loudly, refusing to buy into her words. All the money in the world couldn't give me what I wanted, what she still managed to receive despite all the odds being against her. A loving childhood and the sole attention of a supportive mom.

Realising I'm only punishing myself; I reach over to turn on the radio which causes her cuffed hand to graze my knee. This is going to be the longest drive of my life. The chorus of a new pop song begins to play but Meg immediately turns it back off, reaching over to rest her hand on my thigh. Throwing her a side glance, I force myself to focus on not crashing the car rather than the heat building along my leg as if her palm were on fire.

"I saw you in the streets a few times growing up. I used to hang over our balcony every time I heard the chaos from below, desperate to see what new gadget or designer outfit you had. I remember complaining to my mom how unfair it was that some people get everything they want when I had to save my allowance and wait for sales. Do you want to know what she said?" I don't react, pretending I haven't heard when I'm actually hanging on her every word. "She said, 'You're only rich once you have all the valuable things money can't buy.'

My heart is slamming a powerful beat in my chest as I finally roll up the driveway, I've dreamt of returning to. Rounding the central fountain, I pull up right outside the front door and leave the engine running for someone else to park the car properly. The richly dark exterior matching the wealth of crime happening within, yet nowhere has ever felt more like home to me. Taking the small key from my pocket, I slip it into the lock of my handcuff and release myself from a peacefully sleeping Meg. She's curled up like a cat, her head laying on the armrest and eyelashes fanning her cheeks, blissfully unaware of the evil lurking nearby. Ignoring a strange tug in my chest, I hop out of the car as a couple of Ray's men appear in the stone arched doorway.

Dressed all in black with guns slung across their bodies, the pair stride towards me in unison, one shoving past to take possession of the car and the other leaning into the passenger seat. Jolting awake as meaty arms enclose around her, Meg's screams fill the quiet estate as she's dragged out of the seat by her hair. I look around the open courtyards either side of the mansion curiously, wondering if anyone will notice her high-pitched shrieks. If there are any neighbours close by, I'm sure this isn't a rare occurrence and they either know better than to interfere or are paid handsomely for the inconvenience.

Clawing at the arm holding her in place, her eyes find me, a plea in their sea of blue as if she thinks I might help. I scoff inwardly and follow as she's hoisted over the guard's shoulder and carried into the house. She scratches his bicep, bangs her fists on his back and even tries to bite him but if he felt any of it, he doesn't slow or seem bothered. Despite my first thought being to run into the house and find Rachel, a nagging pull draws me after Meg, some stupid notion making me need to see that's she's delivered to the underground chamber safely. Passing through the hidden door behind the grand staircase and trotting down the stone steps, I tell myself I'm feeling arbitrarily protective since she's been in my charge the last two days. Besides, if this meathead is anything like the rest of them, I need to make sure he remembers to lock the cell door.

Throwing her inside the third unit on the left, he slams the medieval door closed and pulls a wooden beam down. Producing a brass padlock from his pocket, he then winds the thick steel chain hanging on the wall around the beam and secures it in place with the lock, shoving the key into my hand as he leaves. The electric lanterns have been switched on, lighting a dim path down the long corridor. A shiver rolls through my spine with the plummeting temperature down here, and if that wasn't enough to make me want to run back upstairs then the scent of desperation and death certainly is.

My eyes land on Meg as she assesses me closely, her hands coiled around the bars in the centre of the wooden door. I could close the grate, so she's trapped in her worst fear, but I reckon she's suffering enough right now. Anyone would think surely by now, she'd be crying and begging for mercy, but there's no sign of panic or alarm in her face. Just a determination to see out this inevitable fate with a sense of dignity I have to respect. Without having a reason to stay any longer, I throw her one last smirk and move to leave the makeshift dungeon.

"I honestly thought, deep down, you were better than this," her words carry to me as I reach the first step, halting in place to hear the rest of what she's burning to say. "Only the weak turn cruel, blaming the world for their bad luck instead of having the strength to overcome the challenges they need to face. And if that means I'm in here and you're out there, so be it."

The vein in my forehead begins to pulse as I stomp up the rest of the steps, slamming the door behind me as if that will banish her words from my mind. I couldn't give less of a shit what others think about me, so why does her opinion affect me so much? My mind is whirling as I turn into the living room and collide with an eager looking Rachel.

"Wyatt, there you are!" Her words turn into a squeal as I bend to hug her and lift her right off her feet. The raspberry and vanilla scent of her shower gel wraps around me at the same time her arms do, holding me tightly as she hangs suspended in the air. A tear slips from my eye which I hide in her hair, the fractures that have grown at an all-consuming rate slowly knitting back together. This is the kind of hug I need every day for the rest of my life, one filled with pure unadulterated love. Placing her down with a sniff, Rachel cups my cheek and looks at me worriedly.

"You look drawn, have you been sleeping okay? Eating properly?" Taking my hand, she pulls me towards the kitchen without waiting for a reply. Taking a moment to compose myself whilst she isn't looking, I look through the patio doors to the tiny dots beginning to twinkle in a darkening sky, thanking them for finally providing me with a real parent. I don't need matching genetics or a piece of paper to tell me Rachel is more of a mom to me than I've ever known.

Planting me down on a stool, Rachel busies herself making me some dinner and fills me in on every little thing I've missed since being away. From unwanted squirrel's in the attic, building a nest and chewing through electrical wires, to Charlton defending some big-shot celebrity in court which was broadcasted on mostly every channel. I simply listen and watch, a smile fixed to my face as she moves around in cropped jeans and a simple t-shirt. Despite clearly having an excess of money, Rachel never dresses in fancy clothes or flaunts her worth. She's humbly content being the perfect housewife and nothing more. No social hierarchy or faked humanity and it's the most refreshing thing in the world.

"-business in Seattle so he will be away for a few days.

I've told him he shouldn't be travelling at his age, but you know what Ray's like. He always has been on the bull-headed side." Rachel swings her brown eyes over her shoulder to smile sadly at me. I've never seen her and Ray together and I can't picture it to be honest, but surely there must be a reason she married someone twenty years older and it clearly wasn't for his money. Finishing with a sprinkle of grated cheese, she turns and plants a steaming bowl of tomato and bacon pasta in front of me. The smell is divine, my mouth watering with the lack of decent food lately.

"Now, be honest with me. How are you doing?" Rachel props herself on the other side of the island, watching me eat as if it's the most fascinating documentary she's ever seen. I think about spinning her a lie or shrugging off her concern, but I won't lie to her. Not when her undivided attention feels this good.

"I ache," I confess on a sigh. "My soul aches. Every time I think I know how to overcome my pain; it only gets worse. Like a mountain that keeps growing with every step I take, the peak never in sight. Being happy shouldn't be a struggle, but I can't even remember what happiness is anymore." I flinch as Rachel's arms wind around my neck, having been too consumed by my thoughts to realise she had moved. Leaning into her chest, I let her reassuring whispers and gentle strokes ease my thoughts for now, knowing the second she steps back they will slam back into me tenfold. Thoughts of vengeance, death and the blue-eyed girl beneath my feet who is unknowingly now at the centre of it all.

Avery

"Oh, my poor boy! What have you done to him?" Axel's mom has sauntered across the room to inspect the botched shave job we had just finished, reaching out to run her finger across a few missed long hairs. Garrett's hand shoots across from the other side of the bed, snatching her wrist tightly in his grip.

"Don't you dare touch him *Sharon*," he hisses her name through his teeth. His hazel eyes are blazing with fury, his arm trembling from the firm hold that has the slender woman whimpering. After a tense second, which has even the doctor hovering in the doorway frozen with anticipation, Garrett releases her with a shove and moves to sit on the bed. Sliding his arm beneath Axel's neck, Garrett tenderly pulls him close like a lion protecting his sleeping mate from outside threats.

With a roll of her eyes, Sharon turns around to face the rest of us and holds out her palms expectantly. Doctor Breeson jerks into action, rushing forward with a clipboard I hadn't noticed he was holding, pulling the pen from his jacket pocket and handing them both over. Her eyes roam over the words upon the paper, lips pursing before scrawling an elaborate signature with her manicured fingers. The glint of an outrageous diamond fixed to her skinny wedding finger catches Garretts attention; his eyes narrowed as he tracks the jewel back down her side.

"There," she hands the clipboard back to the doctor, his forehead dripping with sweat making his black hair look even greasier. "I've already made the necessary arrangements." He nods quickly, his eyes flicking back to Garrett before ducking out of the room like a bomb is about to detonate.

"What arrangements?" I ask when clearly no one else is going to speak. Dax's muscles are bunched by the bathroom door, his locked jaw matching Huxley's, who has edged around and slyly stepped in front of me. Sharon's pale brown eyes light up further as she takes in Huxley, scanning his handsome features, broad frame and pausing over his crotch for a beat too long.

"Axel's coming home with me."

"Like fuck he is!" Garrett roars, gently placing down Axel's head before leaping from the mattress to join the rest of us by the foot of the bed. "I refuse to let him out of my sight, especially around the likes of you. You're not beyond pimping out his unconscious body for the right price." His chest is heaving, fists clenched ready for a fight that Sharon doesn't seem interested in having.

I clearly don't know as many details of Axel's past as everyone else in this room, but I know enough and the woman before me isn't the monster I envisioned. Axel has her full lips and heart shaped face, although that's where the similarities end. Her hair sits perfectly at the back of her slender jewel-covered neck, her breasts too perky to be natural in an expensive pantsuit. She easily could have been a model or boutique owner, but I suppose marrying into money was more her speed. Twisting her lips at Garrett's comment and checking her watch, she looks to the ceiling as if her patience is being tested.

"Axel is still a minor and, by law, needs to return to my care whether I want him to or not. I have a lot on my plate at the moment, so by all means, tag along and play happy couples or whatever this is," she waves her hand vaguely between the two of them, "He's being transported within the hour, with or without you." Her heels click loudly across the floor as she moves to leave, my mind whirling with questions, concern and an idea.

"We're all coming with him." She halts at my demanding tone, looking back over her shoulder, although she isn't looking at me. A smirk pulls at her lips as she holds Huxley's gaze and shrugs.

"I'm fine with a bit of extra eye candy hanging around," she winks at him and leaves, her hips slinking with much more vigour than before. *Well, that was disturbing.* No one moves for a while, watching the empty space in the doorway as our minds reel.

I'm the first one to turn, finding Dax's blue eyes fixed on me with a note of longing in them. For a split second, I could have easily run into his arms and allowed his spicy scent to wash away my worries. His gentle hands and soft lips to take control of my pain and wipe it from existence, but that's the weakness in me breaking through. I don't need a man to fix my problems for me and I definitely don't want to depend on one to. That's the slippery slope many fall prey to, losing the power to correct their own mistakes and lay the blame for their misgivings on others. At least if I try and fail, it's on me. I need to be good enough, strong enough.

Focusing on Garrett instead, whose neck so taut it looks like it might snap itself at any moment, I close the space between us and take his fists in my hands. "Nothing will happen to him. You heard her, she'll be preoccupied and it's the last place Wyatt would think to look for any of us." Some of the tension ebbs from his shoulders at my words, his concerned gaze flicking back to Axel. On a large sigh, he whispers his agreement and shifts back to the bedside, brushing his fingers along Axel's jaw. Peacefully sleeping Axel, blissfully unaware that he's about to return to the place of his nightmares.

Watching through the Nissan's windscreen, Axel's bed is pushed into the back of the ominous black van in front. Garrett is also on the bed, his arm and leg hoisted over his lover, hissing at anyone who gets too close like a pissed-off cat. The two porters struggle to move the extra weight on the silver ramp, using their shoulders to stop it from rolling back down, I have to snort at the ridiculousness of it all. Finally managing to secure the bed in place, flip up the ramp and slam the back doors closed, one of the porters bangs on the side window for the driver to pull away with us right behind. Luckily, we were in the habit of keeping all our belongings in the trunk in case our motel rooms were ransacked while we were away, so no time was wasted on our end.

In the driver's seat, Dax's expression is focused as he follows the van through the busy streets, refusing to let any vehicles push their way in between us. Huxley and I are spread across the back seats, my legs lying across his since he is manspreading so much, it was this or huddle in the corner. Kicking my Converses off, I relax against the black leather in my yoga jumper that sits off one shoulder and push my hand into the open bag of Starburst sitting between us from the hospital vending machine. Picking one out, I unwrap the pink cube and lean over to pop into Huxley's mouth, earning a brief confused glance from Dax in the rear-view mirror.

The dynamic between Huxley and I have changed massively since we left the safe house. I had worried this latest attack would send him spiralling back into the dark place he was only just managing to claw his way out of, but in fact the opposite has happened. He barely utters more than a few words, even to me in private but his actions speak volumes. The first night in the motel, I'd been about to turn in for the night, exhausted and defeated by the day, when Huxley had dropped to the floor in a one-handed push-up.

"What are you doing?!" I'd asked curiously and more than a little disturbed.

"I'm getting Meg back." That one statement meant more to me than any profession of love ever could. No promising to try his best or pretending everything's going to work out, just pure determination. In his silent observations, Huxley has realised I don't need pretty words or reassurance, I need action. And even though when it comes to it, I won't let anyone else suffer in this quest except me, the least I can do is to make sure Huxley continues on this path to a full recovery. Mentally and physically.

That night I'd jumped straight out of bed and begun running drills with him, rounds of squats, push ups and sit ups, some light sparring practice and even a midnight run around the city, Huxley's comforting presence by my side the entire time. The burn of my muscles is a balm to my anxiety, the only productive way to soothe my helplessness. And if the grunts of exercise through our thin motel walls screw with Dax a little, I'm fine with that. Not to be a passive aggressive bitch, but the more his feelings for me dwindle the better because one day very soon, I'm going to risk everything to save my twin and I don't care what happens to me in the process.

A motorbike pulls up beside us in a queue at the traffic lights, a woman's figure in hot pink leathers and matching helmet leaning over a custom painted Kawasaki Ninja. My eyebrows rise and I openly gape at the black machine with fuchsia lightning bolts decals, the gritty sound of her exhaust filling my ears as she speeds away. My eyes track her, weaving through the vehicles with ease and a sense of freedom I could only long for. Slumping against the window, I watch the world blur by knowing I have no place in it, my self-esteem taking a mental battering. Soon enough, we've left the city behind and settled in for a long drive in the typical silence we've been sharing lately.

It's times like this I wish I had my phone to scroll through all the photos of Meg and I. Camping trips, movies nights, college parties. Memories we probably won't get a second chance to enjoy together, the future looking bleak for both of us. If I can somehow contact Ray Perelli and convince him to take me instead, let me pay the debt he feels he's owed, then maybe for Meg it doesn't have to be the end. Dax's deep voice pulls me from my thoughts.

"Axel's not gonna be happy if he wakes up in- "I kick the back of his seat hard, causing the car to swerve before he rights himself.

"*When* he wakes up," I growl. "The surgery went well, he's just.... taking his time to recover. Resting is the best thing he can do." I meet the brief narrowed glance he throws back at me with a look of venom, refusing to consider his words.

"What I was going to say was – if he wakes up in his old house. Resting to Axel means being trapped in his past, replaying the same night over and over. Physically he'll pull through, but I doubt he'll be the same Axel knew when he comes around. Especially back there." Oh, well that's different. I slump back in the seat, already restless despite having barely made a dent in our long journey. This is the exact reason I was home schooled and kept everyone at arm's length, I can't handle losing those I care about. And losing the Axel I knew will leave a scar on my already damaged heart for sure.

"He's got Garret," I reply weakly. Dax scoffs and even Huxley glances to me with uncertainty. I'm praying Garrett pulls through on this, takes Axel's offered heart and treasures it like the precious gift it is. They could heal each other in ways no one else can, their connection clear enough for anyone to see. Needing to escape my own head for a while, I lean through the centre of the car and turn the radio's dial until a string of pop songs are blaring through the speakers. Losing myself to the music, I snuggle into Huxley's side and feign sleep. His protective arm rounds my body, his fingers finding my hair to make repetitive strokes.

Sometimes, I wish I were the type of girl to let someone take over for a while, to wake me when everything is back to normal. But that seems too easy. Pain is what lets me know I'm awake, the raw ache in my chest reminds me life doesn't stop for anyone. We must brave our own storms and cling to the hope a brief ray of sunshine might peek through the clouds before our last sun sets. No shortcuts, no cop outs, no mercy.

Meg

Holy shit, I'm going to die down here. The instant Wyatt walked away from me; the realisation dawned that this is all real. For some reason, I thought things wouldn't go this far, that some part of him wouldn't dump me in the hands of a murderous gangster and walk away. I should have fought harder, I should have unleashed the true ferocity of my struggling, maybe even sobbed and pleaded.

How could I have been so stupid? I reckon I subconsciously allowed myself to be put back into Wyatt's clutches, figuring it's my turn to suffer in the revolving cycle he can't seem to break free from. Everything is so unnecessarily fucked. Wyatt feels more than hard done by; he genuinely believes he's missed out on something due to my existence. But if it came to between me and Avery, then I'll gladly take this round. She's been through too much, and as much as I can pretend, she has a chance to flee and start over, I know she'll be running straight towards me.

An electronic lantern shines through the steels bars I'm clutching onto, the grate allowing me to look along the dark corridor and see the bottom of the steps I was dragged down. Trailing my fingers down the grooves of thick beams, my shoulders sag forward until my forehead is pressed against the wood. My body begins to shiver in Wyatt's t-shirt, the dampness in the air seeping into my bare skin. Slowly turning, I glance around my new home with tears brimming my eyes.

Bleak stone walls glow dimly from the lantern's fake flame, the empty space barely big enough for me to lie down in. If I hadn't had my crash course in battling claustrophobia in the trunk of the sedan, I'd be in fits of hysterics by now. But if the light remains on and the monsters stay on the other side of the door, I reckon I can handle this. For now. A metallic toilet sitting in the corner makes me grimace but at least it's better than alternative, lounging around in my own filth. One single toilet roll has been placed on the tank and there's a matching sink beside it which I promptly check has running water. After splashing my face, I slump down onto the floor and hug myself. *What happens now?*

The stone floor is unforgiving, no chance of finding a comfortable way to sit or lie. Rolling the clicks out of my ankles, I pull my hair loose from the tie holding it up and flick the band back in forth in my fingers. If I manage to get a guard close enough to the door, I reckon I could use this bad boy to catapult small stones right into his eye, for no other reason than my sole amusement. One point for each curse word and ten if I manage to cause some retina damage. Feeling alongside the wall, I start to build an ammo pile whilst singing my way through the Sweeny Todd song list. Seemed fitting.

Lesson 101 of survival, you're only as screwed as your mindset. Even if such a time comes of me giving up on escaping, which isn't likely, I need to promise myself I won't let Wyatt see me crack. I'm unsure why it's so important, but if there is one thing still within my power, it's that I can't let him see he's won. He can do what he likes to me now, but he won't have the satisfaction of my misery. And who knows, if breaking me becomes his main focus, hopefully it'll buy more time for Avery to get as far away as she can. And I swear to everything I hold dear, if she's not then I'll…give her a firm talking to, maybe a slap.

It's inevitable my morale won't last forever, but at least I'm a vivid daydreamer. Leaning back as comfortably as I am able, I focus on my breathing and bring a vision to life around me. The cell transforms to a field before my eyes, luscious green grass splaying across the ground. The sun is beating down on my face, a flurry of sparrows flying freely overhead. A small ball rolls towards my foot, followed by the lacrosse team. White vests and skorts hug their lean bodies, displaying each of their individual numbers in red. Mesh sticks in hand, they smile down at me with blue gumshields fully on show and I chuckle. We've played some killer games the past few years, returning as victors with huge trophies for the college display cabinet. But we've also lost too, had our asses handed to us time and again, but we never gave up.

A faint creak sounds down the corridor as I begin to envision the goaltender scooping up the ball- Wait, I hear real footsteps! I jump up to my feet, my legs already turning numb on the hard floor and I grip the steel grate to peer around. "Hey, is there someone else down here?" I ask hopefully, able to just about see four doors across the opposite side. A short, plump woman comes into view, looking around nervously as she makes a beeline for me.

Her dark hair is loose on her shoulders, the curled ends bouncing with each hurried step. She glances at the doors either side before focusing her attention on me. "Oh, my love," she breathes, reaching out to stroke my hair but deciding against it at the last moment. Withdrawing her hand, I watch suspiciously as she kneels in front of the door. Sliding back an opening I hadn't noticed; she proceeds to push an oblong box into my cell. Crouching down, her hand shoots through the gap to grab mine as I accept the box. Her thumb caresses the back of my hand and I resist yanking back, sensing she isn't here to harm me.

"I'm so sorry you are the price that needs to be paid," she murmurs before pulling back and closing the slat between us. I weirdly miss the heat of her hand instantly, my short time in here clearly already influencing me. Her footsteps scurry away as I sit wondering what the fuck all that was about. Opening the box, I squint to see the items crammed inside and use my fingers to feel out what's in there.

Firstly, there's a small plastic bag containing a toothbrush, paste and bar of soap. Then I pull out flattened item that confuses me until I feel an air toggle on the underneath and blow up to discover it's an inflatable pillow. Next comes a handful of energy bars, an empty bottle I imagine I'm supposed to fill using the sink and a large bar of chocolate. Seriously, who is this lady and why is she sneaking me chocolate? Lastly, the padded nylon material spread across the base of the box unfolds to reveal a sleeping bag and my imprisonment just became much more manageable.

Two energy bars and a whole bottle of what I'm sure is not drinking water later, I slip into the sleeping bag and rest my head on the pillow with a sigh. The light from the corridor is enough to take the edge off, but my claustrophobia is lingering beneath my skin. I need to keep calm, allowing my fear to consume me will only hurt myself. The four walls feel like they are shifting closer, the darkness pressing in on me like a heavy weight leaning on my chest. Goosebumps prickle across my entire body, my breath fogging in front of my face as nightfall has the temperature plummeting. Pulling Wyatt's collar up to my nose, I inhale his heady scent with the sole purpose of banishing the stench of damp and faeces. *Yeah right.*

Maybe being a therapist's daughter has made me too understanding, but I know I don't hate Wyatt with every fibre of my being like I should. During our journey, I learnt his indecisive glances and conflicted expressions, noting all the times he didn't know why he was still ploughing ahead with someone else's plan. The human mind is complex enough without being at war with itself. But if this is what he truly thinks he needs; I do find myself hoping he's right. Maybe that's why I didn't fight hard enough, because in coming here maybe I could save both him and my twin from miserable fates.

Not even a scurry of rats or a dripping tap sound to fill the silence around me. Just the drumming of my fingers on my collar bone and the unsure thump of my heart. I should be used to my own company, considering I was an only child up to a few weeks ago. But for one moment, between early morning yoga sessions and midnight chatting in bed, I'd never felt so complete. And now I lay staring at the shadowed lines across the ceiling with the cold biting at my cheeks, I'm no longer able to ignore the anguish I've been trying to pretend hasn't been tearing me in two since I woke up in the trunk of the car.

If I can just hold onto the hope that Avery is safe, that'll be enough to withstand anything thrown my way. I yearn for her company, her strong yet comforting presence to bolster me, but I will gladly give my life to never see her down here. She's suffered enough at the expense of Nixon's decision to have us adopted so I suppose it's my turn.

Axel

Why can't I move? Shrouded in darkness, only the thump of my heartbeat in my ears tells me I'm not dead, not that I feel reassured. My body feels like I've been buried in concrete, every muscle too weak to push against the weight holding me down. My mind slipped through the fog to rouse a little while ago, but my eyelids are still too heavy to lift. What the hell happened to me? Using all my focus, I push every drop of my energy into twitching each of my fingers one by one. Satisfied my fingers are in working order, I slowly begin wiggling my toes back and forth to banish the pins and needles sending tingles up my legs. A shudder rolls through my restricted spine, making me want to groan at the involuntary movement but no sound passes my lips. Finally, an eternity of lying in the pitch black of my own panic, I manage to crack my eyelids and blink a few times to focus.

A sea of stars greets me on the other side on my vision, glowing softly in a mix of pale yellow and green. There's something so familiar about the perfectly pointed shapes, something blaringly obvious lingering on the edge of my mind but I can't quite grasp it. A solid weight beside me suddenly shifts, a hand slinking over my chest and heavy breath fanning my ear. *Fuck.*

A scenario I've played out a thousand times before slams into me, a pained noise actually leaving me this time. A hand clasping my mouth, painted lips whispering to 'shh' in my ear. Perfume so strong clogs my throat, the scents of smoke and alcohol filling my nostrils as fingers brush across my exposed skin. Those glow-in-the-dark stars are my only anchor to reality, the only constant in this repetitive nightmare. How am I back here? Did I ever even escape or was it all a dream?

The figure clinging to my side sits upright, flicking on my space-themed nightlight to assess me. I will my body to move but I'm stuck, glued to the mattress and only able to scream in my mind. Soft hands touch my cheeks, the tears slipping from my eyes landing upon delicate fingers. Please no, not again. I can't be here again. My name is being said but it might as well be miles away, battle cries of useless determination filling my ears as I stare at those damn stars. By the time I've counted the five points of each one, this should be over. Sitting upright, the darkened silhouette looms over me until I can no longer count, and I recoil until a sea of hazel catches my attention.

Garrett. The invisible binds holding me in place snap at the same time my chest bursts with relief and I lurch upright to grab him. A shot of agony slices across my mid-section, pain blazing a trail through me until I'm slumped back and writhing in discomfort. "Shit stay still Axel. I'll be right back." Garrett's gone before I can beg him to stay, my outstretched hand desperately grabbing the air as agony of a different kind swallows me whole. He's barely left the room and I'm already contemplating jumping up to chase him, not giving a shit about the repercussions. The small unloved boy in me would do anything for a simple hug, and the broken man I am only wants it from him.

The pain in my abdomen has lessened to an intense throbbing by the time he finally returns, flanked by a bearded man in flannel pyjamas holding a black bag. What the fuck is happening? Garrett re-joins me in the bed and presses a kiss to my sweat-covered brow before pulling down the cover to expose me. My eyes begin to swim with unshed tears, the vulnerability of this moment sending tremors along my skin, but I remain as still as possible, trusting his steady gaze implicitly. My body jerks as the strange man lifts my top, my breathing hitched in suspense.

“W...what’s going on?” I manage to croak, keeping my focus directly on Garrett as something is peeled back from my stomach. He links his fingers in mine, gripping my hand tightly every time I hiss or wince from whatever the fucks being done to me. His eyesight doesn’t flicker from mine the entire time, his undivided attention pulling me through. The sharp scratch of a needle is pushed into the crook of my free arm, a rush of cool liquid filling my veins which has my muscles tensing. Almost immediately, I can feel the pull of drowsiness starting to drag me under, away from him. Droplets pool in the shell of my ear as tears stream down my face, my vision blurring in my desperation to stay in his warmth. “N-no, please don’t make me go back Gar- “

“-an abundance of krill attracts other visitors to the Peninsula in the summer. Antarctic Minke Whales. They use their pointed heads and short dorsal fins to give them endurance- “

“What the actual fuck are you talking about?” I grumble, my head already starting to pound before I’ve even opened my eyes. Garrett’s voice has filtered through the depths of my slumber several times before, but this is the first time I’ve been able to rouse enough to ask him why he’s telling me that frogs can’t vomit or kangaroos can’t fart. His chest rumbles as he chuckles, my hand clutched in his over his heart. Breathing causes enough discomfort that I don’t bother trying to move my limbs, each inhale burning the back of my throat.

“Well good morning to you too, Sleeping Beauty. How are you feeling?” His hand cups my cheek, a huge dimple-framed smile waiting for me when I manage to open my eyes. The room is a thousand times too bright, the permanent grogginess embedded into my skull magnifying tenfold.

"Like a sack of shit." I grumble. "Tell me I'm hallucinating and I'm not where I think I am." Garrett's smile drops, his brows pinching as if he was expecting me to say something else. Instead of answering me, he releases my hand and shifts to slowly lift me up by the shoulders. After stuffing his pillow behind my back, I sink back in my new elevated position and look around the room from my childhood. Yep, I'm really here. The midnight blue painted walls and solar system project I made in fifth grade hanging by astronaut-themed drawn curtains. Not that they are doing anything to block out the sun's powerful rays which leave me squinting.

"There was nothing I could do," Garrett says under his breath and flicks off a huge TV he must have carried in whilst I was asleep. Snuggling up to my side, black lounge pants cover his long legs and I unashamedly run my finger over his bare abs. It's so easy to get caught up in moments like this, Garrett's body warmth seeping into me and his eyes completely focused on mine.

My pain ebbs away with the rest of the world, a fantasy of him being solely mine teasing me with its impossibility. Garrett will never tie himself to one person when there's so many others falling at his feet, and who can blame them? To anyone else, he's a handsome college kid with honey streaks in his hair to match his light eyes, a natural on the basketball court, always has an easy smile and joke dancing around his full lips, cash to burn on whatever he desires.

But none of that is what I see. I see the barely contained monster living beneath his flesh, the one that craves affection but strives to push it away. The one that refuses to believe he deserves more than rough sex and empty promises.

His eyes drop to my lips briefly which I lick on cue, making him swallow hard and turn away. "Anyway," he continues, "Sharon's barely even here half the time. She's married some rich dude and is playing secretary at his firm. Besides, I won't be leaving your side, not even when you need a piss." As if on cue, all the fluid in my body floods south and I groan in discomfort. Nudging Garrett to prove that statement, I start to push myself up despite the anguish it causes me.

"Hey, relax - you have a catheter. You can just go whenever you feel like it." Garrett tries to gently push me back down, but I refuse, nausea rolling through me. I don't want to picture my junk all rigged up but now it's all I can think of and I throw up in my mouth a little at the thought.

"Well get it the shit out. I'm not using that." I scoff, slowly swinging my legs off the side of the bed as Garrett runs from the room and returns a moment later with a bearded man I vaguely remember, his black bag in hand again. Only the stethoscope around his neck tells me he's a doctor of sorts, his black t-shirt and jeans nerving me. Who is this guy peeling off the duvet to inspect my dick and is he even qualified to do it? This could be some random that bought a prop and-

"Holy fucking dicksickles!" I roar as he starts to pull the tube out with excruciating slowness, falling back into Garrett's lap on the mattress. Tears leak from my clenched eyes, my hands ripping holes in the bedsheet and chest heaving in the aftermath of the worst pain I've ever felt. A soft snigger reaches my ears which has me hunting for its origin. Garrett's eyes glazed are with mirth as he bites down on his fist, bubbles of laughter escaping him regardless. "You're rubbing that better," I sneer when I start to breathe normally again, thumping his thigh pathetically.

"Deal," he winks playfully. The doctor stays between my legs and takes the opportunity to check on the dressing strapped to my abdomen. I push up onto my elbows with curiosity, wanting to see what the fuss is all about. The bandage is lifted to reveal a thinly stitched line below my belly button, pink and raised. A glint of metal flashes in my mind's eye, some beefy guy dressed in black lunging for me, a high-pitched scream.

"Avery!" I suddenly shift, searching the room as if she'll magically appear and groaning in reaction. "Is she- "

"She's safe, she's here in fact. I'll tell you everything soon enough, just focus on getting better for now. I'll take care of everything else." Garrett soothes me by stroking my head, his lop-sided smile leaning over me. His undivided attention sends a flurry of butterflies through my stomach that have nothing to do with the re-dressing of my wound and everything to do with man who will definitely be my downfall. A faint click from the door closing sounds as he bends forward, his hair tickling my cheek a second before his lips press against mine with the softest brush. A gentle caress that brings every nerve ending to life, electricity coursing through my body.

The rest of the world melts away, the movement of his mouth on mine pulling every morsel of raw emotion to the surface until I'm left tingling and breathless. His tongue darts across my bottom lip as I break to inhale, my hand snaking up to pull him back down forcefully. Our tongues tangle as if they never thought they'd get this chance again, feverishly fighting for more and more. My discomfort is a distant memory, only me and him in this moment I never want to end. For one brief minute in time, he's wholly mine. Pulling back slowly, Garrett kisses the tip of my nose and smiles with that dimple popping, heart stopping smile I could happily drown in. *Damn, I might get stabbed more often.*

Huxley

Avery moaning in her sleep distracts me from the hardback in my lap, Meg's name falling from her lips. I'd woke hours ago in my makeshift bed on the floor, restless and unable to drift off again. Luckily, this particular guest room in Axel's home has been used as the storage space for all his dad's possessions. Boxes of classic literature, ornaments, even some of the finest suits I've seen line the opposite wall. Ignoring the morbid truth that someone's life can be packed up and stashed away as if they never existed, I'd gone in search for a reason to stay beside Avery while she slept and found the entire works of Truman Capote in perfect condition. Axel doesn't speak of his father often, but I do know he was beyond rich and surprisingly humble about it.

Another shuffle and groan sounds to my left, Avery gripped in the throes of the nightmare she's had every night since Meg was taken. Placing the book onto the floor beside me, I kneel up to soothe the crease from between her eyebrows with my thumb. Her face relaxes on a deep exhale and she leans into my touch for a moment. If she were awake, she'd have lurched back and refused any comfort I could offer. That's why I offered to sleep on the floor beside her, close enough to protect her but far enough away to not let anything happen in the night. She'd only hate herself for it in the morning.

Once her breathing has deepened again, I take one last look at the serenity in her features. Long eyelashes fan her pale cheeks, her golden hair shining in the early morning rays. *Get some rest my angel.* Grabbing a fresh set of clothes from my bag, I sneak out into the corridor and close the door with a soft click. The bathroom is only the next room along but I stroll slowly, letting my eyes roam over the interior bathed in daylight after arriving in pitch black last night. I'd stayed in mansions before, but this one is by far the grandest.

Wooden beams line the ceiling in a geometric pattern that matches the marbled flooring beyond the bannister. A glimmering chandelier sits central above the winding staircase, its crystals bathing me in a shimmering sea of light. Pointed archways frame either end of the hallway adding to the thick, wooden doors giving the building a gothic feel. Trailing my finger along the mahogany bannister, paint fumes travel to me through the maze of corridors. The butler who showed us to our room last night briefly spoke of the recent renovations in an irritable tone that matched the way he spoke about his employer and her new husband.

After a quick wash and change in an equally lavish double bathroom, I go in search for breakfast. Not that I'm hungry in the slightest, but I promised myself I needed to make the effort and restore my strength if I'm going to stand a chance of protecting Avery. Twice now I've been beaten down and rendered useless. My masculinity took a bashing the first-time round, but I refuse to sink any further into the rabbit hole. I need to be better. Her life could depend on it.

Turning towards the wide staircase, a door at the end of the hallway catches my eye. Not because its white unlike all the rest which are a range of the deepest and richest browns, but because there's a small rectangular sign on this one. Creeping forwards, curiosity filling my veins, the sign comes into focus. A starry background sits behind a suited astronaut with 'Axel's Room' scrawled in the centre. My heart squeezes and I have to turn away, the innocence of the boy who endured so much torture behind this door making me feel sick.

Shuffling sounds just as the door swings open, an exhausted looking Garrett appearing in the doorway with a towel clutched in his hand. His hair is long enough to cover his eyes when he allows it to flop forward like this, a yawn pulling his mouth wide open. Scrubbing a hand over his face, he pulls the door closed behind him and almost crashes into me. Jumping out of his way, he continues up the hallway without looking back. My gaze flicks to the door handle, wondering if Axel might be awake yet.

"Don't even think about it," Garrett shouts back to me, entering the bathroom and slamming the door shut. *What an asshole.* I don't know why I'm surprised Garrett is still as much a possessive dick as always, maybe I figured he'd have realized by now we're his family and we're not going anywhere. But no, Garrett takes what he wants, pisses on it like a dog marking his territory and then leaves it chewed up and worthless to anyone else. I hope Axel manages to escape with his heart intact, but he's a grown ass man and it's not my problem. I'll just be here to pick up the pieces.

Jogging downstairs and emerging in the kitchen, a whole team of staff lift their heads to greet me kindly. A guy around my age with a top knot hiding beneath a netted cap grins at me while stirring a huge pan of pasta. Beside him, a group chat easily as they make subs in a production line and another pair are preparing tubs of salads on the far end of the middle island. It doesn't escape me they all seem to be of college age, cementing my suspicions that Axel's mom is still every bit the predator she used to be. A busty brunette in a maid's outfit I'm sure is from a sex shop strides past, giving me a seductive side glance as she walks past.

"You guys know its barely 8am, right? Forget pastas and salads, where's the bacon and pancakes?" I slip on an effortless smile and slide into a stool opposite Top Knot. It's been too long since I was social, and I hope I'm pulling off the easy-going friend-to-all I used to be. Top Knot grins wider while a girl to his right balks, quickly turning to whip out some flour and eggs. "No, I didn't mean- "

"It's cool man, whatever you want – we can do. Anything for a friend of Axel's, we've heard so much about him. He's like Steve Jobs and we're his apples." Okay, that's officially strangest thing I've ever heard. Feeling eyes on me, I glance around to the others who quickly drop their awe-filled gazes and giggle like schoolgirls, even the men. "To answer your question, its Sunday. We prep lunches and meals for while we're at college during the week and return on Fridays to stay. Although Sharon requested extras to be made for while you and your friends are staying." I narrow my eyes at his first-name basis with Axel's mom, feeling like I'm missing something obvious.

The girl beside him lifts a saucepan onto the hob and pours in pancake batter. Other than the maid, they are wearing their own clothes with the additions of plastic gloves and hair nets. A white t-shirt hugs her curvy frame with a Gucci logo displayed across the front. A heart shaped diamond hangs from her neck that dangles forward as she checks the pancake I'm now going to have to eat out of politeness.

"This weekend job must pay really well," I say, gesturing to the Rolex sitting on Top Knot's skinny wrist with a splash of pasta sauce flicked across the glass face. The permanent smirk on his face remains but no more words pass his lips, the twinkling of a secret held within his eyes. Dax slips into the stool beside me, sliding his arm around my shoulder to pull me in for a quick hug. I enjoy the contact more than I should, my chest instantly loosening with his presence. I hadn't realised how unnatural it's been without Axel initiating the hugs and gentle touches between us, or the growing void we are all drifting in.

Throwing my inhibitions out the window, I reach over and drag his head down onto my shoulder. Snaking my fingers into his Afro, his muscles relax on a contended sigh. Several pairs of eyes shoot our way, but not with judgement. Hints of jealously and encouragement flare to life in the staff's faces, Top Knot frozen in place with a look of longing to join us. I clear my throat to pancake girl, jolting her back into action to serve up my stack of pancakes and push them towards me while nibbling her bottom lip. I move the plate between Dax and I, sharing the fluffy goodness with him in silence.

The staff refocus on their tasks, busying themselves with the various meals before packing them into individual portioned boxes. Each container has a white sticker with today's date placed on top and is stacked into the double doored refrigerator neatly. Dax is still slumped against my body as they all finish up and mostly leave. A few hang back, Top Knot included, clearly waiting for some kind of invite to join us which I can't help but snarl at. The sound leaving my throat has them scattering like cockroaches after a light has been switched on, leaving us in peace at last.

"How is she?" Dax mumbles, not needing to say her name for me to know who he means. There's a lot to be seen from the outside of a conflict, the pining stares and misconstrued intentions. Each squandered opportunity to fix their issues and petty words covering their true feelings. I also notice how Avery is desperately trying to ignore the attraction and the way Dax refuses to beg for her forgiveness. All of which have nothing to do with me and I won't be dragged into their squabbles like a referee whose team is falling to shit.

"Ask her yourself." I mumble, slipping from the stool and leaving him to mope alone. Turning the corner, I come face to face with a snooping butler that I recognise. His thinning dark hair is combed over, a grey speckled moustache lining his upper lip. He's the only member of staff I've seen who is above college age, his pressed white shirt, black slacks and shiny shoes showing years of professionalism. I raise an eyebrow and square my shoulders, waiting for him to stop spluttering over himself.

"Oh, er – excuse me, Sir. Mrs Barrett has requested your

presence." I frown, wondering why Axel's mom thinks I would come running because she clicked her slender fingers.

"Are you sure it's me she wants?"

"Unless you know of another 'stacked blonde' staying here at the moment?" He air quotes with a roll of his eyes, his posture speaking volumes of his attitude towards Sharon. I tap my chin with my index finger, pretending to be lost in thought.

"Maybe she means Avery, that girl is tougher than bull picking a fight with a red brick wall."

"I'm willing to bet my life she means you," he mumbles before turning and leading the way. Forced to follow, I drag my feet and take the opportunity to glance out of the floor-to-ceiling windows lining this side of the mansion. A perfectly green setting lies before me, rows of automatic sprinkles spraying across the manicured lawn. At the far end, a metal cage is just visible which houses the tennis courts. Passing through an extravagant and barely used living area, hammocks swing gently in the breeze on the patio. The butler leads me through the spider web of hallways, passing various rooms before turning sharply and opening a door at the far end.

The space inside is dim, electric lanterns descending alongside a hidden staircase. Sulphur tickles my nose and a brush of humidity makes me thankful I opted for a simple vest and shorts combo. The butler ushers me towards the steps before closing the door, leaving me in almost complete darkness. Squinting and trying not to fall, I feel each step with my bare foot before stepping down until I find myself in an underground chamber.

The room has been decorated to look like a cave, the bumpy walls and curved ceiling painted stone grey. Sounds of the rainforest echo from hidden speakers, insects chirping and frogs croak between the hollow droplets of rain. Two leather massage tables sit to the left, below shelves of small bottles and rolled towels. Artificial vines have been draped around blue lights which reflect on the water filling the centre of the room. At the back of the round jacuzzi Axel's mom is eyeing me hungrily.

"I thought you could use some relaxation. I can see from a mile off how tense you are." She licks her cherry red lips and unashamedly tracks each my biceps with her pale brown eyes. Fighting the impulse to cross my arms defensively, knowing it would only make me appear more muscular than I really am, I stand loosely with unhidden hatred filling my features. If I wasn't worried she would kick us all out and Axel would be trapped in a house alone with her again, I wouldn't have been able to restrain my tongue from spilling every curse word and name I have rolling around my mind at her.

"I'm good." I shrug and turn to leave, splashing behind telling me she's rushing to stop me. I manage to jerk back before her wet, slender hand lands on my shoulder, growling for her to step back. In no versions of this world would I have ever found her attractive, regardless of the things she's done. A black bikini top barely covers her huge, clearly fake, breasts, her stomach unrealistically slender. Her thigh is covered with black ink in the shape of a large cat, it's body on the prowl and fangs exposed in a hiss. I'm almost certain it's supposed to be a cougar. *Shudder*.

"You seem so stressed. Why don't you let me help relieve you?" she tiptoes to whisper into my ear but is careful not to touch me. Yet.

"What about your husband?" I try to play the loyalty card, not that I thought it would work. Her chest brushes mine before I take a step back in time, bile rises in my throat.

"Oh, don't mind him, he's banging his secretary."

"You are his secretary," I deadpan. She giggles like life is some big fucking joke. She can screw who she wants, abuse who she wants and will never face any repercussions.

"Handsome and intuitive, what a catch. Seriously, have a

massage on me." She winks, sashaying her hips across the room to stroke the massage table. Her talons lightly scratch the leather, the cocky smile her face showing she actually thinks I'll be persuaded. Reaching over the table, pushing her ass high into the air, she pushes a button on the wall I didn't notice. The sound of a door opening reaches my ears although I can't see it from this angle, a man appearing a moment later. He doesn't spare me a glance, his eyes trained on Sharon. His dark skin is well oiled, muscles flexing with each step in nothing but a tiny pair of purple briefs. *Oh, for the love of emasculation, tell me that's not his uniform.* I can't hold back any longer, the audacity of it all overwhelming me.

"You really are a vile creature, you know that?" The falter in her practised smile makes me smirk in turn as I leave her behind. Jogging up the stairs, I shake off the vibes of overaged smut and shift my mind back to the girl I care about instead. The only one that really matters. We've got work to do to save her sister and get out of this house as soon as possible. It's time to wake up Avery.

Wyatt

"You don't have to wait on me hand and foot, you know," I tell Rachel yet again after she plants a tray of breakfast on my lap. Lashings of bacon and thick sausages sit upon a bed of fluffy scrambled egg with crispy hash browns balanced on top. My mouth is watering just from the heavenly smell as I push myself upright against the headboard. I woke naturally a little while ago from the best sleep I can remember having, and I don't think the memory foam mattress is the only reason for that. Back in the black dress with white collar and apron she likes to wear during the days, Rachel has a skip in her step and huge smile spread across her face as she rounds the bed to fluff my pillow.

"I know, but I've missed this so much. Please don't take it away from me." She mock flutters her thick eyelashes and pouts her lips, causing me to smile. Rolling my eyes, I stab a sausage with my fork and push it between my teeth as she releases a school-girl worthy squeal. I didn't miss the double meaning in her words, her natural motherly nature having been suppressed since she lost Sydney all those years ago. I can't fathom how she has managed to pull through such a loss and not withered up inside like I would have.

While I eat, she potters around my room. First, opening the black-out curtains to almost blind me with the sun's rays, then scooping my worn clothes from the cream carpet. I've never been one to tidy up after myself since I was mostly raised by staff looking for a pay rise or had a wealth of girls at college eager to please me. Rachel disappears into the en-suite and a shadow catches my eye by the triple wardrobe, green orbs gleaming out of the undefined shape. Following the figure's eye-line, I glance down to the two rounded tablets on my tray beside a glass of orange juice. Indecision pulls me in two directions, not seeing the harm in keeping my mom around now I've made my peace with her presence and wanting to pretend I'm a normal guy that isn't going insane.

"Rachel," I call, unable to keep up the pretence they are vitamins any longer. Her ponytail swings as she bounces back into the room, halting at my uncertain expression. "Why have you been drugging me?" I point to the pink pills and watch the frown pull at her lips. Slowly sitting on the edge of the bed, she turns to me with so much grief in her eyes, I can barely stand to look.

"Oh, my darling boy, I hope you won't be angry with me." She sighs and hangs her head, a tear trickling down her cheek. Pushing my tray aside, I pull her into my arms so her head rests upon my shoulder and reassure her that will never be the case. "They are antidepressants from my personal stash, I've been on them for longer than you've been alive," she huffs a laugh.

"So why are you giving them to me?" I whisper, still not understanding.

"I love having you here, you know that right? But a part of me wishes you never came. You're too pure for this place, but joining Ray is a lifelong commitment which will eat away until there's nothing left. I've seen it happen to so many, all traits of their personalities drained until they are mindless drones with 'Perelli' branded on their asses. I thought if I could intervene before you started to be affected by the terrible doings that happen here, I could shield you from the same fate." Stroking the tears from her cheek, I simply hold her as those words churn in my mind. Rachael has told me before she stays out of Ray's business, but clearly, she is still touched by it. Before she even knew me properly, she saw someone worth saving and fuck if I don't love her all the more for it.

"Anyways, I'd best get on. Ray is due back at some point today. Be sure to take this down to your friend, I reckon the guards are watching me a little too closely now." Rachel picks up a styrofoam container she'd left on the bedside table and places it into my hands with a wink. A wave of steam escapes the box as I open it, a miniature version of my breakfast concealed within. Raising an eyebrow and opening my mouth to refute the 'friend' comment she made, Rachel whirls out and clicks the door shut behind her.

After a good stretch and a quick change, I glance back at the container on the bed with a frown. It must have been days since Meg ate properly, and its fricking cold down there. She could have hypothermia already, not that I care. But if Rachel is prepared to ease her suffering before Ray has his way, then the least I can do is aid her too. Besides, I've done my part – I delivered her here. I never agreed to torture her pointlessly too. She's a part of someone else's plan, a means to someone else's end.

Pulling a second pair of cotton pyjama pants and socks on, I also don another top layer and head out of the room with the box in my hand. Taking the central stairs two at a time, I notice several guards pacing outside the lower windows as if they are expecting an attack. A man walks across the entrance hall, grinning at me shrewdly as if he recognises me but I'm sure I've never seen him before. His eyes are different colours, one brown and one blue, with a scar etched into his right eyebrow. He's a strange mix of scrawny arms and legs, but with a rounded gut and slouch to his posture.

Waiting on the bottom step for him to pass with a '*don't fuck with me*' scowl imbedded into my features, a soft chuckle escapes his crooked lips and he disappears. Creep. Rounding the bannister and reaching out for the hidden door's handle, I can already hear Meg's singing. Inching down the stone steps, I take a moment to listen to the eerily beautiful words leaving her lips, speaking of unfulfilled dreams and forgotten wishes. The electronic lanterns I left on are still faking flickers across the grey walls and casting shadows within Meg's cell via the open grate. Reaching into my hoodie pocket, I remove the padlock's key and unhitch the chain before slipping inside.

"Good morning," Meg halts mid-lyric to beam up at me from her place on the floor. "Well, if it's even morning? I slept like the dead so who knows. Oops, maybe I shouldn't be using that metaphor – yet." She giggles to herself, sitting upright in an electric blue sleeping bag. Foil packets glint in the dim lighting and an empty bottle is beside her head. Oh Rachel, your big heart is going to get you in so much shit.

"It's morning," I confirm gruffly and hold the container out for her, ignoring her jab about there being no coffee. Shutting the door behind me, I reach through the grate to secure the padlock in place and slump onto the hard floor. Meg groans loudly, chewing on a rasher of bacon with her eyes closed. Her hair is a ruffled mess around her shoulders like she's been fucked each way until Sunday, and I hate to admit I prefer it that way. My t-shirt still hangs from her, the short sleeves making me feel cold even through my two layers of clothing.

Remembering why I'm doubly dressed, I pull a rolled-up t-shirt from the pocket of my extra hoodie before shedding it, along with my top pyjamas and socks. Throwing them across to Meg, who is too huddled over her food to notice, I watch her with fascination.

"Does anything ever affect you?" I have to ask, knowing I would be going insane already if the roles were reversed. Is she incredibly resilient or has she in fact already floated about with the fairies? Snapping off a chunk of the lid to use as a scoop for her eggs, she shrugs at me.

"Only if I let it. But I'm more interested in why I'm being

honoured with a visit from Perelli's puppet himself. I thought you'd be too busy being patted on the head for being such a good boy to show your face down here again." My eyes slide away, refusing to be goaded, noticing the toothpaste and soap on the sink, and shaking my head slightly. Shall we just order her a personal masseuse and get it over with?

"I was bored, thought I'd come to torment you for a little while. Or we could wrestle again, that was good fun." The devil is definitely present on my shoulder today, pushing me to play a dangerous game I might actually end up enjoying.

"If you are looking to have your ass handed to you again, I'll always be ready. But considering this cell is small enough without you slumped across it, how about I beat you at something else?" Placing down her empty container, Meg now sees the clothing and hurries to dress.

Standing before me, she lifts the hem of my shirt she's wearing and slips it over her head in one movement. My jaw literally drops, finding her bare underneath. I'd tried to avoid looking during our shower but now, with the light bouncing from her hardened nipples and the shadow curving beneath her full breasts, my tongue is threatening to hang out of my mouth. The hourglass dents to her waist sway as she stretches for my benefit until I manage to grit my teeth and look away. A shudder rolls along my body and through the hardened length of my cock as she dresses, my fingers itching to stop her.

A small rock bouncing off my chest has me swinging back to see her sitting once again, cross legged and grinning ear to ear. She's tucked the pyjama legs into my socks which reach halfway up her shins and zipped my hoodie all the way up to her chin. Leaning forward with her own rock in hand, she uses it to draw a grid on the stone slab between us and puts an 'X' in the top left-hand corner. Is this seriously what it's come to?

Snorting, I place a 'O' in the centre. She sniggers as if I've already made a mistake and plays her next turn while rolling her tongue across her teeth. A challenge lights in her eyes, daring me to try and beat her. I continue to thwart her every move until I realise my mistake, seeing too late she has three corners and will win by default. Refusing to see that happen, I draw a new grid next to it and we start over. And over. And over. Until the floor is covered and we've shifted onto the walls.

I'm too distracted by her body language to concentrate, losing game after game of fucking noughts and crosses because she's pushing her tongue into her cheek or nibbling her bottom lip. Pushing up onto her knees, she leans across me to place her damn 'X' on the space next to my mark, her body pressing against mine. My mouth is too close to her jaw, filling me with notions I shouldn't even be considering.

"Wouldn't it have been nice if we'd could have had a chance to do this, you know...before." She turns her head, the gleam of her eyes looking directly into mine. I sit back on my feet to put some distance between us, needing to clear my head.

"You wouldn't have spent time with me willingly before you were forced to." I respond not liking how desperate I sound. Dropping the rock, I swivel to sit on her sleeping bag and pull my knees up to my chest. That's enough games for today.

"Ha, well I briefly thought I was dating you at one point. How idiotic is that?" My eyebrows raise in surprise as she nudges down beside me, urging her to explain. I hang off every word as she relays her catfishing story, unable to hold back my laughter when she describes the scrawny ginger guy who eventually turned up in my place. Her joyful presence is so alluring, especially in her final days. The thought kills my mood as I wonder how I thought eliminating such a bright light from the world would set me free.

"What if it had been me?" I ask quietly, knowing this conversation is fruitless.

"Well, at the time I had wanted it to be," she admits shyly. I can't tell but from the way she ducks her head into her shoulder, I imagine she's blushing.

"And now?" I press on, needing to hear her answer for some unknown reason. It's pointless but feels important to me all the same. I need to know if there was a chance I could have been saved from this fate, guided down another path.

"Now...I don't think you even know who you are anymore so I can't make that assumption. You don't have to live up to whatever these people expect of you, you can still-"

"*These people* accept me for who I truly am, a cold-hearted monster. I've done things you wouldn't even believe." My eyes cut across to the hunched figure scratching at the wall in the corner. She shouldn't be down here, not after what she suffered in a cell like this because of me. I need to get her out. Standing suddenly, my fingers begin to shake as I pull the key from my pocket and hurry to unlock the chain on the outside. A cold sweat beads on my forehead, guilt shredding my insides. Meg is talking but I can't hear her over the blood rushing through my ears, and when her hand lands on my shoulder, I shrug her off roughly.

"Don't go thinking I can change, Sweetness. I was born from a crackhead, there's poison running through my blood stream. This is exactly who I was always destined to be, like you were destined to rot down here."

Avery

My fist connects with Huxley's jaw, pain slithering across my knuckles. "Stop holding back," I growl, bending low to throw my shoulder into his abs. I manage to push him a step backwards before he twists sideways so I stumble forward. Catching myself before my face becomes best friends with the floor, I swing out my leg and groan as our shins crash together. "Fuck!" I shout, hopping on my good leg and holding the other to my body. This isn't working. I'm so far off my game, I can't concentrate and Huxley's not even trying to retaliate anymore.

"Maybe we should take five, have a short rest?" Huxley offers, helping me to hop over to the wall. I slouch back and rub the latest addition to the mass of bruises and bumps on my leg. Rolling my grey leggings back down, I peel off the matching vest and square my shoulders in a hot pink sports bra.

"I can't rest; I need to be ready." For what, who knows but it helps me from feeling restless. Useless.

"Burning yourself out won't do anyone any good either. We've been at this for two hours now. Let's get some lunch." My eyes slide past Huxley's head to see the sun has almost drifted directly overhead beyond the skylight, not that time has any concept to me anymore. Sleep is no longer a blessing while my mind is plagued with visions of Meg suffering, so I was happy to be woken by Huxley and dragged down to the gym. The space is clearly one of the newly renovated rooms in the house, each machine sparkling in chrome with no sign of use.

"You go ahead, I'll be out soon," I lie. Moving over to a rack of dumbbells, I lift my usual weight before deciding against it, putting it back and selecting the next one down. I need to improve, push myself to uncomfortable limits. Huxley sighs loudly as he leaves, grabbing his t-shirt from the floor on the way out. The samurai scene splayed across his entire back shifts as he walks, the flex of building muscle beneath making me envious. It's been so easy for him to bulk up while I'm struggling to even feel stronger.

Falling into a routine of lifting the dumbbells into the air and dropping into a squat, sweat runs a line down my spine and my thoughts consume me. I know Meg's alive; I can feel it in the pit of my soul, but that's where my certainty ends. The lengths Wyatt will go to in hopes of proving himself to Perelli are my biggest concern. The second she's safe, he's a dead man walking. No matter what it takes, I'll be ready to make sure of that. Huxley's been a godsend, helping me train and keeping me busy because he understands. I don't need saving, I need support.

A shadow to my left makes me flinch. Cursing under my breath that I wasn't focused enough to notice him approaching, I turn my back to Dax and continue squatting. This time, as I rise, I lift a leg, so the opposite elbow meets it in the middle and crunch my core tightly. My hair has fallen free of its bun, the hairband hanging loosely on the end, but I won't stop. I can't stop. Large hands land on my hips, holding me still as Dax closes in behind me. His hair tickles my ear, whispering for me to take a break.

For a moment, I yearn to step back and let his warmth envelope me. Let his hands roam my flesh and lips erase my thoughts for a while. Sensing my defeat, his head leans onto mine and his thumbs paint slow circles over my leggings. What a pretty world he must live in, where hugs can heal wounds and words can grant wishes. But I learnt long ago, wishing is pointless. No one genuinely cares and no one fixes your problems without an ulterior motive. Clenching my jaw, I decide to allow

Dax to give me exactly what I really need right now – target practice.

Dropping the rubber weights onto the blue mat at my feet, I twist to throw an elbow into his ribs. An oomph of shock leaves his lips as I wheel around, slamming my palms into his chest to put some distance between us. A black tank top hugs his muscles like a second skin, his biceps falling loosely either side and baggy shorts hanging to his knees. Tearing my eyes away before I do something stupid, like lunge at him for a whole different reason, I turn to leave. His hand suddenly fists into my hair as he pulls me back into him with a yelp of surprise, his lips brushing against my ear.

"Isn't this what you wanted? To hurt me?" His voice is gravelled, as if he's drowning in anguish, he has no right to feel. He made his bed, and I'm gonna make sure he stays in it. Stomping like a spoilt brat, Dax releases a bark of pain as my boot slams onto his bare toes. Jerking forward, I manage to escape his hold, ducking across the room to retie my hair high onto my head. His piercing blue eyes are locked on mine while we slowly prowl around each other.

The air around us stills, the tension begging to be broken. Quickly rushing forward with a battle cry, I leap into the air to lock my legs around his middle, tugging on his Afro in the bitch move he used on me. I'm thrown onto my back with his weight crashing on top, causing the air to whoosh from my lungs sharply. I wriggle, not letting him grab my wrists like he's trying to and throw punches into his side in quick secession. Somehow managing to shift my knees into between the cage of our bodies, I push him aside and roll away quickly. Scrambling up to my feet, his hand catches my ankle and drags me back down.

Throwing my free foot backwards, it connects with his face and I still. Glancing over my shoulder, Dax is smirking around his busted lips like a crazed lunatic. Its then the truth hits me. He wants me to hurt him, wants to be punished. And knowing I'm playing right into his hand ruins the appeal to me. "Let go," I huff, shifting to sit on the mat and glare at him irritably.

"You can't just decide to quit when Perelli's men are after you," he growls, tightening his grip on my ankle. Dragging me closer, Dax shifts to crawl up my body until his heaving chest is brushing mine. "You can never stop fighting, even if you feel like there's nothing left to fight for." My eyebrows remain dipped, a scowl cemented into my features for him. I attempt to swiftly jerk my knee upwards to catch him in the balls, only to find my thighs are pinned beneath his. Pushing at his chest, he catches my hands and lifts them above my head, leaving me open and vulnerable. He grinds the bulge in his pants against my core and I hate myself for the flood of heat that pools there.

"If it comes to being me or Meg, I won't fight at all." I breathe, failing to keep my eyes away from his lips. Those lips that promised to protect me, begged me to be his. They press into a hard line, his frustration clear but I simply shrug. "I'm just a means to an end. I've been telling you this whole time; my life has no worth."

"To me it does! I couldn't protect my mom from my dad before she died, so I won't let you throw your life away." He grits through his teeth, pushing himself upright with a slight shove at my restrained hands. I lie still, watching him stalk from the room with his posture more rigid than a metal rod. Sighing, I shift my hands beneath my head as stare at the sun-kissed skylight above until I'm seeing spots. Dax will learn soon enough; not matter what he says I'll never value myself. That vague level of self-appreciation most people should have was stamped out of me and I've been ready to leave this world for a long time. He'll move on, eventually.

A tabby cat pads across the glass above me, the pink pads of its paws leaving dirty marks across the windowpanes. I chuckle to myself, following the animal until plops itself down and proceeds to lick itself. I bloody love cats. They don't give a shit about anything other than eating good food and staying dry, knowing humans are inferior to their constant whining. A sparrow flies overhead, drawing the feline's full attention until it takes chase. Running on agile white feet, the cat leaps high into the air off the edge of the building and falls out of sight. "Oh shit- "

"Don't worry about Comet, he's fucking invincible." A familiar voice I've missed draws my attention to the doorway. Axel is leaning against Garrett, their arms draped over one another like they can't get close enough. Shadows of hair growth are starting to show in certain spots across his head, emphasising how much of a shit job we did, and I stifle a laugh behind my hand. His amber eyes are twinkling, his smirk soothing a slither of my stress.

"Comet?" I snigger, pushing myself upright. The urge to run into his arms is overwhelming but the dressing strapped across his abdomen stops me. His torso is bare and black lounge pants hang low on his hips, the slight clench of his grip around Garrett's shoulders betraying his relaxed appearance.

"Don't judge me, I was six-years old and I've always been a nerd at heart. The brain needs exercise too." If it hadn't been for current circumstances, I'd have dropped my panties right there and thrown them at him. The heat-filled side glance Garrett's gives him tells me he feels the same, a mental image of Garrett in a matching pink thong to mine making me laugh out loud. A stitch pulls at my side from the strange tug of happiness, I can't pull back now it's been set loose. The pair eye me curiously, huge grins stretching across their faces as the laughter brings tears to my eyes. Damn, I really needed that.

Slinking across the room, Axel tugs me beneath his free arm, and we move into the living room. Garrett slowly places him down on the white sofa before sitting with a cushion on his lap and guides Axel's head down onto it. I take the end with his feet, carefully lifting them to slide underneath. The mansion is like a show house, everything pristine and beautiful, yet without a single trace of character. White sideboards hug the edges of the room, a shaggy rug fills the centre to take the cold edge off the marbled flooring. Opposite the sofa is a huge plasma TV and every console anyone could wish for, but the lack of cables in the back shows they've never been touched. I wonder if young Axel was even allowed in here or if he was kept locked in his room.

"Have you seen your mother yet?" I finally ask, filling the silence as we all spiral into our own dark thoughts. Garrett's jaw is clenched hard enough to crack a tooth, his usual relaxed demeanour seeming worlds away.

"I'd rather my eyeballs were removed than to see that woman again, although it is inevitable. For now, Garrett is doing a fantastic job at being my guard dog." Axel reaches up to scratch Garrett's jaw who begins to pant with his tongue hanging out in return. The pair share a sweet smile which I turn away from, feeling like an imposter in their moment and longing for a similar one myself. I must be seriously lonely to crave affection since I usually prefer my own company. Axel's foot nudges my stomach to bring my attention back to his amber eyes. "So, what happens now?"

"Now, you recover." I reply evenly. "That's all you need to focus on. I'll worry about getting Meg back."

"And how do you plan on doing that?" Axel's eyebrow quirks and Garrett turns to face me, his tired eyes laced with worry.

"I don't know yet," I grumble, looking away from the pair staring at me. "Meg knows I'll find a way, she's just gotta hold on. She's tougher than she looks." A sad smile graces my lips, knowing Meg will be giving anyone who dares come near her absolute hell. I'm just not sure what lengths her captors will go to in order to keep her in line.

Meg

"Okay, just one more...perfect!" Avery's blue doe eyes are twinkling from the fairy lights around her bed as she makes the final brush stroke across my cheek. Dipping the brush into a cup of water, she closes the lids on the face paints and turns me by the shoulders to face the mirror. I can't help but smile at her artistry as she gets straight to work on my hair, braiding it down the length of my back. Half of my face is a mask of colourful flowers ranging in all sizes from a large rose across my temple to delicate hidden daisies amongst the blossoms on my cheek and chin. The other side of my face is a decorative skeleton, jewels lining my whitened forehead with a hollow eye and invisible nose. Tying the two sides together is a toothy smile painted across my lips. She places a floral crown onto my head and claps excitedly. "This is going to be the best Halloween ever!"

"Only if you are ready, stop worrying about me and go get dressed," I giggle, although eternally thankful for all the effort she's made on my behalf. Skipping across the room to her walk-in wardrobe, she flicks her blonde hair over her shoulder to smirk at me.

"We both know your crush is going, and you need all the help you can get," she winks and disappears in time to avoid the cushion I throw at her. She's right though, he said he'll be at tonight's Halloscream frat party and I wouldn't have been able to replicate Avery's vision for me. Standing in the skin-tight jumpsuit, the polyester glued to my curves like it was also hand painted on, I push my feet into a pair of skinny black heels. The costume features a skeleton across the front and back, roses nestled into the bones with a raw,

bleeding heart in the chest cavity. Hot and dark, perfect.

Avery returns a moment later, effortlessly looking incredible. A PVC cat-suit covers her body except for the unzipped V flaunting her cleavage. There's a cute pair of cat ears upon her head, her golden length of her hair hanging across one shoulder to her waist where a coiled whip has been attached. Slinking over to the vanity in full feline mode, she paints three lines on each of her cheeks and turns to me with a grin. I now notice the yellow slits covering her irises which must be contacts and release an appreciative whistle. "Well aren't you the cat that got the cream?"

"Ugh, you sound like my mum when you say shit like that." Pushing her feet into leather biker boots in true Avery style, we leave the mansion arm in arm and hop into the waiting Rolls Royce. Jenson regards us in the rear-view mirror before easing the car down the driveway. A shiver rolls down my spine and I feel the strange sensation of being watched, which has me looking back to the looming building as we pull onto the street. A trick of my imagination sees a figure step out of the front door, which is absurd since we were the only one's home.

Avery uses her phone to crank up the music filtering through the speakers and the figure filters from my mind as she begins to dance in her seat. Falling into her swaying, we sing the rest of the short journey to my college campus and park a street over from the frat house. After thanking Jenson, we follow the thumping bass the rest of the way to avoid the chaos that comes with a 'Hughes' child in their midst. It's impossible to enjoy ourselves when the paparazzi are pushing a lens into her face and jumping down her throat for a drunken slogan to splash across the newspapers in the morning.

Rounding the house, spiderwebs hang from the bushes and carved pumpkins line the path, candles flickering inside. Strobe lights are leaking through the windows in time to the music, figures jumping inside with their fists firmly pumped in the air. In the top central window, a shadow is standing behind the glass pane, seeming to be staring at us as we strut up to the front door. Wow, these guys have really gone all out this year. Pushing the door open, I brace myself for the onslaught of music that is about to blast into me, but nothing comes.

Five figures in blood-red robes stand at the bottom of the staircase in front of us, the rest of the house is dark and empty. Their hoods are pulled low, casting their faces in shadows as we wait for something to happen. I reach out to grip onto Avery's hand, but my fingers meet the air and I spin around in search of her. She's gone. Twisting back, panic seizing my heart, the figures have also vanished, all expect for one. I know I should turn and run, but my feet stay rooted to the floor as I wait to see what will happen next.

My body is pulled closer of its own accord, my toes dragging across the wooden planks. I struggle and fight back but it's no use, the force of a thousand hands shoving me forward. Only when my chest is pressed against his do I stop, my breathing rapid and ice clawing into my bones. The house around us falls away, nothing but stone and shadows skirting my vision.

His hand suddenly reaches up, making me flinch as he drags a calloused hand down my cheek. There's longing in his touch, a wishful craving for something more. I can't help but lean into his touch, the warmth melting frost coated skin. His fingers trail lower, a path of heat skimming across my neck. The air around us changes a second before his hand clasps around my throat in an iron-tight grip, a choked noise leaving me in response. He applies more pressure, squeezing until I cannot draw breath and I feel my windpipe closing.

But the sense of dread I expected doesn't come, no flash of life before my eyes or praying for a miracle. Staring deep into the shadow beneath the hood, a pair of green eyes begin to glow with a blinding intensity. Despair and misery fill their empty depths and my last thought is how I wish I could have intervened sooner.

I jolt upright, sweat clinging to my skin and my breathing laboured from my nightmare. What the fuck was all that about? I try to grasp onto the important details my mind was trying to show me, but the dream slips away before I get the chance. Resting a hand on my chest, I focus on evening out my breathing and slump back against the wall. My mom would have a field day with me right now, she would have grabbed her 'Dreams and their Meanings' book from her impressive bookcase and flicking through the pages to analyse what I can remember.

A pang of guilt blooms in my chest for all the years I withheld my dreams and emotions from her. She's always been ready to delve into my mind, but I had worried she might not like what she found. The daughter of a therapist should be the straightest of arrows, no dark thoughts, or fantasies of running away like I've had multiple times over the years. She's been right there, willing to teach me coping mechanisms for the never-ending spiral of shit life dishes out and now I'll never get the chance to tell her how sorry I am for shutting her out.

Footsteps ring out from the steps beyond my door bring me back to reality, butterflies bursting to life low in my belly as I anticipate Wyatt's arrival. Wait, no. Clearly, they are fluttering around in dread, their wings singed and heavy with unease. That would make more sense than the former, otherwise I'm really messed up. But I have always had a thing for the wrong guys...

The chain is pulled free, its rattling vibrating through the cell and the door is yanked open. Wyatt's green eyes regard me for a second and I have the insane urge to run to him instead of away, until he steps aside to permit an aged man and his two guards' entry into my temporary residence. Shuffling forward with the support of a cane, the older man's shrewd eyes drag across my body in a way that leaves me feeling exposed and the ghost of a smirk appearing on his thin lips. His thin hair has been gelled back, the dim orange lighting emphasising the scars scattered across his leathery skin.

"Meg, is it?" I remain still, not fooled with his pleasantries. I know who this man must be by the loyalty seeping from the guards who refuse to leave his side as they all clamber into my cell. He's the reason I'm trapped here, his twisted vengeance bringing my life to an early end.

"Ray Perelli, I suppose you've come to kill me now. Get it over with then, the stench of death clinging to you says we'll be having a shared funeral at this rate." I square my shoulders boldly, even though I'm quaking inside. Will he use a knife to slit my throat or a gun to end me quicker? Or maybe he'll flood the cell with gasoline and set it alight. Perelli chortles, having to hold his side to keep his hip from snapping at the jerky movement. His guards remain statue still, no lights appearing on upstairs and I notice Wyatt hovering in the door nervously.

"Not yet, my dear. There's still two pieces of this puzzle missing. But I assure you, I'll hold you as long as it takes." My heart squeezes at his words, the thought of Avery still being hunted enough to shatter my resolve. Tears well in my eyes, a silent prayer resounding in my mind. *Run far, beautiful lady, and don't turn back.* Perelli seems to notice the mess around my cell, his eyebrows creasing as if he's going to reprimand me for not tiding my room.

"Who brought her these luxuries? This is a prison, not a fucking hotel." He slides his cane beneath my sleeping bag and chucks it towards the sink with as much strength as he can muster. The man before me isn't the mob boss I envisioned, but he doesn't need to be because he has something much more potent – power and money. That deadly combination is what keeps this place swarmed with armed guards and loyal men I won't be able to escape so easily from. I keep my mouth clamped shut, not owing him anything.

"I did," Wyatt's deep voice filters in from the corridor and my eyebrows rise. How interesting Wyatt should take the fall for some woman he barely knows, which leads to the questions of who is she and why does he care for her? Perelli growls dangerously, shunning me with his back and retreating. The guards step out shoulder to shoulder behind him, creating a wall of muscle I couldn't slip past if I tried. The door is slammed closed and chain locked back in place, my heart sinking with the knowledge I'm stuck in here for a long while yet. But as long as it takes for Avery to flee the country or whatever she had better be doing is fine by me.

The echo of skin on skin sounds and has me running to the steel bars to see Wyatt's head whipped sideways. Turns out the old man has more bite to his bark than I gave him credit for. His emerald eyes slip to me, the resounding misery from my dream confined within them. I'm failing to see any reason Wyatt would ally himself with this man or was he so adrift any option seemed better than being alone.

"Seems you have a soft spot for our prisoner, son. We don't have time for your weakness. As soon as Avery has been located and brought here, we will release the hydrogen chloride rigged up in each of the inner vents and burn them both from the inside out. Only then will Nixon know of the pain I've felt for the past twenty years." So, poison it is, real classy. Perelli smiles wickedly and reaches out to clasp Wyatt's shoulder who still has his eyes locked on me.

"Should we be speaking of the specifics in front of her?"

"She won't alive long enough to tell anyone." Patting Wyatt, Perelli begins to shuffle past with the guards hot on his heels. The trio slowly slink away into the darkness in the opposite direction to the stairs. My eyes track them until they've disappeared, the realisation that there must be another way out of here lifting my shattered spirits. Before I can start to hatch a plan, Wyatt's hands whip out to catch mine around the bars. His palms crush my knuckles against the steel, a whimper leaving my lips before I can stop it. His features are rigid with the promise of more pain etched into his face.

"If you ever tell anyone of the undeserving kindness Rachel has shown you, I'll kill you myself."

Avery

A knock at the door saves me from picking at my cuticles, although I was quite invested in making my chipped nails look longer after another day of sparring with Huxley. Readjusting the towel around my chest after a recent shower, I jump down from the bed with a sigh. Swinging the door open, two garment bags are thrown into my unsuspecting arms. The butler has turned and left before I can ask what these are for, a note on the bag catching my attention. '*Dining Hall 6pm.*' Frowning, I place the items onto the bed and unzip the first to find a black suit. Moving onto the second, I find a beautiful dress in navy satin staring back at me. The straps are strings of diamonds which follow the low dipped neckline to a sapphire-coloured gem at the bottom of the V.

Huxley joins me in the room a moment later, a matching towel hanging on his hips as he strides over to assess his suit. "I was ordered to change by that butler, he can be quite handsy when he feels like it." I snort a laugh, sifting the silky material through my fingers. I have no interest in dancing along to Sharon's tune, but my rumbling stomach protests loudly on cue. *I guess we're doing this.* Dropping my towel, I reach for the dress before feeling Huxley's eyes on my bare skin.

Straightening slowly, I meet his chocolate gaze and lick my lips on instinct. Huxley's been my rock these past few days and for a brief, selfish minute I'm prepared to throw my morals away and allow him to ease my troubles. Pushing up on my tiptoes, I press my palms to his chest. My fingers graze the circular scar by his collar bone, the steady beat of his heart thumping beneath my right hand. Strong and powerful, like him. We hold eye contact, our breaths mingling as his arms wind around me. Pulling me into the safety of his body, my eyes flutter closed as I close the distance between our lips.

His mouth moves against mine slowly, his hands holding me as if I'm made of glass. Too gently for my liking. Snaking my arms around his neck, I pull on his waves to make him open his mouth and slip my tongue inside. His tongue piercing scrapes against my teeth, our mouths meshing awkwardly. The coiling heat I was expecting in my core doesn't come and I end our kiss on an internal curse. Ugh, damn my stupid body for not giving me this. Stepping back, I offer him a weak smile as if nothing's wrong, but I can see by his expression there most definitely is.

"It's not the same anymore, is it?" he asks softly, his eyes already filled with understanding.

"No," I breathe. On paper, Huxley is an ideal catch. Roguishly handsome, beach blonde waves and pools of melted chocolate in his eyes, muscles for days, incredibly smart and beyond protective. But my lady-parts seem to be craving something a little darker, the twisted part of me preferring a little more damage to work with. He leans forward and presses his forehead to mine, the citrusy scent from the shower gel we've both used coiling around us.

"I care for you and I'll protect you with everything I am, but I'm not the one for you."

"There is no *one* for me." I whisper. He pulls back with a roll of his eyes and disbelieving smirk, dropping a kiss onto my nose. We step out of our embrace that's bordering friendzone and begin to dress. Pulling the dress over my head, I let the material cascade down my body. It weirdly fits like a glove, the floor length skirt flaring out when I spin side to side. A pair of glittering, silver heels are at the bottom of the bag, a small jewellery bag tucked inside one which I leave on the bed. Walking over to the mirror on the vanity in the six-inch heels, I brush out my still damp hair and braid it over my shoulder.

Huxley's reflection dresses quickly, the extra-slim fit shirt barely fitting over his broad shoulders. His slacks are also too skinny, an unladylike snort leaving my nose as he turns to reveal his accentuated bubble butt. "What the fu- "he mumbles, straining to pull on the black blazer. I can only imagine Huxley's clothing choice was all too intentional as my outfit fit so well, every one of his muscles outlined through the suit. "No way, nope. Not doing it," he starts yanking the material off vigorously. Buttons fly and seams rip as I snigger, a naked again Huxley rummages in his bag for his dark jeans and white polo top.

"She's not going to be happy," I sing across the room. This only seems to spur him on, as he ruffles his hair into a shaggy mess. Smirking, I pick up my lip balm from the vanity's white surface and gloss a coat over my lips as Huxley moves in behind me. He drapes a heart-shaped sapphire around my neck and gently eases the matching studs into my ears, dropping the velvet bag onto the table in front of us. "You ready for this?" I ask, sharing a look of determination with him in the mirror. After a sharp nod, Huxley offers me his arm and we leave the room with two minutes to spare.

Butler Bill, as I started calling him in my head, is waiting for us at the bottom of the staircase. Dax, Garrett, and Axel are already by his side, their suits reminding me of the night they converted my dance studio into a nightclub. A sad smile pulls at my lips, simpler times seeming so distant now. Each one has gone for their own take on passive aggressive defiance – Dax has used his tie to fix his hair back in a fluffy ponytail, Axel's sleeves are rolled up to the elbow with his shirt only buttoned over his navel and Garrett is wearing his entire suit backwards.

Reaching the bottom step and feeling left out, I bend to grasp the side of the navy material in my hands and pull hard, ripping a slit all the way up to my hip. The guys break into cheers while Butler Bill seems to have an aneurysm, his eyes wide and breathing on pause. I reach over to adjust Garrett's tie knot at his nape and Axel turns to plant a kiss on my cheek, my heels making me almost eye height with the group for a change.

"Come on then, let's get this shit show over with." Axel prompts, striding forwards to lead the way. Garrett hurries to his side, complaining that he should still be resting while the rest of us follow them. My heels click loudly on the gleaming marble floor as we stroll from one side of the mansion to the other, every wall pristinely white with no homely additions in sight. No artwork, pictures of Axel, clocks, mirrors, nothing. Just closed wooden doors that match the network of beams crisscrossing overhead. Butler Bill shoves past me as we near a double doorway, rounded black iron doorknobs matching swirling decorations covering the timber.

"Ahh, Master Axel, your mother has requested we meet in the ballroom to begin-"he quickly fumbles for the handle, but Axel slams his palm on the door loudly. An echo of ringing silence follows, everyone holding their breath to see what happens next.

"No." Axel's quiet tone is laced with a deadly authority which surprises me, his amber eyes flicking back to me. "She's never going in there." I remain still except for an understanding nod, trusting his reasons without needing an explanation. Axel has so many demons within these walls, I'll do whatever I can to alleviate his struggle of being here. After a tense moment, I step forward to link my arm in his and gently pull him onwards to the open doors at the end of the hallway. A long dining table surrounded by lavish chairs is visible, so I take a lucky guess and hear the others fall into step behind us. We enter the room as a tight unit, ready to play out this charade and get back to our rooms as quickly as possible.

Velvet curtains in the richest shade of plum are drawn

over a row of windows, a similarly coloured shaggy rug beneath the table which has been set for ten. Gold flourishes line the ceiling and surround the chandelier hanging in the centre. At the far end next to a lit fireplace, a dark piano reminds me of home. Huffing behind us draws my attention to an approaching Sharon, an emerald green bodycon hugging her surgically enhanced body with a young man on her arm.

"Never one to follow the rules, were you Axel?" She mumbles, her lip peeling back in disgust as she assesses Garrett's outfit. "Ugh, do you ever take anything seriously?"

"Life's all shits and giggles until someone giggles and shits," he shrugs, and I snort loudly. Deciding to ignore him, Sharon pushes her way through us with her lapdog on her heels and turns back with her fake smile back in place.

"Well, no matter. I'd like to introduce you all to my husband, Richard Barrett." The pasty man puffs out his chest arrogantly, not intimidated in the least by the four guys that are all easily a foot taller and glowering at him like he's pissed in their milk. He's slim, his blue suit probably from the children's section, with blonde hair and a grotesquely large mole on his neck.

"Pleasure to meet you at last Axel," Richard has the balls to outstretch his hand, which I give him props for. Not that Garrett feels the same, stepping in front of Axel and slapping the offensive limb away with a snarl. Unphased, Richard slips his hand around Sharon's waist and pull her into his side possessively.

"I don't even know why I imagined you'd marry some rich bastard on his death bed, again. Of course this piece of jailbait is enjoying the house Axel's father worked so hard for." Garrett puffs out his chest in a challenge while Axel is happy to let him take the lead, no doubt thankful his personal bodyguard is blocking his view from the woman glaring at him. I shift closer and force my fingers into Axel's clenched fist, grief for his father clear in his tone.

“For your information-“ Sharon begins but Richard places a hand on her shoulder to cut in, an usually kind smile on his lips.

“There’s no need for the hostility *boys*. If you give me a fair chance to introduce myself, you’ll learn I have my own company, can provide more than enough for Axel’s mom and I’ve already started making some improvements on the house. This place will feel like a real home for all of us soon enough.” If Richard notices the way all four men surrounding me bristle and take a dangerous step towards him, his permanent smug grin doesn’t let it show.

Gently pulling on Sharon’s waist, he leads her over to a seat at the far end of the table. After she is seated and he’s placed a kiss on her head, he moves around the room towards the head of the table. I notice the chair in front of the piano is slightly different to the others, the back is higher with black armrests and a darker shade of purple cushioning. Axel spurts forward, clutching his side as he beats Richard to the chair, his stare alight with a challenge.

“Not fucking likely,” he growls, lowering himself into the seat carefully. Richard shrugs with his carefree smirk and takes the place by Sharon instead. Garrett settles himself on one side of Axel and Dax places his hand on my lower back to guide me to his other side. Tension clogs my throat, the tremors of an oncoming panic attack trickling down my spine. Family reunions aren’t my idea of fun anyway, but the friction in the air is unbearable. As Dax pulls my chair out for me, I have the strongest impulse to turn and run until my eyes flick back over to the piano.

Longing grips me. The glossy coat of black beaconing me over, a tune already sounding in my mind that has my fingers twitching. It’s been so long since I’ve felt the calming press of keys beneath my fingers, the soothing notes of my soul transforming into music. Twisting away from Dax, I cross the space and click my heels off without a care. I need this, and I'm pretty sure Axel could do with a distraction too. Draping my skirt behind me on the leather stool, I lift the lid and smile at the ivory keys. My old friends. Closing my eyes and tipping my head back, I let my fingers drift across the grooves until a melody sounds in my mind. One I've never played to an audience before but suits my mood perfectly.

My index finger presses down on the first note, a rigid cord in my spine snapping at the sound as the rest of my fingers join in. I wrote this piece myself, the soft flutter of notes reminding me of my mum on a summer's day. Her billowing skirts and loose hair twirling around her as she dances across the garden, the sounds of nature her only music. Full of light and life. With each chord that reaches my ears, I picture her land on pointed toes, her arms high in perfect arches like she would prod me to do during my ballet lessons.

The clouds overhead begin to darken, their fluffy texture growing heavy to match the weight pushing on my chest. My movements speed up, chasing the keys in an effort to save her. Large green eyes flick to me worriedly, pure panic gripping her delicate features. A fork of lightning flashes in the distance as my heart pounds in time with my fingers, the sweat covering my body coordinating with a sudden downpour of rain in my mind. She turns and runs, taking my soul with her as I use the melody to mourn her once again.

The crescendo I created lessens, my eyes cracking open to stare into the dancing flames carefully contained with the fireplace. I'm hot everywhere expect the empty hole in my chest, my hands shaking as I bring the piece to a close. The last few notes linger in the air, my fingers desperate to hang onto her memory for a few moments more. Dragging myself upright, I close the piano lid and inhale deeply, recovering from the onslaught of emotion that has left me blissfully numb.

"Holy shit," Dax's voice reaches me, but I ignore him. I

may have played in their company, but that release was solely for my benefit. The door opens abruptly, slamming back against the wall as a strikingly gorgeous blonde enters on painfully tall heels.

"Sorry I'm late, hope I didn't miss the fun."

Axel

My eyes remain glued on Garrett's face, the strength passing through his hand on my thigh the only reason I'm still in my seat. I'd happily bust my stitches to launch myself across this table and choke out that conceited son of a bitch tripping over himself to please my mom. Visions of each and every way I could hurt him are soothing my twisted soul after Avery's beautifully haunted music has brought every emotion I refused to feel to the surface. I could pummel him with my fists, smash a vase over his head, strangle him with the curtain tie. I appreciate he would be taking the brunt of my anger on behalf of my mother, but I don't hit women – even if they are psychotic bitches. And he must have known about our stained relationship when he married her, so I'm willing to bet he'd take any punishment I wish to deliver on her behalf. 'Til death do they part and all that.

The chair beside me scrapes back, a leg knocking mine beneath the table and I know instantly it's not Avery's. Garrett is looking at the unwelcomed guest curiously, but I honestly don't give a shit who it is. I knew my mother was up to something the second she requested my presence down here. We only ever had family dinners in this room on Christmas Day, my father sitting in this very chair while I built by recently unwrapped model rockets by his side. A high-pitched squeal draws me from my memory, breaking my intent focus on Garrett's lips to see Avery dragging the girl from the seat by a handful of her blonde hair.

"You're in my seat," Avery says calmly, shifting into place the second the leggy guest has scrambled out of the way. I smirk over and she throws me a subtle wink back. Without needing to be asked, Avery has my back and knowing that has my mood lifting instantly. I'm not the vulnerable kid I use to be, I'm the real man of this house now and with my Shadowed Souls around me, it's time to have some fun. Straightening her red dress with more composure than I'd have expected, Blondie moves further down to sit beside Dax just as a round of champagne arrives. Garrett immediately reaches over to remove the champagne glass that's place in front of me over to join his, catching the retreating waiter to request an orange juice for me since I can't drink on my meds. *Swoon.*

"This is Sasha," my mom speaks directly to me. "She is Richard's niece and is very- "

"I don't give a fuck," I interrupt, staring her dead in the eye. My plan to actively avoid her may have floated straight down shit creek but that doesn't mean I will be courteous. My mom pouts her pink lips as if that would change my attitude.

"I'm sure you two would hit it off if you gave her a chance. She's studying aerospace engineering and already has an apprenticeship waiting at NASA when she completes her degree." Huh, that does sound pretty cool but unfortunately for Blondie, she is associated with the devil incarnate by rubbing shoulders with my mother. "Maybe you should accompany her to the annual Caudwell Gala next month?" Blondie's dark eyes flick to me uncertainly and I can't tell if she's actually interested or also being forced into this farce.

"*If* I was going to attend some stupid gala where you will no doubt be, my preferred date would have a little more packaging between his legs." I reach over to slip my hand into the backwards collar around Garrett's neck and pull him close to rub noses with me. *Eskimo kisses.* Cocking his eyebrow, he stares at me expectantly until I've realised my mistake and a laugh escapes my lips. "Sorry, *a lot* more packaging."

"Come now, Axel. Stop being ridiculous, I want grandkids while I'm still young enough to enjoy them." I release Garrett to roll my eyes, finding a missed cobweb in the corner of the ceiling to stare at.

"Valuable goods, you mean," Garret scoffs. His grip tightens on my thigh, more likely to restrain himself from flying into a rage rather than in support of me but I still love that he's come to my aid. However, I know for a fact his vicious words or even breaking a bunch of valuable shit won't phase my mom. No, the way to get under her skin is by taking away what she really cares about – her money and popularity. That's why she hates me. I ruined her precious reputation when I refused to be her pretty, angelic boy and transformed myself into a menacing skinhead that bites back.

"There's no need for that, Gary," Richard chimes in. I instantly shift my gaze to Garrett's face, his expression turning murderous and I fight to hide my smirk. This should be interesting.

"Call my Gary again," Garrett twists to glare at him, "and I will yank your small intestine out of your mouth, rip your large intestine out of your ass and use you as a human skipping rope." A full bellied laugh leaves my throat, Richard's cool façade shattering with a look of horror. Avery fist bumps Garrett across the table as a line of waiters enter the room. A bowl is placed in front of me as I wipe the tears from my eyes, the mix of sweet and salty scents drifting around the room. Three scallops sit in the middle of celeriac soup, my mouth already drooling.

"Oh, I'm actually vegan." Blondie at the far end lifts her plate and hands it back to the waiter, muttering her apologises as if it's her fault. I can guarantee my mom forgot to inform the kitchen of her guest's dietary needs, yet she still has an eyebrow cocked condescendingly and a scowl ready for the poor waiter.

"Oh shit, you poor thing!" Garrett jerks up from hovering over his plate, speaking with his mouth full. "Do you have an epi-pen, should we have a doctor on stand-by?" The whole scallop between his teeth bursts, juice seeping down his chin while he continues to stare at her with genuine concern. Blondie flicks her mortified eyes to my mom who tells her to pretend he's not in the room. That's fine by me, pretend he's not here while I lean over and drag the pad of my tongue over the salty juice from his chin to his lips. Garrett swallows loudly, his tongue sticking out to tangle with mine.

"Oh, for all of our sakes Axel, stop that! I'm fully aware of what you're doing and that it is all for my benefit. Well, it won't work!" Cutlery clashing loudly against her bowl mixes with her exasperated sigh. I keep my eyes on Garrett's hazel ones, our breaths mingling as I reply.

"What am I trying to do, Mom?"

"The same as always. Acting out, showing off. Whatever it takes to anger me." I turn my head to see her shoot out of her seat and Richard places a hand on her arm, trying to calm her with quiet words. *Moron.*

"Why on earth would I give a shit what you think? You broke me in so many unfixable ways, used me for your personal gain no matter the cost to my sanity. I'm rebuilding my life; you're just pissed your cash mule has left you far behind." Our eyes remain locked in a stare down to the death until Richard somehow manages to coax her back into her seat. Dabbing the corners of her mouth with her napkin, she throws it into her empty bowl and leans back on a sigh.

"You're always were such a spoilt shit; do you know that?"

"Spoilt? Spoilt?! Ha! How do you figure that one in that fucked up head of yours?"

"You got all of your father's money." The flare to her nostrils makes me grin, my eyes floating upwards in fake thought. When my father died, he left her absolutely nothing like she deserved. I, on the other hand, received a sizeable trust fund, pre-paid college fees and a yearly allowance.

"Oh yeah you're right. And guess what – I gave it all away." Her face turns to a shade of beetroot, the crazed look in her eyes reminding of the night she'd found me freshly shaven and finally free. If I had thought writing those cheques to abused children's charities had helped to alleviate some of my grief, it's nothing compared to how watching my mother's internal seizure is healing old wounds to my battered soul.

The waiters return at that moment with our main courses balanced on the palm of their right hands, this dinner party suddenly much more pleasant from my perspective. Minuscule versions of duck confit are placed in front of each of us, my mom too busy twitching and seething to notice. Blondie receives a plate of sliced tomato with some diced onion sprinkled on top and licks her bottom lip excitedly. She can add 'easily pleased' on her résumé.

Spearing a teeny tiny carrot on my fork, I notice Garrett glaring at his food it as if it will magically transform into a pizza for him. On his right, Huxley fails to fight a yawn behind his hand, and I feel his pain. Guilt swamps me that my brothers and Avery fell the need to stay in my childhood home with me, but at the same time I can't let them leave. I won't survive staying here on my own, if boredom doesn't kill me first, my nightmares sure will. Dax is also pushing his food around his plate, every so often sneaking a glance over to Avery who is obviously ignoring him. I know I need to do something to break the uncomfortable silence but don't know what. On my third mouthful of delicious yet microscopic dinner, an idea pops into my mind and I fight to hold back a grin. Knocking Garrett's leg under the table to grab his attention, I bob my eyebrows mischievously for him to play along.

"Never have I ever said the wrong name during sex," I begin, leaning over to lift Garrett's champagne glass to his lips. He chuckles, knowing full well he called me Alex once by a slip of the tongue but that shit counts. In my peripheral vision, I see Avery take a sip from her glass too, much to Dax's shock.

"Never have I ever received a lap dance," Avery plays along with a grin. All four of us guys sip from our glasses remembering Huxley's birthday at Strip 'N' Tip last year.

"That's a wrong we need to right," Garrett smirks across the table. "Come on Dax, give her a show." The other end of the table is still eating formally as if they are above us, although from time to time, Blondie glances over in clear hope to join in.

"Never have I ever had a threesome," Dax counters bitterly. Garret and Avery cheer loudly, holding their glasses in the centre to clink with mine and I sip my orange juice with pride.

"Never have I ever faked an orgasm," Huxley takes his turn, looking across to Garrett expectantly. Avery alone downs her entire drink and we all stare at her, clearly thinking how much of a crying shame that is.

"Never have I ever..." Garrett begins looking up in thought. I can't even imagine what's churning in that mind of his and I'd be dreading it if I wasn't finally enjoying myself. "Sent a naked photo to someone holding Huxley's cowboy hat over my junk while he was asleep in the same room." My eyes bulge and mouth drops wide open before curving into a smile and punching his arm.

"You asked for that photo, it was Valentine's Day and you promised you'd never tell him!" I half shout jokingly, although Huxley doesn't look very impressed.

"That's my favourite hat," he complains, running a hand through his hair as if he knows my balls were lying on the inner felt for that photo and he can scrub my sack germs from his scalp. The moment of feeling myself again soon ends, my meds beginning to wear off and abdomen starting to ache. Our empty plates are cleared, and I use the table to push myself upright.

"You can't leave yet, you haven't had dessert," my mother instantly chastises me. The tightness of her lips and twitch in her left eye tells me just how annoyed she is with my behaviour, and I bathe in that small victory for one moment more. Her outer shell is tougher than ice but once it cracks, it shatters.

"It's my house, I can do what I like." My reply sends a further flare of anger through her brown eyes, her mouth opening and closing a few times like a fish out of water. Another fun clause of my father's will, this mansion becomes mine the day I turn twenty-one and I won't waste a second putting it up for sale. There're too many memories in these walls that need to be forgotten. "Besides, I've got my dessert right here." I stroke the length of Garrett's throat with my finger, tipping his chin up to be captivated by his smile and dimples. Finishing his drink, he rises and links his fingers through mine. Turning towards the door, a sea of blue catches my attention and a wicked thought flares to mind. Offering my free hand out to Avery, she blinks a few times before accepting, a knowing smile lifting her lips as I gently tug her to her feet. "You're coming too."

Wyatt

Pacing around my room, I'm about a minute and a half from erupting. Weak. That's what Ray called me. As if I'm not the only one who follows his requests without complaint and delivers actual results. And maybe the enigma that is Meg Connors did manage to breach my walls with her unshakable resolve, but I haven't shown a shred of weakness in all the time Ray has known me. He should try guarding a girl that fills his dreams with sultry looks and impossible suggestions, only to have the reality match once awake with the bonus of her body warmth constantly too close. Well that ends now. Consider the walls re-erected and my outer armour impenetrable.

There's a groove in the carpet from my black socks, spots of fluff scattered through the cream tread marks. I need to get out of here. Away from the guards and Ray's expectations and the shadowed figure in the corner and my fucking dreams and *her*. Yanking a pair of black designer jeans from the wardrobe, I pull them over the boxers I donned after my recent shower and hunt for a shirt. Not black, I'm not going to a funeral – yet, or white because I'm not a domino, not in the mood for lilac or mint. I'll go burgundy for a change. Slipping a gold Rolex onto my wrist, I slide my feet into my Nike's with the matching gold tick and laces before giving myself a quick spray of cologne.

After a quick goodbye to my mom's eerie shadow, I stride from the room with a roll of cash and Meg's cell key in my pocket, so no one can gain access to her while I'm out and head in the direction of the garage. Rachel is wiping the TV stand in the living room as I pass through, dust collecting from lack of use no doubt. After a quick gush over my appearance, she runs a hand through my damp hair to push it back from my eyes and tells me to be safe. I kiss her cheek and promise not to get into any trouble with a wink, feeling more myself already.

I duck into the kitchen quickly to grab an apple for the time being and stroll through the connecting garage door. A skinny man in a black suit with matching flat cap nods to me in greeting, a cigarette hanging from his lips as he opens the back door of the limo. Word sure travels fast around here, but I can't complain. This beats driving around in the sedan for hours without a destination in mind anyway. Dropping into the leather seat, the door is closed for me while I lean over to grab a bottle of whiskey from the mini bar.

"Where are you headed?" the driver asks from the front, eyeing me in the rear-view mirror.

"Surprise me," I reply, pushing my finger onto the button that closes the glass partition between us and lean back with a sigh. Tonight, I'm going to drown myself in whiskey until the old Wyatt returns, the one who doesn't give a shit about anyone or anything except having a good time.

Strolling down a busy street in central Chicago, the night life is buzzing even for a weekday. Skyscrapers all around stretch towards the full moon, their office lights switching off for the night as if there is a power cut sweeping from building to building. A sea of people bustles around me, half scraping their heels on the concrete, trying to delay the journey home whilst the other half shove past them eagerly in search for a good time. For once, I enjoy blending into the masses and take pleasure in simply being outside and carefree. No rushing to make a reservation, no deadlines to ignore, no family ties holding me back.

A pair of Lamborghinis races by on the highway, their passengers hollering as they dodge traffic to best the other. The traffic lights at the far end turn red and the sounds of their wheels shredding across the tarmac fill the air, stopping just in time to allow masses of people to scurry over the crossing. I continue wandering along this side of the street, surveying the unique range of nightclubs before selecting which one I'm most in the mood for.

Country music floods through the open doorway of a club on the smaller side, a jukebox sitting proudly beside a fully stocked bar and an indoor waterfall visible at the rear of the space. Next door is an establishment illuminated by red lighting, the dance floor already filled with headbangers as rock spills onto the street. Excited roars drag me a few bars down to halt in front of an enormous gaming bar, displays covering every free space of wall with a different console from several eras stationed at each. A crowd has gathered around a particular screen by the bar, two minimally dressed female fighters against a Japanese-style dojo background leaping towards each other with their front legs raised. Excited mutters escalate into cheers as the fighter on the left gains the upper hand.

I'm about to step inside for a closer look when a group of guys burst through the doors to my left. Laughing hysterically and huddled arm in arm, something about them has me pausing to watch. They are all dressed in shirts and jeans, the overpowering scent of their aftershave hitting me like a slap to the face but that's not what catches my attention. Their smiles are wider than their cheeks can accommodate, clearly drunk and having the time of their lives. It's when the blonde with glasses reaches over to pluck a hot dog from his comrades' hand and stuffs it into his own mouth that realization dawns on me. It's like seeing a memory float before my eyes, the resulting sidewalk scuffle of his actions exactly like my Shadowed Souls have done so many times.

My relaxed attitude sours immediately, an ache I've been able to avoid up to now taking root in my chest and expanding until I can't breathe. A visceral desire consumes me as I remain rooted to the pavement, my eyes tracking their every movement. I've been able to prevent the thoughts of my former friends filtering through my mind whilst immersing myself in Ray's orders, but now they flood back into me sharply. They'll never forgive me for the things I've done, not that I'd ask them to, but then my thoughts drift onto Axel. He didn't deserve the fate he received, and I can only hope my part in it enabled him not to suffer needlessly. It's a small reprieve, but one I need to cling onto.

No longer in the mood, I turn away and stuff my hands in my pockets. Trying to decide where to head to now, my eyes halt on a red mini parked across the road, the female behind the wheel trying to slip out of sight even though our eyes have already connected. A hand lands on my arm, spinning me back around forcefully.

"Dude! We're sole mates!" My eyebrows raise as the skinniest of the group stands before me, his appearance contradicting the firm clutch he still has on my bicep. His dark hair is swept across his forehead, invisible braces lining his teeth which aren't living up to their name. Shrugging out of his grip, I'm about to tell him to fuck off when I see he's pointing to our sneakers. Sure as shit, he's wearing a matching pair of Nikes and I now understand his declaration.

Bracing myself on his shoulder, I twist my leg into the air which he mimics until the bases of our sneakers are pressed against each other. "Sole mates," I agree. Howls of excitement sound as the rest of the group bundle into me, a beer is placed into my hand as I'm crushed in a bear hug. Barking out a laugh, the group drags me inside the bar they recently vacated without another word. This club is the type I expected to end up in tonight, complete with a sticky dance floor and brawl taking place in the back corner. The DJ in his elevated booth ignores them as he jumps in time to his music, fist raised, and a monsoon of people crammed beneath copy him.

Forced into a bar stool, my hand is grasped in multiple sweaty ones as introductions are passed around – not that I can hear anything over the techno racket thumping through the speakers. I've already made up my own nicknames for each of them anyway, shouting my own name back to Glasses, Braceface, Freckle Features, Bull ring and Elf Ears.

A barman walks over to us and points to a yellow badge pinned to his polo top, *'ID Needed'* printed across it in black. My new friends pass nervous glances between themselves and I decide to spare them the embarrassment of leaving the town's shabbiest establishment without being completely smashed. Standing on the stool's lower bar, I lean across to speak into the barman's ear.

"We're all twenty-one and you're going to keep the drinks flowing until we can't stand," I push the roll of cash into his hand and sit back with an eyebrow raised, the ball firmly in his court. After a stunned beat, he swallows thickly and pushes the money into his pocket, quickly retrieving us a tray full of shots. Hands clasp my back before we clink our tiny glasses together and throw them back, reaching for the next without pausing. The taste of oblivion skates over my tongue, leading a path through my body which I encourage to spread until it devours me.

"Hey, that's you! You're Wyatt Hughes!" Freckle Features shouts into my ear, drawing my attention to a small flatscreen above the bar. A female reporter is relaying a story I can't hear with exaggerated hand gestures, the headline 'Where is Nixon Hughes?' scrolling across the bottom. In the top corner of the screen, my god-awful mugshot is on display for everyone to see. A cut on my temple is pissing blood down my face and onto my shirt, my blackened eyes barely recognisable but the sign I'm holding with my own name splayed in white lettering is undeniable. Shoving my two fingers into my mouth, I whistle sharply over to the bartender. His eyes swing to me instantly, abandoning his punter to rush over and switch off the TV at my instruction. I've only just forgotten about the shitshow that is my life, I'm not nearly drunk enough to deal with reality right now.

Several bottles of tequila and a fall off my stool later, I'm hoisted up and swaying in my companion's arms. Fuck, I've missed this. Having people to lean on, emotionally and physically, and not being alone all the damn time. I've spilled every miserable secret and damaged thought to these five strangers, and the best part is they haven't heard a word of it. Just nodded along and sensed when to hug me, which is exactly what I needed. Bull ring has his arm slumped around my shoulders as he drags me into the throng of people on the dancefloor, his central nose piercing glinting in the strobe lights.

An ass grinds up against my crotch in an instant, a blonde smirking over her shoulder at me. I remain still for a little while, praying her snaking hips and roaming hands can stir a response out of me but I already knew it was useless. She's extremely pretty, slim yet busty and squeezed into a tiny pink dress, but everything about her is all wrong. Gripping her by the waist, I plant her in front of Elf Ears and shove my way to the door. With a glance back, I notice five sets of concerned eyes focused on me, my new friends staring longingly but I give them a simple salute goodbye, not wanting to be followed. My skin feels too tight and the room is beginning to spin, a rise of vomit threatening to explode from me if I don't flee the overcrowded space.

Spilling onto the street, I lean over with my hands on my

knees and gulp in the crisp air. Why did I think this would be a good idea? A pair of shiny loafers become visible beneath my face, a glance up showing me the full length of my limo driver. *Stalker much?* But I can't deny that I'm done for the night and thankful to have a quick escape. Concentrating on following his exact footsteps, I misjudge my step into the limo and fly across the back seat in a slumped mess. My eyes flutter closed, consciousness drifting in and out as a pool of drilling collects beneath my cheek. Streetlamps blur past my closed eyelids, the door opening by my feet jolting me upright.

I stagger back to my room, my eyes unable to focus. I almost fall down the stairs, my hands slapping against the stone wall to stop myself. Pressing my back against it instead, I slide further down into the darkness below. This is fine, I'll just sleep it off on my comfortable memory foam mattress. Back to normal tomorrow. I fumble in my pocket, withdrawing my bedroom key and twisting it in the shiny padlock. The clang of the chain hitting the floor makes me wince, my head throbbing as I bend to pick it up. Stumbling inside, I praise myself for remembering to hook the chain back onto the wall before flopping onto my bed.

My face connects with a hard floor and pain flares to life in my body. *Fucking ow.* I'll have to tell Rachel my bed is broken when I wake up. I'm rolled onto my back, the hands of an angel gripping my pulsating cheek. Her face is hidden in shadow but there is an orange glow around her head, her halo firmly in place. "Hey you," I grin stupidly, heat seeping into my chilled flesh. This is what the girl in the club couldn't give me, this feels right. I lean into the gentle touch, reaching out to drag the angel down onto my body. Mmmmm, she smells all soapy. I wrap my arms around her tightly, never wanting to let go because she'll have to go to heaven soon. But she can't leave yet, I need her.

Her arms wind around my neck, her hug reaching a place in my heart I'm too embarrassed for her to know about. It's not pure enough, not worthy of her. Sleep tries to drag me under, but I refuse, something telling me I need to savour this moment for as long as possible. Shifting onto my side, I pull her with me so I can memorize her face. Those thick eyelashes over icy blue eyes, that cute button nose and full lips. Enticingly soft lips that are every man's desire. But no one else can have her, even if I know neither can I. Her eyes are staring into mine widely, too much clarity in their depths for me to handle.

"Stop seeing me," my speech comes out slurred, but I know what I mean. She's peering deeply into my soul and making me ashamed of it. Shutting my eyes, I lean my forehead against hers and take one last inhale of her scent, knowing everything will be back to normal in the morning.

Avery

Despite his obvious discomfort, Axel pulls Garret and I into a darkened room with an iron tight grip on our fingers. A familiarly sweet, yet musty smell of aged paper and ink washes over me, moonlight shining through an arched window to illuminate a personal library. I can make out the outline of a long sofa, its black leather catching the light, with two matching armchairs on the opposite side of the room. My bare feet step onto a circular rug, my toes flexing in the soft sheepskin texture. Axel flicks on a tall lamp, slowly lowering himself into one of the armchairs beside it whilst clutching his stomach.

"No offence Axel, but you don't really seem to be ready for…this." I point between myself and Garrett, knowing he couldn't be gentle even if he tried. When Axel had offered me an early exit from the most awkward dinner party to have ever happened, I'd gladly taken it. Between Dax's longing puppy-dog glances and Sharon's narcissism, I could have had more fun walking across a sea of Lego.

"Oh, I'm not going to be joining in, physically." The shadowed smile that takes root on his face would seem more appropriate for someone plotting a murder, his hands linking over his stomach as he casually slouches back to watch us. I throw a look to Garrett, who's standing rigidly straight beside me with a determined clench to his jaw.

"No, not without you."

"Well I'm right here, and I didn't tell you the best bit. I command, you obey. Got it?" A tremor of surprise mixed with excitement ignites within me, although Garrett's posture only tightens further. Flickers of confusion and uncertainty pass across his half-lit face.

"I don't understand. You said you didn't want me to be with other people."

"I never said that; I just didn't like you dragging me along like a third wheel, choosing where we went, who we fucked, how it happened. Tonight, I'm in control. Now, both of you, strip."

I lick my lips, a concoction of anticipation and champagne fuelling my actions as I push the thin straps from my shoulders one by one. Keeping our eyes locked of Axel's, Garrett pauses for a few seconds longer before pulling his tie over his head.

He yanks his jacket and shirt off, buttons ricocheting around us as my dress pools at my feet. Stepping out and kicking the material aside, I ease my thumbs beneath my lacey black thong and push it down while Garret hastily removes his slacks and pants. Standing gloriously and unashamedly naked before him, Axel's amber eyes drag over the length of our bodies, desire clearly swirling in their depths despite the lack of light.

"Kiss her," Axel orders, bringing his thumb up to rub across his bottom lip. Garrett turns and drags me into his body in the same movement, a gasp leaving my lips which he uses to push his tongue into my mouth. There's never soft caresses or gentle kisses with Garrett and this is what I need right now. A moan escapes me, desire zipping through my core the way I'd expected it to earlier with Huxley. Garrett's tongue devours me hungrily, his fingers digging into my underarms and his solid erection already nudging at my abdomen. Molten heat sets me on fire with the need for a brief escape from the world.

"Is she wet for us?" Axel's voice drifts across the room,

Garrett's hand immediately sliding down to my ass and dipping between the cheeks. We both groan into each other's mouths at the feel of how wet I am, Garrett's long digit easily pushing inside of me. I nibble on his bottom lip and trail kisses down his neck as he pumps his finger in and out, adding a second for good measure.

"She's soaking for us," Garrett's voice is strained, his muscles bunched beneath my fingertips. "What's next?" He asks with clear desperation on his voice.

"Put your hands behind your back and keep them there while Avery does whatever she wants with you." Garrett's fingers still inside of me but he doesn't let go, his nails digging into my hip and his chest heaving beneath my lips. When I'm sure he's about to refuse and bend me over like a rag doll, he removes his hands so quickly, I gasp at the sudden loss of contact. Clasping his hands behind him, Garrett's stares upwards, trembling with desire. I cut a glance to Axel who is smirking like he's having the time of his life and gestures for me to continue my assault.

Firstly, I graze my teeth along his collar bone and place kisses across his chest. I run the pad of my tongue over his nipple and he hisses, holding himself surprisingly still as I repeat the process on the other side, giving the bud a little bite. Carving a path through his valley of abs with my mouth, it doesn't escape me he's fully shaven as I drop to my knees on the soft rug. Starting from his ankles, I slowly scrape my fingernails up his calves, along the inside of his thighs and stop short of his balls. His frustration is clear by his growls but I'm having way too much fun to stop. Painting featherlight circles across his groin with my fingers, I lean forward as if I'm going to take him in my mouth, stopping short and smile up at him wickedly.

Snarling, Garrett's hands unexpectedly shoot out to grab the back of my head and hold me in place as he plunges his cock straight into the back of my throat. Holding me helplessly still,

Garrett fucks my mouth like his life depends on it, his smooth head gliding over my tongue at an impressive speed. Gripping his thighs, I can only hold on for the ride as Garrett's true sexual demon is finally unleashed. I slide my fingers across to scratch his balls, his grip on my hair tightening enough to leave a bruise on my scalp.

Releasing me as quickly as he started, Garrett lifts me to my feet and uses his hand on my nape to guide me over to Axel's seat. Pushing me back down onto my knees in front of the chair, Garrett lifts my wrists and plants them either side of the armchair before shifting down behind me. The head of his dick slides against my entrance, his hand snaking around my body until his palm is pressed against my clit. With his fingers holding me open for him, he slides his whole length into me in one smooth movement. Crying out, his free hand curls around my neck and settles under my chin, pushing my head up to lock eyes with Axel's.

Axel has released his dick from his pants, his fisted hand slowly pumping up and down his shaft as he watches our every move. Although not together like before, the three of us are bonded in this moment, our pleasure and ragged breaths mingling in the air. My cries echo around the room as Garrett builds up a vigorous rhythm, each thrust hitting my G-spot. His fingers tighten around my neck and groin, purely animalistic noises sounding behind me, but Axel is the opposite. Calm, composed. Legs spread wide, casually stroking the impressive length of his cock, his eyes churning with yearning at the scene being played out for him.

My eyes flick down to the bead of precum glistening on top of his dark purple head, my tongue instantly darting out to wet my bottom lip. Smirking down at me, Axel runs the knuckles of his free hand across my nipple and I arch my back in response, desperate to be closer to him. Every drag of his fingers sends sparks flying throughout my body, my toes curled, and fists clenched. Abandoning his dick, he gives my tits his full attention, rolling my nipples between his thumb and forefinger with the occasional sharp pinch. I try to lean into his touch, but Garrett has me locked in place, pounding relentlessly, and filling me completely.

An orgasm rips through me like a tidal wave, delicious destruction tearing me apart on a scream. Garrett's hand shifts towards my mouth and I bite down hard on the fleshly part between his thumb and forefinger, riding out the intense waves with muffled moans. My walls are gripping Garrett's shaft so tightly, he's momentarily forced to slow while I bathe in the euphoric feeling, I hadn't realised I'd missed until now. My limbs is a mixture of tingling yet heavy. If Garrett wasn't holding me, I'd have melted into a blissful puddle on the floor and refuse to get back up again.

Axel's eyes haven't wandered from mine, still smoothing his hand up and down on his dick. I shift my hands from the edge of the seat, drifting across the leather to rest on his thighs. Garrett tries to yank me backwards into his body until Axel warns him off, a silent conversation passing between the two which I'm too distracted to concentrate on with Axel's cock straining for my attention.

"Gently," Garrett whispers into my ear almost threateningly. He slows his pace and curls my braid around his hand to keep control as I lean forward to take all of Axel into my mouth. His velvet softness eases across my tongue as I carefully pull back, licking every drop of saltiness from his rounded helmet. Axel's leaned all the way back, groaning and urging me to continue with his palm on my head. Garrett grinds deep within me, a sensual shift in our usual dynamic which I'm not complaining about.

Keeping my pace slow, I take Axel between my lips again and again, swirling my tongue around his tip each time. Gripping the base tightly in my hand, I pump alongside my steady movements until the desperation in his groans call for more.

Sucking and occasionally scraping my teeth along his length, I take him deep into my mouth just as he explodes on a curse, warm salty cum squirting directly down my throat. Garrett holds me in place by my hair, forcing me to take everything Axel wants to give, not that I would have moved anyway.

The second I pull myself free following Axel's release, Garrett picks up his punishing rhythm. His hands wind around me like a cobra pinning its prey in place, driving into me at such a speed I can barely catch my breath. Each slam of his body against my ass feels like a spank, his movements harsh as if he needs to teach me some sort of lesson. His mouth finds my neck, biting down sharply which has me crying out in protest a second before another orgasm rakes through my body.

Stars burst behind my eyelids, my inner walls rippling with pleasure. Still he doesn't relent, using me to vent all of his pent-up sexual frustration. My nails rip into the arms of the chair, Garrett's shouts joining mine as his cock swells and pulses within me. Finally freeing me from his hold as he chases his release, I slump forward onto Axel's thigh. I'm definitely going to ache in the morning, but I don't regret a second of it. At least, not right now. Garrett grinds against me one last time, prolonging his pleasure before leaning over me. His fingers interlink with Axel's, the three of us absorbing the last few moments before our troubles return with a vengeance.

Before long, Garrett lifts his weight from my back, his arm around my middle taking me with him. Passing me his discarded boxers, I hold the material between my thighs as he pulls out of me and leaves me to clean myself up. Slipping his shirt over my shoulders, I see he's already pulled on his slacks and left the button open. There's a tight clench to his jaw, concern brewing in his eyes as he silently lifts Axel to his feet and helps guide him towards the door.

Leaving my dress and the cum-covered boxers crumpled on the rug, I push my arms through the shirt sleeves and button it all the way down to graze my thighs. The guys exit the room without even a glance back, leaving me alone in the dark. *Well, fuck me, I guess. Quite literally*. Shame washes over me, the feeling I've been used twisting uncomfortably in my chest. But who am I kidding? I used them right back. Even Axel during his recovery, which was completely selfish of me. I've been so caught up in training and not sleeping, I forgot it's not just me who is hurting, emotionally and physically. I needed a distraction and I took it, no strings attached. Surely there are worse ways to destroy your morals than trapped between two insanely hot guys.

Dax

The morning rays piercing through the glass skylight hurt my tired eyes, forcing me to squint and rub them even more than my reckless night's sleep already was. Blasting Fall Out Boy through my wireless headphones, I tap the treadmill's digital screen to speed up my causal jog to a full-on run. Pumping my arms in time with my burning calves, I relish the sweet pain of pushing myself for a change. We're due to return to Waver-sea soon, which would include gruelling 5am training sessions on the basketball court before class. Not that I can see us going back if nothing has changed around here. We were supposed to use Axel's place as a hideout while we came up with some sort of plan and ensure Avery stayed hidden away from harm. I don't want to be that dick who leaves in a time of need to finish his degree and move on with his life when everything is going tits up, but with Avery still ignoring me, it doesn't seem like I'm wanted or needed here either.

The elastic holding my hair back snaps, my blonde curls exploding around my face and sticking to my sweat-covered neck. I keep running, refusing to stop until these unwanted feel-ings are dulled enough to give me a short reprieve. The pound-ing of my feet matches the heavy bass streaming into my ears, the bloodthirsty lyrics starting to make me feel invincible. If only I knew what I was running towards, I could implement the steps to get there sooner and save my stress. Unless I'm subcon-sciously running away from something instead.

The last song in my playlist comes to an end so I shut off the machine, gasping for breath and struggling to remain upright on my trembling legs. Abandoning my trusty mp3 player and headphones on the treadmill's handle for later, I grab my hand towel from the weight bench and scrub the rough material down my face. Lifting my head to the skylight, I nearly jump out of my skin at the creepy ass cat sitting directly above me, his yellow eyes zeroed in on my every movement. His striped tail flicks back and forth casually while his tabby shoulders flex as if readying himself to pounce on me straight through the glass. I edge my way out of the room, not breaking eye contact the entire time.

Every window in the mansion has been designed with the purpose of drawing in as much daylight as possible, but when there is this much space and practically no one in it, the point seems mute. I've yet to find a room I could imagine as being homely and can't help but think how dreary it must have been growing up here. It's always eerily quiet, the staff only around on weekends and Sharon accompanies Richard to work on weekdays. Not that I expect she does much other than eye-fuck his employees and pass her menial tasks onto interns. Strolling through most of the lower level, each room as grand and unused as the last, I finally enter the kitchen to find Garrett slumped over the kitchen counter.

"You alright, man?" I ask, pulling a bottle of water from the refrigerator and leaning against the same counter. He groans loudly, slowly sitting upright on the stool to face me. Damn, he looks like shit. Dark circles cling to his bloodshot eyes, his hair is a straight-up mess which is saying something considering he never styles it normally. Next to him on the black surface, he's laid out a large mixing bowl, scales, flour, butter, eggs and sugar.

"I don't know what to do," he mumbles, his widened eyes looking pitifully desperate. Pushing off the side, I wash my hands in the sink and return a moment later to help the usually arrogant fuck that probably wouldn't have done the same for me. Nah, he'd have laughed and called me an asshat.

"When I was a child, my mom used to bake with me every Sunday. She swore by this trick, match the ounces and half the eggs. So, if you use six ounces of flour, butter and sugar, you'll want three eggs. Or four ounces each and two- "

"I know how to make a fucking cake, Betty Cocker. You're not the only one who had to learn to fend for himself young. I meant I don't know what to do about Axel." I still halfway through measuring the flour, torn between throwing the bag into his face and wondering what's going on with them two. Although, I've already made up my mind to help my brother when he needs me and place the flour down on the counter, gesturing for him to continue.

"He said he should be enough for me, made it sound like he wanted to give whatever this thing is a real shot. And I've tried to open up, given him my full focus, everything a monogamous moron would do. But then Avery's on the end of his dick and I'm just there thinking this is exactly why I don't let people in." I stare into his troubled hazel eyes, swallowing the jealously of Avery being with another and try to focus of Garrett's problems. My shit can wait until later.

Reaching for the mixing bowl, I take an egg from its cardboard home and crack it evenly on the rim. Tipping the contents in and discarding the shell, I pull Garrett up by his white wifebeater so he can see properly. "Imagine the yolk is your heart, and all the white is the bullshit you hide behind. Now here comes Axel," I pick a fork from the cutlery drawer and stab it directly into the middle. The yolk pierces and its yellow centre spills around the bowl.

"Letting him in will make you vulnerable, you might even bleed for a while. But if you persevere through the bad times, you can become something more, better." I whisk up the egg vigorously until its massively frothy, happy with myself for that on-the-spot analogy. Garrett continues to stare at the bowl for a long moment, watching the top layer of bubbles pop and fizzle.

"Congratulations, that is officially the most ridiculous thing I've ever heard and seen all at once." He leans across me to dump the pre-measured flour into the bowl along with a huge scoop of butter and pours a ridiculous amount of sugar in straight from the bag. Setting the bowl into a chrome, electric whisker, I huff and stalk out of the room, leaving him to his shitty problems and even shittier cake mix.

My foot hits the bottom step of the staircase before I still, the thought of returning to the emptiness of my room thoroughly unappealing. There's only so long I can lie in the four-poster bed that sits in the heart of the room on a raised step, surrounded by chunky furnishings all in mahogany which give the space an ominous feel. No, shutting myself away will only make the void between our once tight-knit group grow and fester. I miss heading for pizza after ball practice, playing video games at full volume whenever Garrett brought a girl back to our house on campus, hosting Dungeons and Dragons every Sunday evening so we could unleash our inner geeks.

The thought of those days being over hurts me more than I care to admit. Despite one of us missing, I must believe we are able to band together and find a glimpse of happiness in each other's company to grab on to. Even though I am the only one, I could forgive Wyatt if he walked through the door right now and asked to re-join us. Everyone gets misled sometimes, it's his choices from here on out that will determine if he's redeemable or not. Spinning on my heel, I stride across one of the many living areas and exit through the patio doors. The sun is hiding behind a cloud-covered sky, a slight chill in the air which I relish against my heated skin. A set of hammocks are on my left with a square, steel fire pit placed between them.

My sneakers leave footprints in the low-trimmed lawn as I stroll around the grounds, heading east first. Following the sound of trickling water, I find a rounded wall mirroring the curve of the mansion, dozens of wicker tables and chairs covering the outside space. A gap in the low wall gives way for a flight of stone steps, leading down into a well-designed garden. The slanted hillside holds multiple tiers, held in place by wooden slates to house flowers of all colours and varieties. A large water feature sits centrally at the bottom, pathways leading away from it in a maze-like pattern through tall hedges.

Winding through the tables, each one holding a closed parasol in the middle, I notice a platform at the far end framed by a wide wooden arch. The ballroom I haven't seen before is visible through a set of double French doors, making this the perfect area for holding lavish parties. Continuing past, I skirt the mansion and find myself nearing the front gardens. Strips of luscious green follow a long, concrete driveway to the tall gates at the end.

A flash beyond the gate catches my attention and the long lens of a camera is yanked back into the half-open window of a red Mini Cooper. Fucking paparazzi, probably looking for a follow up on Axel's return. Nothing stays quiet when you are rich. I start sprinting down the driveway, the brunette in the vehicle hastily speeding away with a loud screech of the tyres. I'll get you next time. Turning back to the grand front door, Ionic columns standing proudly either side, I re-enter the house and circle back to the kitchen in search of food, hoping Garrett has cleared out by now.

Thankfully, the kitchen is empty as I find myself a banana and grab a couple of cereal bars from the cupboard. I glance at the oven to find it off, no deliciously sweet smell filling the room like I expected. The sound of chatting filters in from the living room along with the mystical soundtrack of Harry Potter. Deciding to investigate, I find Huxley, Avery, Garret and Axel sitting in that order across a lengthy cream sofa, the curtains drawn and plasma TV screen in front of them playing the opening scene from The Philosopher's Stone.

"Oh hey, we're gonna have a movie marathon, if you wanna chill with us?" Axel offers, spotting me lurking in the open archway.

"Where's the cake?" I ask, ignoring his question since I don't really want to answer. I appreciate the sentiment but don't particularly feel welcome, especially since no one else has bothered to look my way.

"What cake?" Garrett replies, focusing on the screen and raising a metal whisk to his mouth. Shifting forward, I see the mixing bowl full of mix in his lap, Axel with the other whisk in his hand and Avery leaning over to take a spoonful. *Who the fuck…just, ew and…. why?*

"Fucking barbarians, the lot of you." Avery's giggle reaches my ears as I'm about to turn away, the sound so pure and light. I hadn't released how much I'd missed it, needed it. My heart hitches in the hopes that small glimpse of joy was directed at me. I crave to put a smile on her face that never wavers, cause laughter to spill from her lips as easily as breathing. I know in this moment I can't leave the mansion until she's found happiness in her life again. I'll take online courses, I'll attend night school to make up the lost time, but for now I'm staying right here.

Rolling my shoulders back, despite aching to join their home cinema set-up, I stride straight back into the gym and shove my hands into a pair of red boxing gloves. Throwing my fist into the punching bag in the far corner, I hop on my toes, ducking and swinging with a new sense of determination.

"What are you doing? Come and join us." Huxley catches my wrist as I swing back, halting my movements with a surprising amount of strength. In fact, his whole body looks broader, his chest filling a white t-shirt and his biceps straining against the short sleeves.

"What's it look like? It's not just you that needs to bulk up." Huxley sighs deeply, his blonde waves having grown enough to almost lie on his chest.

"But this isn't you. You don't use your fists or rely on violence. Out of everyone here, you need to keep a level head." I grunt, shoving him back a step and continue my assault on the punching bag.

"Yeah well, look how far that's gotten me. Avery hates me, my brothers think I'm unable to help. I have to do something." This time Huxley moves to stand in front of me, blocking my access to the punching bag and challenging me with his brown eyes.

"Then make it something worthwhile, go to Avery. Don't let her leave until you've patched things up. When she got back from her place, don't think it went unnoticed how she sought you out first. Whether she admits it to herself or not, she misses and needs you." He looks so sure; I wonder if Avery has said as much to him. If there is a chance I can fix our fragile relationship. But even as I think about it, I know she will never be able to forgive me for the things I've done, no matter what the outcome is.

"She doesn't need me, she needs Meg. And I'm going to do everything I can to save them both."

Meg

Wyatt's snores aren't the only reason I've laid awake watching him sleep beside me. He hadn't even managed to find the sleeping bag in his drunk state last night, collapsing in the middle of the floor instead. I unzipped the outside and dragged it across us in a makeshift blanket and lifted his head so he could use the pillow. He'll have enough to regret with his killer of a hangover when he wakes without the added strain of a neck injury. I know it's foolish and that only his inebriated state brought him down here, but I can't deny how good his warm embrace felt against my skin. Maybe it's just been too long since I've had human contact. Or maybe…

Stopping that train of thought at the station and switching off the engine, my eyes flutter to the door, a flicker of hope igniting within me. I'd been so stupidly caught up on my feelings, I'd momentarily forgotten the fate that awaits me here. I need to stop being ridiculous. If I remain here, I'm doomed to die by poisoning. This isn't the time to add Stockholm syndrome to the list, I need a plan and I need it now. Wyatt is on his side facing me, his hot breath mixed with hints of whiskey fanning my face. The answer I've been looking for is right in front of me, hidden in the safety of his pants. *No, not his dick you slut* – although I wouldn't say no, but the key!

Smoothing my fingers across the stones separating us, I reach beneath the blanket for his jeans. My hand lands on his waist and I gently reach down to feel out the groove of his pocket. The denim is rough beneath my fingertips, the curve I was hunting for presenting itself to me. Wyatt's hand abruptly shoots between us and grips my wrist tightly, his eyes flying open with a snarl.

"What are you doing?" he growls, the confusion in his gaze clear as he takes in his surroundings. Well damn, no backing out now.

"What do you think?" Ignoring the painfully tight grip on my wrist, I reach forward for his belt buckle and flutter my eyelashes at him. He remains still, not pulling me in but not pushing me away either. Conflict pulls at his features, his morning glory shifting beneath my fingers and making me smile. Whether he'll admit it or not, I affect him and that will be my ticket out of here. Shoving me onto my back roughly, he suddenly stands with a slight sway and backs towards the door as if I might pounce on him. Keeping my smirk firmly in place, I stand and wait for his next move.

"Why would I ever lower myself to be with you when I could have anyone I want?" he grits through his teeth, the lie evident by the bulge in his jeans but his words hurt nevertheless. "I'll sooner have a few ribs removed and suck myself off than let you near me."

Closing the distance between us, I press my chest against his in a challenge. If he wants to upset me, he can go right ahead, but he'll look me in the eye and see I don't give a shit while he does it. Wyatt thinks the world revolves around pain and fear, but those are not the ways to crack me. If he wants me to shatter at his feet, he'll have to dig a lot deeper than that. Inclining his head to regard me with shrewd eyes, I seize the moment I've been waiting for and press my mouth against his.

He freezes beneath me, but I've come this far so I wind my hand around his neck and pull him into me. His lips jerk into action, punishing me with their kiss. Heat rolls from his body, his hands slipping into my hair and yanking roughly. On a gasp, he takes over control and I gladly let him. His tongue duels with mine, twisting and battling to get even closer. Electricity zips through my body like my tongue is wrapped around a live wire, filling me with a current that has all the hairs on my body standing on end.

Reining myself in, I focus on taking back the upper hand. My fingertips skim his solid chest through his shirt, the smooth material sliding beneath my touch. Following the mouth-watering abs, my hands land on his waistband, jerking him forward to grind against me. He is rock hard, his dick straining to be free. Popping open his jean button, I slide my hand beneath his boxers and take him in my palm. He hisses against my mouth, strung up tighter than a wind-up toy.

Stroking his veiny length, I push my hand deeper to cup his balls and shift their heavy weight in my palm. His hands are still knotted in my hair, holding me roughly in place against his lips despite not kissing me. Instead, he's watching me carefully as if this is a trick or I might disappear at any moment. Placing one more soft touch against his mouth with mine, I lick a path with my tongue to his square jawline and along the side of his neck.

Unzipping his jeans further, I hook my thumbs beneath his boxers and push them both down and I drop to my knees before him. His dick springs free, an impressed smirk taking root on my face. Forcing myself to focus, I wiggle his jeans the rest of the way past his shins and dip my hands into the pockets in one, smooth move. I dig deep, my heart pounding heavily as I find them empty. Shit.

Buying myself some extra time, I nibble at his thighs and tease him mercilessly, enjoying myself more than I should. His hands remain locked around my head, but they don't hinder any of my movements, his head falls back against the door on a frustrated groan. Feeling around the edge of his pants, I find the back pockets and nearly whoop as my hand clasps around the key.

Coyly pushing it into my sock, I need to finish what I started to not seem suspicious. *Oh no, how will I survive?*

Shaking my head at my inner sarcastic bitch, I take the base of his cock in my hand and slide my lips over his tip. Pushing onwards, I take him all the way into the back of my throat in one long movement. His involuntary buck beneath me is all I needed to seal my double victory. Not giving him a moment to compose himself, I draw back and repeat the process with a mixture of toe-curling slowness and heat-bursting speed.

Jeez, even I'm getting all hot and bothered in response to his moans and gasps, wetness spreading between my thighs that I need to keep clamped together tightly. I can't let my lady parts drive my actions when I have an ulterior motive. And screwing with socks on is just a big no-no, so this will have to do for the both of us. Gripping onto his muscular thighs, he grinds against me as I build up a steady rhythm. he is groaning loudly to. His hands are splayed in my hair, pushing me on in encouragement.

Suddenly the dynamic between us changes, an invisible string snapping which has Wyatt holding me still so he can thrust into my mouth. The spell I'd had him firmly under has reversed, his legs pump against my palms as he chases down his own release and all I can do is hang on for the ride. The smooth ridge of his cock gliding across the roof of my mouth has me imagining all the ways he'd take me, and luckily my mouth is too full to suggest any of them. My resolve has deserted me, a hint of saltiness from his precum making me heady.

Fuck, I want him. Just a little, in this moment. I want him to take everything he needs, use me in the worst ways and leave me thoroughly satisfied and shamed. I want to be his dirty little secret. A loud moan fills the cell a second before his cum spurts into my throat on one final thrust. He grips me tightly, bucking and groaning as he rides out his orgasm. Swallowing his load that was threatening to choke me, he gasps and finally eases me off him gently. His fingers coil around my chin, tilting my head upwards with the small trace of a caress. His face is shrouded by shadows, his mindset unreadable as I remain on the uneven ground bruising my knees.

He moves so quickly; I can't help but flinch. Using his grasp on my jaw to shove me aside, his jeans are pulled up and he's out the door without buttoning them up. The chain rattles loudly as he hastily locks me out of sight and stomps up the stairs. The door at the top slamming closed echoes throughout the dungeon and I allow myself a second of hurt from his rejection. Okay, second over. Reaching into my sock and producing the padlock key, I grin widely despite the hint of trepidation cutting through me.

The chances of me escaping are slim, extremely slim. But if I remain here, I'm going to be killed anyway and no one wants to sit around wondering what death will feel like. My mom didn't raise me to wait for a miracle to find you, you have to get up and find it yourself. I would rather wait until my clit isn't throbbing with need and the household is mostly asleep, but I don't have time to waste. Wyatt could realise the key is missing any second and my chance would be lost for good.

Pulling on the hoodie, I slip my arm through the bars on the door and search for the padlock. The chain is much thicker than I expected as my fingers trail further along it with no avail. Standing on my tiptoes and using the bar to hold me up, my fingers graze the padlock but it's too far down the chain for me to grab. Panic starts to filter through me, my heart beating wildly as I weigh up my options.

Going with option A, don't think – just do, I grip onto the chain and hoist it up. Yanking with all my strength, I manage to pull it high enough to draw some of the steel manacle through the grate. The padlock is closer now, my hands able to reach out and unlock it without a moment to lose. As soon as the lock is free, the chain begins to slide back through the grate like a recoiling snake. I desperately grab to stop its descent but the heavy weight slips through my fingers and crashes to the ground. No going back now, I reach around to hoist up the wooden slat covering the door and dash out into the corridor.

My limbs are tingling and I'm on the verge of a heart attack, but I force my legs to move as I begin to run. Leaving the staircase behind, I follow the tunnel which seems to be slanting at a downward angle. The lanterns have either not been placed this far down or not turned on as I'm plunged into darkness and keep running all the while. I really hope I'm right about this.

Garrett

"Garrett?" Axel's mumble reaches me through a deep sleep. I jerk upright on my front, dread spilling through me that something is wrong. Looking around the room wildly in panic, the dying sun bleeding out into hues of reds and oranges beyond the window, my eyes settle on Axel. There's an amused hook to one of his eyebrows, those dazzling amber eyes filled with mirth and his lips slanted up into a smile. It's then I notice my hand is firmly clasped around his balls, obviously getting carried away during our midday nap session.

"Although I appreciate the massage, I'm not ready to take this any further with you at the moment." Retracting my hand, I roll onto my back to stare at the ceiling. I didn't miss the way he specified 'with me', because we both know he's more than ready to let Avery into his pants. I get he's recovering, which is exactly what he should be doing, but he didn't even ask me if he needed relieving. I've been by his side every moment of every day, nursing him back to health with my blue balls tucked firmly between my legs and he lets Avery suck him off because she knows how to be *gentle.* It may not be my forte, but I could go easy for Axel. I'd do anything for him. And holy fuck, am I jealous?

"I'm sorry, it won't happen again. Until you're ready," I grumble, not liking the worried look I can see him giving the side of my face. He pulls on my far shoulder, rolling me onto my side to face him.

"You don't have to wait for me, you know. If you want

to go and find someone to relieve you, I'll be fine. You've been amazing with helping me recover, but you're still you. Nothing's changed." *Ouch*. I must fail at hiding my reaction as Axel's brow furrows further, his hand reaching up to cup my cheek. "I didn't mean it like that, you know how you get. You're practically a sex addict and I can't give you want you need right now."

"Maybe I only need you," I whisper, a rare glimpse of my vulnerability rising to the surface.

"We both know that'll never be the case." He snorts and looks away from me, staring at a spot beyond my shoulder while I quickly shut down my stupid fucking emotions. Clearing my throat, I nudge his hand from my face and leave the bed. Throwing my legs into a pair of blue tracksuit pants, I grab the matching jacket from the arm of a nearby chair and leave the room, blood rushing through my ears too fast to hear Axel's protests.

I hate I let him deep enough to be able to hurt me. Why did I do that to myself? Guess I'm still aching for punishment, the same way I was as a boy who stubbornly waited for someone to care for him, despite the long-term effects it would have to myself. A part of me wanted Axel to care, maybe even more and I was ready to gut myself at his feet to let him piece me back together or crush me beneath his boots.

What if I've been wrong this whole time? What if Axel likes being with me because I don't usually do ties, he would have been free to leave and come back whenever he felt like it. My heart's a revolving door; many pass through but there's no emergency stop button for anyone to stay long enough to hurt me.

Turning the last corner before the kitchen, Sharon collides with my bare chest. She steps back on her ridiculously tall heels with an 'oomph', clutching her Louis Vuitton handbag like a lifeline. Her eyes flick to my abs quickly, darting back to my face as I growl like a pissed off panther. I've been waiting to catch her alone, and boy is now a better time than any when I'm spiralling through hatred and self-doubt. Stepping forward, I force her into the cage of my body, leaning my hands against the wall either side of her head with a death stare, her wide eyes filling with the type of fear I strive on.

"If Karma doesn't come for the abusive piece of shit you are one day soon, I'm going flay you alive and spit-roast you on a barbeque. Then I'll force feed you to every single one of all your paedophilic friends that have ever dared laid a hand on Axel." A shudder rolling through her skin-tight pantsuit makes me smile the kind of smile a psychopath would give his next victim. Pushing away, I round into the kitchen until her already-composed voice stops me in my tracks.

"You're worse for him than I ever was."

"What the fuck did you just say?" I whirl around to see her smug shitting face back with vengeance, one hand casually on her hip.

"At least Axel always knew what I wanted out of him, but you're just dragging him along to prove something to yourself. He's a passing novelty to you, so who's the real abuser here?" Sharon spins so fast, her ponytail whips around her viciously and she strides away with confidence. I stand there, mouth hanging open and a heat rising to my cheeks as if I've just been slapped. I can't move, can't think straight.

Red curtains my vision. I want to smash everything in close range and scream. To beat the living shit out of the closest possible person, feel their bones crack beneath my knuckles and hear them beg for mercy until the beast within me is sated. But none of that will matter now I understand the problem. Fuck, I hate Sharon is the one to put things into perspective, but I realise why Axel doesn't believe I can change. No one will ever believe it because I've never given them cause to. But I'm gonna prove them all wrong. So, fucking wrong.

∞∞∞

"Yes, there. It's perfect." I glance around the patio, excitement rippling through me. Avery has just finished dotting candles around the hammocks, Huxley following to light them while Dax works on lighting the fire pit. He nudges the burning wood with a steel poker and places a mesh cover on top, heat already radiating around us. Night has fallen, a thick blanket of the deepest blue acting as our canopy, thousands of twinkling specks covering the moonless sky.

Avery retrieves some thick blankets and cushions from inside, adding homely touches to my master plan. When I'd gone in search and found the three of them in the gym earlier, I'd been more than surprised with their instant agreement to help me. I hadn't given any of them enough credit, having been too focused on Axel to remember these fuckwits are still my family. The only one I've got.

The grandfather clock inside chimes, announcing the arrival of the late hour I asked Axel to meet me down here. I quickly shoo everyone back inside, putting a pin in thanking them as I tell them to fuck off. Running a hand through my hair, I smooth it over and frown at my tracksuit. Maybe I should have changed. Axel steps into view, the sight of his muscular frame in his basketball kit and slanted smile instantly banishing all my doubts. If he's with me, nothing else matters.

"You look amazing," I breathe. His brows quirk as if I'm exaggerating but I've never been more serious. From his freshly shaven head to the single mole on the sole of his right foot, he's perfect to me. Sliding my arm into his, I lead him outside. Wood crackles within the firepit, a faint line of smoke drifting upwards. The scent of fresh cut grass drifts to us, Axel's favourite smell, after I forced the butler to skip serving Sharon's dinner and mow the lawn instead.

"What is all this?" Axel asks, his tone laced with surprise.

"I wanted to talk," I mumble, suddenly and ridiculously shy. I don't usually handle opening up very well, but the whole bottle of Jack Daniels I downed a short while ago has definitely taken the edge off. Holding the double hammock still, Axel settles himself inside carefully. Nudging in beside him, I cover us with a checked blanket and slide my arm beneath his head, so he's forced to snuggle into my side – not that he needed any encouragement. We stare up at the stars, all the words I want to say muddling in my mind, yet nothing spills from my lips.

"What did you want to talk about?" Axel finally asks the question I knew was coming but was still dreading.

"So much has happened this past week. We didn't get to finish our conversation from before..." My eyes drift to his stomach, wishing for the millionth time I could have taken his place.

"We argued, it's what people do." Axel shrugs. "We're back to normal again now."

"No, it's what couples do. And we've never been normal. So where does that leave us?"

"I thought you didn't do labels," Axel grins up at me but I can't return it. He's acting as if we can still be carefree fuckbuddies like before, but surely he can sense everything has changed. This soul consuming, heart pounding pressure I've been carrying around can't possibly be one sided.

"You said when I was ready to say the words out loud, you'd be ready to hear them. Is that still the case?" I hedge around what I really want to say, fearing his answer. If Axel rejects me, I don't think I'd survive it. Shifting onto his side with a grunt, he stares into my eyes, searching for truth in my words.

"I don't want you to get confused between caring for me

and feeling for me. Maybe you've got caught up in being with me too much, but when we return to Waversea, think of how you'll feel with all the ladies fighting for your attention again. If you continue down this path, I fear its only me who is going to get hurt." I grind my jaw, focusing on a bright star directly above. He was all for us before but it's like he's trying to push me away. I must make him see how badly I want this.

"You know you're the only one I've ever had meaningful sex with and the connection is real. But I want to be more than physical with you." A glaze covers his amber eyes, so much hope held within their depths that I long to fulfil.

"People don't change overnight Garrett. I can tell you want to, but I don't think it'll be enough. Why can't we keep things the way they were?" The strangest notion to cry pricks the back of my eyes, something I haven't done in so long I thought my tear ducts had seized up. I can sense I'm losing this battle, but I can't give up.

"I'm not the same person I was, even just last week. I nearly lost you and, in that moment, everything I wished I'd said to you nearly consumed me. I want more, I want you. And I need your help to get there." My free hand winds around his neck, my thumb stroking his strong jawline as I tilt his face up towards me further.

"Gare, I can't- "

"Please Axel. We can do this, be a proper couple."

"I don't believe you." He breathes, my heart hitching on half a beat. I can tell I'm hurting him, but I can't stop. If I close myself off now, I'm certain I'll never be able to open up to another again. I'm ripping out my bloody, charred heart and offering it to him on a platter.

"Then believe this." I close the small distance between us to press my lips against his. Kissing him tenderly, drawing him into my body to tell him I'm all his. His lips are achingly soft, my raw heart beating in time to his as we lose ourselves in the moment. Breaths mingling, stubble grazing. A salty wetness seeps into my mouth, Axel's tears glistening in the candlelight. I kiss a trail up each of his cheeks, banishing his doubt and saying a silent vow to never make him cry ever again.

"I promise to never hurt or let you down. Be my boyfriend Axel, just mine and I'll be all yours. Only yours." I turn into his body, our chests pressing against each other and I place a hand over his heart. I draw a line across his jaw with my nose, nuzzling into his neck the way he likes. I won't stop until he understands how much I need him. Kissing back up to his ear, I rest my forehead against his to stare straight into his incredible eyes.

"Say yes," I whisper against his lips. It feels unnatural to let so much vulnerability show in my features, the only person I've ever deemed worthy of fighting for holding my future in his hands.

"Yes."

Avery

Usually I hate the rain, but as I lie in bed pretending to be asleep, I'm thankful for the cover its going to provide me for what I'm about to do. With everything that's been going on, I'd almost forgotten what today was, but luckily a whisper came to me in a dream and jolted me awake. The day has just broken although no one would think so with the looming, grey clouds filling the sky though our net curtain. Sliding silently out of the bed, Huxley's light snores still sounding from the opposite side, I crawl to the chest of drawers I've claimed and pull out some black jeans and a long-sleeved top. Piling my underwear and biker boots into my arms, I creep around the edge of the room, unhooking Huxley's jacket from the back of the door before slipping out.

Only the constant ticking of a grandfather clock below the bannister sounds as I rush into the bathroom to wash and change. Dragging my fingers through my hair, I quickly braid it down the length of my spine and I pull the large hood low over my eyes to conceal most of my features. Feeling the heavy weight of the jacket's pocket in my hand, my head starts to spin with anticipation. Taking a steading breath, goose bumps line my arms between the cotton, I tiptoe back into the hallway and down the darkened staircase.

Butler Bill rounds the corner by the kitchen, my heart lurching as I dive behind an unnecessarily tall vase. He passes in his full butler attire, coattails, and all, too focused on the shaky tray in his hands to notice me. The scent of buttery toast and sweet tea coil around me, my stomach grumbling in protest, but I don't have time for breakfast. If any of the guys discover what I'm doing, they'll tie me to the bed and won't let me out of their sight for a long time.

Carefully checking each corner before continuing, I move through the mansion as quickly as I dare and come to a halt at the front door. Glancing back at the stillness behind me, I leave the safety within and escape into the pouring rain. Fat droplets pelt onto the jacket instantly as I fumble in the pocket to remove the Nissan's keys, briefly wondering if I should have left an apology note. I sprint over to the flash of headlights as I unlock the doors, diving inside as a flash of lightening bursts overhead.

A tiny part of me is screaming it's not too late, run back inside, slip into bed and pretend nothing happened. But I can't do that. My conscience will never forgive me. Pushing the key into the ignition before I can chicken out, the windscreen wipers begin swaying frantically and I slowly ease the car out of the driveaway. The loosening of freedom I thought I'd feel doesn't come as I pull onto the street, more like a painful tightening of dread. Rain batters against the windscreen, making each traffic light and street name hazy but fortunately, I know exactly where I'm going.

Pulling up against a sidewalk a short while later, the sun has begun to peek through the clouds. The raindrops have lessened to a gentle sprinkling over the stationary car and I trail my fingers along the trickling pathways they create down the windowpanes. I've parked a few streets over, erring on the side of caution even though it takes a little longer, winding through backstreets and circling back on myself to make sure I wasn't followed. Tugging the hood back down to cover the top half of my face, I exit the vehicle without wasting any more time on 'what ifs' and finish my morning adventure on foot.

Halting in front of the iron gates that have kept me safe from outside threats for the past seven years, I stare longingly at the building within. I'd expected the mansion to be deserted but still, the lack of light within and shadows cast over the outside seem sadly cold. No one would believe we hosted the best Halloween parties or danced around the Christmas tree on December 1st, singing at the top of our lungs. The stone walls appear to have long forgotten the lively personality mum once brought, the wilted flowers no longer able to blossom without her laughter around.

Checking either side of me, there's not a soul around except for a red Mini Cooper parked at the end of the street so I discreetly key the pin into the side gate and slip inside. Jogging up the gravelled driveaway, I head to the back of the house and duck out of sight from the main street. Leaves and twigs litter the swimming pool, beer bottles strewn across the patio from our rushed exit.

Dropping to my knees by the French sliding doors, I scramble my way through a thick bush to the left until my fingers graze the hidden key box attached to the outer wall. Without needing to see, I'm able to locate the finger sensor and release the key to let myself into my home. An overpowering stale smell hits me before I notice the layer of dust covering every surface. Tiptoeing, despite being alone, I head for the kitchen first and pluck Detective Vincent's contact card from the refrigerator. Dirty dishes are piled in the sink, the clumps of mould covering them making me gag.

Deciding to call Susie in when I get back to Axel's to sort this place out before it becomes uninhabitable, I move into Nixon's office and settle myself into his leather chair. He always kept spare cell phones in his desk drawer for some reason, although now I understand his need for multiple burners. Plucking out the first one I grab; I switch it on to dial the number on the card. The dial tone sounds on repeat while my eyes drift over the mess of strewn papers and open cupboards the police must have left.

"Hello?" a familiar voice answers after almost a full minute.

"Hey, Detective Vincent. It's Avery." I swing side to side in the chair as a there's a slight pause on the other end of the receiver.

"Oh my, Avery! I've been so worried about you. Where have you been, are you safe?"

"Yes, I'm safe. I've just popped back to my house to do something quickly. I'm staying at my friend Axel's place which is convenient because he lives nearby in Georgia too. I just wanted to see if you had any news on the men that kept breaking into my house?" I ask coyly, not wanting to spill the secret of Meg being my twin but also secretly hoping Perelli has been identified and Meg has already been rescued.

"No leads unfortunately. Have you come across any clues as to who they might be?" I bite my bottom lip, wondering whether to tell her everything I know in the hopes it will save Meg quicker. But Nixon was adamant her link to me was kept a secret, so I must trust I'll find another way.

"Nothing," I sigh. We finish the conversation pleasantly and I immediately power off the cell phone, slipping it into my coat pocket in case I need it for later. I don't know how I'm ever going to find my twin, but I'll never stop trying. I just need a clue as to where Wyatt might have taken her. I know Perelli runs the mob in Chicago, but I can hardly drive there and start asking randoms on the street where he lives. Although soon that might be my only option. Not to give him any credit, but weirdly I think Wyatt has helped me to face the fearsome reality of the world I was hiding from. I'm invincible now, and nothing will stop me from getting my twin back.

A bang sounds upstairs, my heart lurching in panic. My breathing halts as the room starts to tilt, panic seizing my body.

A part of me wants to crawl beneath the desk and hide, I was just praying for a lead and I might have found one. Sliding out of the chair, I dash to the wooden sideboard and lift the lid where a double-barrelled shotgun is hidden. My mum had insisted I visited a gun range once every three months to boost my confidence and learn to protect myself, so I load in the two shells and brace myself to put her money to good use.

Twisting the doorknob, I push the door open with my foot. Both hands are on the gun, my eye trained down the lens as I dash across the hall into the gym. Moving into the hidden staircase at the back, I creep up the stairs and nudge the top door open with the gun's muzzle. Shuffling catches my ears, a figure shifting back and forth in the master bedroom. There's a duffle bag on the end of the unmade bed, wads of cash piled into it. A man walks back to the bag, stuffing several passports and documents into the bag's side pockets. He is almost unrecognizable in khaki shorts and a garishly printed shit, his hairs almost fully silver and a beard lines his jaw. But I'd know him anywhere.

"Nixon?!" I shout excitedly, bursting through the doorway. He whirls around with a handgun pointed directly at my forehead, his blue eyes wide with shock and confusion.

"Avery? Where, what...what were you thinking, I could have killed you!" I can't help but smile, dropping the shotgun as I run into his body for a hug. I was so worried I wouldn't see him for so long and with everything that's happened, he'll know what to do. His strong hands land on my shoulders, pushing me back a step so he can assess me. "What are you doing here?" he growls.

"It's mum's birthday," I shrug like that's the most rational thing in the world. "I had to visit the makeshift grave I made for her by the honey blossom tree." Nixon's eyes flick to the smart watch on his wrist to confirm today's date which makes him frown. He never forgets an important date, but if that's the case this time, why is *he* here? I glance between the duffle bag and the open safe on the opposite wall, most of its contents cleared out. Holy shit, this is what I've been waiting for.

"They've contacted you, haven't they? You're going to pay a ransom to get Meg back." I beam widely, relief washing over me. Nixon doesn't seem as optimistic though, the creases in his forehead deepening.

"Wait, Megan's missing? How did that happen and why aren't you in the safe house where I left you?" The way he said the last bit makes it sound like he wasn't planning on ever coming back.

"Wyatt tricked us. He kidnapped Meg and took her to Perelli. I've been trying to think of a way to save her but you can help me. Where does he live?" The full bellied, sinister laugh Nixon releases makes me feel two inches tall.

"Avery, sweetheart," he pulls me around to perch on the edge of the bed and tucks me beneath his arm. "I'm sorry, but if Perelli has Meg then there is nothing we can do. But maybe this is a blessing, you finding me here. I have a private jet leaving for Tokyo in two hours and I've had false documents for you since we brought you back home. Come with me, we can live without fear." Rising and crossing the room, Nixon pulls out a handful of forged documents and hands them to me, each one with my face but a different name on.

"But Meg needs us. We can't run away and leave her."

"I know it won't be easy, but I think it is best to accept she might already be gone. We have a chance to get out of here, she'd have wanted that for you." I'm already shaking my head, refusing to believe his words. Fury as hot as lava bubbles in my chest that he dared to use the past tense while speaking of her. Meg is a part of my soul; we share a spirit and I can feel she's still alive.

"What kind of cowardly piece of shi- "A crash bellows through the building, the ground beneath our feet shaking viciously. Brick flying and glass shattering are quickly followed by a man shouting, ordering others to fan out and 'find her.' Nixon whirls on me, his features livid and fingers biting into my upper arms.

"Who did you tell you were coming here?" A hiss escapes me from his grip, the man I thought I knew glaring at me as if I've ruined his plans. My eyes land back on the duffle bag as it dawns on me, he hasn't been drawing Perelli's attention away from us like he said – he's been running and hiding this whole time. Leaving us to fend for ourselves in his fight.

"No one," I snarl back, shoving his hands off me. Thunderous footfalls are racing up the stairs, doors banging open as they get closer. My eyes dart to the safe, the large rectangular space probably just deep enough for me to squeeze into. Without wasting any time, I run across and hoist myself into the steel box, pulling my knees up to my chest and cranking my neck. Nixon is there in a second, pushing the door closed with a millimetre gap spare. Replacing the portrait of my mum on the wall, the tiny crack of light I had dissolves a second before the door to the room bursts open.

"Where is she?" A gruff man's voice shouts, a smash reverberating through the wall as I imagine Nixon is thrown against it. More men enter, the sound of shouting becoming deafeningly loud until I'm forced to cover my ears. My mind goes wild, flashing images to match the scuffles and crashes I can still hear. My heart is pounding, a rising panic attack threatening to consume me, but I just about keep it shimmering for now. Nixon's shouts grow quieter until they disappear altogether, leaving me alone and unsure what to do.

"She's not here," the same gruff voice booms through the mansion's walls. I remain wedged in the safe, not wanting to leave in case it's a trick. The darkness around me filters into my soul, a bitter taste left in my mouth. I'm utterly alone now. Every one of my family has gone – mum, Meg, Nixon and even

Wyatt, and I have no way to get any of them back. Tears spill down my legs, my neck stiff and legs cramping but still I remain.

A soothing thought reaches me in the depths of my grief; I'm not completely alone. There are four others that have proved time and again they will fight for me, bleed for me. They've welcomed me into their hearts, but I haven't given them the same courtesy. The Shadowed Souls isn't a name for a bunch of lost teenagers who had shitty upbringings, they are a solid unit. There for each other when it really matters, defending their brothers with a bond stronger than blood. I may not know what to do next, but I know they will have my back. My true family.

Wyatt

Stepping into the scolding spray of water, I instantly grab a sponge and scrub every inch of skin Meg touched. Not because I'm disgusted, because I liked it. What is wrong with me? I had such a clear plan, deliver Ray his revenge and live an easy, quiet life hiding away from the world in a place I'm wanted. But the Meg had to come along with her pale blue eyes that haunt my dreams and stoke my nightmares. Her brown waves felt so right wrapped around my hand as she took me all the way into her mouth with ease. I'm still as hard as granite, nowhere near sated enough when my fingers itch to pleasure her, my cock throbbing to feel her clench around me with my name falling from her lips. Fuck, I'm seriously in trouble here.

My body is rubbed raw by the time I give up, unable to banish her from my mind. There was a connection between us, I'm sure of it and I won't be able to rest until I know for sure if she feels the same. It's stupid of me to consider I could be of worth to someone, especially when I can't have a future with her but the longing look in her eyes couldn't have been my imagination. Even if we have missed the chance to explore it further, I need to know.

Hopping from the shower cubicle and roughly drying my body, I make quick work of picking out a fresh tracksuit and dressing with hurried fingers. I pause briefly, my fingers still on my fly as I glance around and notice there's no shadow lurking in the corner. I take in the whole room, hunting for the figure that's been keeping me company but she's nowhere to be seen. My untouched pill box on the bedside table is staring back at me and I have to wonder what's to blame for her sudden disappearance, and if I'm upset by it or not.

Refocusing on the warm feeling spreading through my limbs and not wasting time with a t-shirt, I zip up my hoodie and leave the room with excitement bubbling within me. I need to lock this shit down, not bound back to her like a giddy school-boy with his first crush. I've never lacked a woman to warm my bed at night, but I've never had anything close to a connection to one.

Suddenly remembering I need the key to her cell, the thought crushing the reality of our situation back into me, I jog back to find my discarded jeans on my bedroom floor. My hands search the pockets, my eyebrows creasing as each one comes up empty. Shit, I must have dropped it. Unless…no. There's no way. She couldn't have used me…

Running down the staircase at a speed my feet are unable to keep up with, I ignore the curious glances thrown my way by passing guards and vault myself into the stone stairwell which leads beneath the house. I slow my steps, my heart beating out of tune with anticipation for what I'm about to find. Please let me be wrong about this. Stepping off the final stair, my eyes land on the heavy chain sprawled across the floor, the key still in the padlock hooked into it. Her door is ajar, only darkness lurking within. I'm aware she acted as any prisoner on death row would, but I still can't help to wonder if it was her fate she was running from or was it me too?

A hard wall shuts down over my emotions, anger at my own foolishness taking over. How could I have been so stupid?! Of course, she'd never want me, I was just a part of her plans, an obstacle in the way. Figuring she wouldn't have risked venturing into the main house, I take off in the opposite direction. The floor slopes a little as I'm enveloped in pitch black, unable to see my hand in front of my face as I trail the wall with my fingers. I creep softly, listening for any signs of life up ahead.

The tunnel twists and winds further than I expected, my hand falling into the air each time I reach a sharp corner. There could be multiple different routes for all I know but I keep following the same wall, trying to keep up a steady pace to find her before Ray realizes she's missing. I don't know why I feel the need to protect her, but if I can manage to usher her back into the cell before the guards bring the slop they call her dinner, she won't need to suffer any more than she already is. Well, until they kill her at least.

My fingers smooth across the brass hinges of a door in time to stop myself from crashing into it. Wooden grooves and a closed metal sheet over the grate tell me this is the same type of door as the cell's, the hint of a light inside visible through a couple of widened cracks now I'm looking closer. A muffled scream sounds from inside, my heart thrashing around my rib cage as I recognise Meg's high-pitch and I heave the door open within needing to think about it.

A faint bulb dangles from the ceiling glowing across a widened cell. A topless figure has Meg pinned beneath his weight on a wooden bed, his hand covering her mouth. I lunge forward on instinct, ripping him off and throwing him at the wall as adrenaline floods my system. Lifting him by the throat, I punch his face over and over until my own knuckles split on impact, his cheekbone now matching his shattered nose. He doesn't fight back or resist, hanging limping while I sate my anger on his face. I only stop when his face is covered in his own blood and Meg's screams finally penetrate the rage that had consumed me.

Rushing over to her, I notice my t-shirt is hanging open across her chest and I step back to attack him again until Meg's hand snakes around my arm. Her fingers are trembling against my skin and not from the bitter cold surrounding us. Shedding my hoodie, I ease her into it and scan her body for any physical injuries, relieved to find I must have got here just in time. Kneeling and taking her face in my bloodied hands, I stare deeply into her glazed eyes.

"It-it's him. F-f-Fredrick Walters," tears spill over as she points over to the man now slumped on the floor. Shock slackens my jaw and momentarily freezes me in place, a war of emotions I can't handle all at once bursting to life within me. Regardless of how I feel about Avery, I would protect her from the piece of scum that stole her childhood any day of the week. Pulling Meg to her feet, I turn to keep her hidden behind my back and link my fingers into hers. To comfort her and to steady myself, the urge to rip his head from his shoulders overwhelming. But first I need to understand what's going on. Having been recently released from prison and hiding in a forgotten crevice of Ray's house can't be a coincidence.

"Why are you here?" I manage to say evenly, despite my hands tightening around Meg's.

"She looks just like her..." his British accent trails off instead of answering me, his eyes fixed on Meg peering around me as he licks his lips suggestively. "Avery was always my favourite. She was different, special...." Unable to listen to him any longer, I step forward and kick my foot directly below the vertical scar lining his chest that Avery gave him all those years ago, making him cough and wheeze. Crouching down, I drag him up by the pathetic bit of hair he has left and growl into his face.

"How are you in Chicago?" I grit through my teeth. His different coloured eyes land on me as if he hadn't realized I was here, too wrapped up in his sick fantasies no doubt.

"I spent six years in a cell like this one," he looks around fondly as I claw at every inch of patience I can muster, "thinking of her. Needing her. But when I came to visit, I saw her in the car with that woman. The one that stole her from me, and I had to free her. But it didn't work. Until Ray found me, he's promised me I can have her one last time before she is…" A tear slips from his brown eye, mixing with the blood coating his skin as his words untangle in my mind.

"You were the drunk driver that killed Cathy Hughes, aren't you?" I whisper in a deadly tone. A fucking smirk pulls at his lips and I snap. Yanking back on his hair, I throw every modicum of rage, grief, anguish, and heartache into my punch to his throat. He splays across the floor, writhing around holding his throat as he gasps for the breath, I've made sure he won't be able to take. Stepping back, I pull Meg into my side and she hugs my waist tightly, burying her face into my shoulder. I stroke her hair gently, my eyes glued on the paedophile before me who is rapidly turning blue, his movements becoming sluggish and involuntary.

Once his body has stilled and the life has drained from his wide eyes, I edge Meg from the chamber without a trace of regret. We slowly walk back through the maze of corridors in silence, her arms locked around my waist the whole way. Her curves feel so right against me, but I must remind myself I'm merely the only person here. If it weren't for her bad luck at finding a way out, she'd be long gone and never think of me again. We return to the lit area by the stairs and I feel like I should say something, but she immediately walks out of the comfort of my body and into her cell without a word.

Pulling the door closed between us, she shifts around inside, and I stand awkwardly, not knowing whether I should stay or leave. Remembering Ray will expect her to be chained inside, even though she would probably stay inside by choice now, I move forward to wind the chain back into position and fix the padlock in place, pocketing the key. Not having a reason to stay, I begin to walk away when her voice finds me.

"Do you see now, the type of people you are affiliated with?" She is slumped down behind the door so I can't see her, although I can hear the sobs she's desperately trying to conceal.

My chest aches and I feel the strange need to help, but it's no use. She's mostly likely hiding away from me as much as anyone else in the mansion.

"I didn't want to do any of this," I confess on a sigh, running a hand over my face, "I just wanted a family. I didn't have a choice." Her face appears through the steel bars, her wet eyes blazing with fury.

"Oh, you had a choice alright, and you chose yourself like the self-centred prick you are. You were saved from a life of who knows what - drugs addiction, abusive pimps, maybe unwanted visitors in your room late night? But like always, you've twisted the truth to accommodate your own feelings because you think you're not worthy of being loved. Have you ever once thought that it was Avery who saved you?" I stand rooted to the spot, unable to deny her words. "She lost the spoilt life you've led, being given to that monster and forced to suffer by his hand for years. And now you've joined an organisation who openly encourages his kind of behaviour, so well done. You win the biggest fuck-up of the century award."

I can't believe she thinks I would willingly associate myself with such a monster, the hurt in her accusation cutting me worse than the betrayal of her escape did. I open my mouth to bite back when the door at the top of the stairs flies open. There's a scuffle of multiple pairs of feet speeding down the steps so I jump out of the way. Two burly guards have a greying man held tightly in their grip: his busted lip almost concealed by the long beard hanging from his chin. Baggy shorts and a boldly printed shirt have me dismissing him, until a pair of icy blue eyes glance up at me. Holy shit.

"Dad?"

Huxley

"What do you mean she's missing?" Dax seethes, bumping chests with me. Garrett and Axel descend the stairs, sleepy eyed and leaning on each other after I tossed them out of bed. A pound of my fist on Dax's door had been enough to draw him out and meet me down in the central hallway.

"I've searched everywhere, I can't find her. And then I realized...my car's gone." I breathe out a sigh, bracing myself for the onslaught of shouts that never comes. Instead, everyone's wide eyes dart around in silence as if Avery will pop up and say 'Psych'. I hadn't thought much of Avery not being in the bed when I woke as she usually hits the gym first thing, but when she wasn't in there or the kitchen or anywhere else I looked, a sense of dread filled me.

"Well it's obvious where she'll have gone, we're in Georgia for fuck's sake." Dax runs a hand down his face roughly before pointing at me. "Find that butler, get him to bring a car around and we'll meet back- "

"She's here," Axel gestures to the orange blur racing past the frosted glass panels on the front door. The tyres screech to a halt as we race forward to open the door, Dax and I bumping shoulders to be the first to give her hell. I rip the door open, a harsh scold dying on my tongue as a blur of blonde runs straight into Dax's body. He's forced back a step, bracing his arms around her as she cries. I pry my keys from her grip, locking my car in its slanted position with a curve of skid marks trailing behind on the driveway.

Garrett and Axel close in either side of Dax, crushing Avery between them all in a group hug. Her sobs lessen while I stand awkwardly on the outside. Fuck it, I shove my way in behind her and wind my arms around her waist, Garrett and Axel drawing me in with their hands on my back. The lime scent of our shower gel fills my nose as I nuzzle into her neck, her body trembling beneath us as she focuses on breathing deeply.

"They've taken Nixon," she eventually murmurs. Dax kisses her forehead, his hair tickling my face and Axel whimpers softly into my ear like a wounded animal. "He was at the house, grabbing fake passports to run and I don't think he ever planned on coming back. But then some men came and I hid- "she hiccups, her choked sobs beginning to return. Dax draws her from the cage of our bodies, leading her into the living room while we follow as if an invisible tether is pulling us along. Tugging her down onto his lap on the sofa, I veer into the kitchen to make her an overly sweet tea.

Returning with the steaming mug in my hands, I find Avery curled into Axel's side with Garrett staring into space on his other side. Placing the cup onto a glass coffee table, I slide in beside her and take her hand in mine.

"Where's Dax?" I ask, only receiving a shake of the head from Axel as he mouths 'don't ask.' I roll my eyes, knowing Avery came to her senses and sent him away like usual. Those two need locking in a room until they've solved their petty arguments and I'm half the mind to do it. A blind man could sense the overriding tension between them, and that level of friction can only form between two people with a real connection, something worth fighting for.

Garret re-joins us in the room, turning his head as if he's only just noticed I'm here. He doesn't hide his scowl at seeing Axel stroke Avery's hair and I could believe he was jealous if he were capable of such emotion. Garrett doesn't do jealously because he doesn't give a shit about anything or anyone enough, he glides through life with no strings to tie him down and I almost hate him for it. How freeing it must be to only care about yourself.

Leaning forward, he lifts the cup and transfers it into Avery's hands, so she's forced to sit upright, before grabbing the tv remote and switches on the large screen opposite us. Axel retracts his arm from Avery's shoulders so she can sit back fully, which gives Garrett a green light to pull him into his own body protectively. A rerun of Fresh Prince of Bel Air has started, filling the silence with Will Smith's fictionalized self-taunting his cousins.

I feel the need to say something, anything that could reassure Avery. But I won't give her false promises. I can't promise to get Meg or Nixon back safety and I definitely can't promise not to kill Wyatt the second I see him again, knowing full well it's Avery's right to make him suffer. Everything is so fucked, but she's safe so I selfishly sit here with the comforting curve of her body pressed against my arm and simply enjoy the moment.

Dead on 5pm, the front doors burst open and the group of teenager's spill into the hallway to work for the weekend. I lean forward on the bannister, watching curiously as they all spilt off to find the rooms they've claimed. Their laughter and excitement make this place feel more like a frat house, a pair of guys pushing and bumping each other to race up the stairs. Top Knot is the last to enter, closing the doors and inhaling deeply, the smile on his face Joker-worthy. Spotting me, he jogs up the stairs and crosses the hallway to clasp me on the shoulder like old friends.

"Hey Huxley! Thank fuck it's Friday, am I right?" He winks, strolling past to enter the bedroom beside mine. Halting in the doorway, he looks back to me with his wicked smile still in place. "You know, you should join us tonight. It's a hell of a thrill."

"Join you doing what?" I ask, my interest piqued.

"In the auction, duh. Friday night is auction night, hordes of thirsty middle-aged women with more money than sense. Some bid for a few of us at once and they pay double if you need to sign an NDA to stop you blabbing to their husbands." His body is practically shaking with enthusiasm as he bobs his eyebrows at me.

"Even if I did need the money, there's no way in hell I'd pimp myself out to a pack of desperate cougars."

"Maybe so, but it's about more than just the money. You can live out your darkest fantasies, nothing's off limits and these ladies are always gagging for more and more. Think about it, we head to the ballroom in an hour. Dress smart." He throws me another wink before disappearing, his cocky demeanour irritating me. Confused and more than a little disturbed, I slowly edge towards Axel's door, dodging streams of excited ladies running in and out of each other's rooms in their underwear. Many stops in their tracks, freely exploring my body with their eyes and running off giggling, leaving me feeling oddly exposed in my gym vest and shorts.

Knocking lightly on the door at the end, Garrett whips his head around the door with a scowl like I was expecting. The pair are known for their afternoon naps, like a pair of cats that only wake for mealtimes. His pissed expression at me shifts when he sees the chaos happening over my shoulder and asks what's going on.

"I think Sharon is up to something. Keep Axel in his room tonight, I'm gonna find out what's going on around here." Garrett nods in agreement, muttering something that sounds a lot like a 'thank you' before slamming the door in my face. Deciding I must have misheard, I head back into my room to prepare myself for tonight.

Avery is curled up on the bed with a cat nestled against her, soft purrs vibrating through the air with each stroke she smooths down its stripy spine. Her bright blue eyes are shining with unshed tears and staring at a spot on the far wall. I close the door as quietly as possible and join her on the mustard-coloured duvet, our foreheads touching. The cat, who's black collar has 'COMET' printed across it in silver, stretches between us and paws at my stomach for attention. I scratch the soft patch between his ears, but my focus is on the beautiful girl with haunted eyes beside me.

"Hey Aves?" I whisper, waiting for her hum in answer. "I just found out Sharon is still running the auctions like she used to, except with consenting young adults this time. Like the madame at a brothel. I'm going to head down soon to play along, and then fuck some shit up. If you need a distraction, you're welcome to join me. We could have some fun," a slanted grin takes root on my face. After a beat, a similar expression shifts into her features along with a cruel edge.

"Let's do it." Comet gets the fright of his life as we both fly from the bed, jumping up with an arched back and hissing loudly. Leaping from the bed with a flick of his tail, I open the door so he can exit while Avery digs through the boxes filling half the room in search something for us to wear. On the third box she flicks open, she shouts 'Aha!' and pulls out a long, suit bag with multiple hangers poking out the top.

Laying it across the bed, she unzips the bag and shifts through the stack of men's clothes, picking out a sharp navy suit for me. After I take the hanger from her, Avery moves over to my bag and rifles through until she finds one of my generic black tops. I watch her curiously as she wiggles out of her pyjamas, standing before me gloriously naked and slips my top over her head and arms until it rests beneath her armpits and on her thighs. She then pulls each sleeve across her bust to make a criss-cross and tucks into the hem around her back. Donning the silver heels and jewellery from Sharon's dinner party/blind date from hell, Avery instantly looks a million dollars and I'll never look at that top the same way again.

I quickly change into the suit, leaving the top buttons of the white shirt open beneath the waistcoat and run my fingers through my wavy hair. Not having any other option, I shove my feet into my white high-tops and shrug on the blazer. Avery turns back to me having tied her hair into a low bun and added a light dusting of make up to her face, looking ruthlessly determined to exact revenge on at least one tyrant tonight. I hear the footfalls of the others descending the stairwell outside and offer Avery my arm, opening the door and slipping into the crowd.

The noise emanating from the ballroom is a powerful mix of enthusiastic chatter and bitchy whispers which I can hear before even entering. Arriving in the doorway, Avery hesitates and yanks me back a few steps. The smartly dressed teens around us take no notice, pushing past to ascend on the room of excitable women. Hands paw over them as they move through, the bidders eager to feel the goods before the auction begins. I flick my eyes to Avery's, pulling her to the back wall of the corridor and bending to speak into her ear.

"If you've changed your mind, we can- "

"It's not that," she breathes against my neck. "I promised Axel I would never enter the ballroom. It seemed important to him..." her voice trails off, her gaze flicking back to the brightly lit room. Being head and shoulders above everyone else, I'm able to see the open set of French doors at the rear leading out onto an equally as packed terrace. Linking my fingers in hers, I guide her along the corridor and through yet another living room the mansion doesn't need, exiting via a patio door at the back. Rounding the side of the building, we re-join the crowd and I smirk down at her.

"Problem solved." Her wide smile beams back at me just as Sharon steps onto a platform at the front. Not a hair is out of place, tightly tied back in a slick ponytail with the deep shade of red on her lips matching her tight bodycon dress. A microphone has been set up at the front of the stage and spotlights shine down on her so brightly, I'm positive she can't see out into the crowd. The staff members I recognise from the kitchen, along with a dozen I haven't seen before, have lined themselves along the wall to Sharon's left. Their chests are puffed out proudly, the finest suits and cocktail dresses dripping from their slender frames.

Sharon is too busy reciting a list of rules she clearly knows by heart to notice us amongst her rich friends while I try to think of a way to slyly ruin her evening. My brain snags on a particular piece of information, that she retains 25% of all winning bids to fund future auctions and an idea cements in my mind. I whisper the plan into Avery's ear, and she suppresses a giggle as someone bumps into me roughly. I look around with a scowl but there's too many women milling around to pinpoint who exactly wasn't watching where they were going.

The first willing candidate is called on stage, a heavily freckled guy of medium build with auburn hair which cause a small group of ladies in the right corner to giggle and bounce with anticipation. I point them out to Avery, and we veer off to approach the small group from either side. Sharon suggests the bidding starts at $15,000 and a plump woman in front of me gets ready to shoot her hand into the air.

"Hey Aves," I whisper shout across them, "wasn't he the one that gave crabs to a whole group last week?"

"Oh, I heard they were fleas and he got them from the cat. That guy sure loves pussy." The women around us balk and gasp, quickly rushing away to filter the rumour through the crowd as

Avery and I fall apart. Sharon calls again for the bids to start, her face dropping as no response comes. Shooing freckle face from the stage, she flaps her hand for the next girl in the queue to jump into the spotlight. A blonde with purple tints in the ends of her long curls bounces onto stage, her skimpy dress exposing her huge chest and tiny waist. Introduced as Vicky, she pushes her cleavage together while I wind my way to another part of the crowd.

"Vagina wider than the Grand Canyon, that one." I murmur loudly enough for a huddle to my left to hear. Not surprisingly, a flow of hushed whispers passes from one end of the crowd to the other and no bids are entered. Sharon stomps across the stage on her black heels, pointing to a girl further down the line and beckoning her onto the platform at once. The brunette is incredibly pretty, an eyebrow cocked over her doe eyes as she nibbles on her bottom lip suggestively.

"Let's start Felicity off at $10,000, shall we? She's rather wild and enjoys sharing partners with a group," Sharon's voice rolls through the speakers dotted around the patio seductively.

"Don't forget how she passes out every time she cums, without fail. We had to call for an ambulance last time," Avery speaks loudly with a broad American accent. Murmurs and questionable glances are passed around, no one bids on poor Felicity either. She runs off stage, holding her face in her hands but I can't bring myself to feel bad. I'm too busy enjoying myself by ripping away the only thing Sharon cares about – money.

"Moving on, a few of you might recognise Karen- "

"Oh, not Chlamydia Karen," I moan, not bothering to disguise my voice.

"Whoever that is needs to report to me at once. There have never been any complaints with my volunteers, and they are all tested for STD's on a regular basis." There's a defiant tick in Sharon's jaw, but still no one raises their hand to bid. Silence falls over the gardens, only the sound of crickets filling the empty void around us. “Well Daniel here- “

“Cries when he cums,” Avery cups her mouth to shout. Holding a hand up against the glare, Sharon squints out into the crowd and demands whoever is ruining her auction to come forward. Edging towards the back of the terrace with Avery in tow, I notice many of the women shift backwards with nervous looks, eager to hear out opinions. Most of the ‘volunteers’ have understood tonight isn’t happening for them and scurried off, all except one.

Top Knot steps onto the stage confidently, widening his stance and crossing his arms in a dare for anyone to challenge his reputation. Plenty of women around us sigh dramatically, clearly familiar with him and Sharon smirks knowingly.

“Ahh, Seamus. Now here is a young man no one can dispute against. He has a perfect track record for satisfaction, always goes the extra mile and is especially well equipped, if I do say so myself. Since it’s been a slow evening, we will start the bidding at $50,000.” Every head in front of us spins around sharply, waiting for approval to bid. So many pairs of eyes are pleading for me to give the all-clear, but it’s not me that responds to their questioning stares.

“Oh yeah, sure. Best night of my life,” Avery says, much to the delight of every woman around us. Their shoulders sag and they share relieved smiles. “Until he asked to do 69 without telling me about his rectal condition. I’ve never been able to get the overriding warmth of shit to leave the back of my throat.” An uproar of cries and gagging gives us the perfect cover to duck out, Avery grabs my hand and drags me through the masses. We don’t stop running until we spill into our room, slamming the door closed and rushing to change back into our pyjamas in case Sharon comes looking for a culprit.

Collapsing on the bed, we roll around in complete hysterics, tears streaming from our ears and my wide smile beginning to hurt my cheeks. At one point, I think the infectious laughter will never end as one of us begins to stop, the other starts back up again. If screwing with Sharon wasn't enough, seeing Avery full of life and happiness is everything. Eventually, we relax until only a few chuckles escape us now and again. Avery excuses herself to the bathroom, her grin still firmly in place as she slips out of the door.

My eyes fall to the discarded suit jacket I left on the floor, something poking out of the pocket which has me rising from the bed to investigate. Pinching the sharp corner, I pull a cream envelope free with a frown. 'Avery Hughes' is scribbled across the front in an old scripted style of writing with 'R.P' printed over the seal on the back. I only take a second to consider if I should hand the letter over to Avery before deciding I need to know what it says first. I can't risk her keeping information to herself that affects all of us, especially now I know she's capable of stealing my car in the night and leaving without a word. I quickly tear the back open and yank out the letter inside.

For the immediate attention of Miss Hughes,

Seeing as you have been smart enough to evade my men on various occasions, I have come to the conclusion you are a clever girl. As such, I believe you will take the offer I am presenting you with this once. Your father stole my daughter from me, a crime which I vowed to see him equally punished for. However, I am nothing if not a fair man and seeing as Nixon has been blessed with two daughters, this is the choice I am giving to you now. Hand yourself over and I will ensure you and your twin a swift and painless death together. However, if you decide to remain hidden, Meg will suffer on both of your behalf's and you will ultimately be free to continue your life. The choice is yours. You have until Monday evening to make yourself known at The Harbour Bridge Casino in Chicago or I will accept you have taken the selfish option.

Yours Sincerely, Raymond Perelli.

The door swinging open has me spinning around, hiding the letter behind my back until I can process what I've just read. Avery smiles at me sweetly, flicking the light off so we are plunged into darkness as she climbs into bed. I shift forward on numb feet, lowering myself into my makeshift bed on the floor and tuck the letter beneath my pillow.

"Thanks for tonight Hux, I really needed that." Avery breathes, rolling over to curl up on her side.

"Sweet dreams angel," I reply automatically. My mind is reeling at a hundred miles an hour, but one truth is blatantly clear. I cannot let Avery see this letter.

I remain curled on top of my sleeping bag, staring at the initials S.P etched into the stone wall, despite the continuous badgering from Nixon in the opposite cell. I have nothing to say, the fact he's here is insult enough. Perelli is one step closer to fulfilling his master plan now. All I can do is lie here and hope Avery doesn't give him the satisfaction of seeing it through. Surely there will come a time when he calls off the hunt and decides to put Nixon and I out of our misery, however long that may be. A week, a month, a year? It already feels like I've been trapped in this stone cell for an eternity, and after my failed escape attempt landed me in even more trouble, it's inevitable I'll only be leaving this place in a wooden box. As if I would be given such a curtesy, I imagine ground up and fed to the pigs would be more Perelli's style.

At least I know, regardless of my body being recovered, Avery will mourn me. She'll most likely plant me a shrine capsule next to our mom in her back yard, if it's ever safe enough for her to return. I'm just thankful to have been able to share a part of her life, to have spent every weekend building memories that will carry over to the afterlife with me. Even if we hadn't known it, our twin bond cemented from the very first time we met. The shy, trembling girl I took under my wing and watched blossom before my eyes. If only she could do the same for me now.

By giving up, I've failed her. I was always the one with the tougher exterior, but the horror I faced in the hidden cell has destroyed every wall I thought I had. His stale breath, his vacant different coloured eyes. The scar on his chest mocking me with Avery's strength where I was floundering, unable to defend myself the way I thought I could. Clearly this is the fate I am due, one way or another this hidden dungeon to be the last place I will ever see.

"Megan," Nixon hisses at me once again. He hasn't once asked if I'm okay, all of his focus on Avery, which has given me lesson 101 on 'Life as Wyatt'. I get he's not a proper dad to me, no matter what my DNA says, but still – I thought he'd at least attempt some useless small talk. Rolling onto my back with a sigh, I stare at the shadows cast over the ceiling by the outside lanterns. My tears have long since dried, two crusted streaks lining my cheeks. My body feels light and weighted down at the same time, an overriding numbness beginning in my chest and expanding until my arms hang limply by my side. "We need to find a way out of- "

"There is no way out," I admit, my bland tone hiding my sense of defeat. I tried and failed, but that's not to say Perelli has won. There's still one way I can ensure he feels cheated, my last opportunity to wipe the smug smile off his face and I've already put the wheels in motion with the untouched tray of muesli and yoghurt by the cell door. It'll take ages and hurt like a bitch, but it's the only part of my life still in my control.

Eventually Nixon realizes he won't get any more conversation from me and leaves me to wallow in my self-pity in peace. Scuffles on the steps come and go, the door hatch opens, and my untouched tray is replaced with another, concerned mutters are passed before the main door is slammed closed. My body clock is so out of whack, not knowing if it's day or night, thunderstorms or sunshine. There could have been a nuclear missile sent to the moon or an apocalypse happening for all I know, while I lay silently forgotten in the dark.

My eyes start to droop, exhaustion from doing absolutely nothing trying to pull me under. Drifting into a half consciousness, an ethereal image of Cathy awaits me. Her brown hair and cream chiffon dress billow in an imaginary wind, a welcoming smile on her perfectly painted lips. She stretches her hand out towards me but for some reason, I hesitate. I'm aware there's nothing worth holding back for, but deep in my soul I feel like there is some unfinished business I need to take care of before I fully give in. Before I can delve into exactly what that is, footsteps before my door rouse me.

The metal clang of my chain being shifted rings throughout my cell, light clinging to a figure who welcomes himself inside and closes the door back into place. Sliding my metal tray aside with his foot, I keep my eyes fixed on the ceiling as he shifts closer without a word. A thick, insanely soft blanket is laid across me and unfortunately my limbs are too weak to shove it off. I hadn't realised quite how much of the floor's icy touch had coiled itself into my skin, but the trace of warmth easing over me causes my body to shiver violently. Strong arms scoop me up like a rag doll and pull me into his firm chest, the solid beat of his heart beneath my cheek.

I don't want to like it, I shouldn't let myself remain, but I must be weaker than I thought. After tugging the blanket into the shape of my body, his hands hold me gently like the most precious belonging in the world. Because let's face it, even though he is the reason I won't ever see daylight again, Wyatt's the first and last man I've ever felt a genuine pull to and for that reason, a part of me will forever belong to him. Even if I do want to take a spade to his stupid, pretty face right about now.

"Things aren't…as clear as they were when I brought you here," he whispers beside my face, his lips too close to my lips.

"Was that meant to be an apology? Because it sucked harder than me, and as you know that's saying something." My voice is raspy, a roughness to my throat akin with swallowing a shitload of sand. His intoxicatingly manly scent wrapping around me in a second embrace makes my head feel light as I inhale deeply. He is sin personified. The type of character an ordinary girl would run screaming from, yet I'm being drawn closer. Like a moth to a flame, I want to be scorched and consumed by his touch.

"Is that what you need from me, an apology? Or would you rather I reserved my energy to save you from this place?" he tilts his head forward to search my eyes for an answer.

"I don't need anything from you. I'm a fucking warrior, so pull up a chair and grab a tub of popcorn while I save myself." He chuckles against my forehead, his luscious lips in the focal point of my eyeline.

"Trust me, Meg, I know you're a warrior. But warriors don't fight alone." His words threaten to have my walls crumbling down, every argument dying a sudden death on my tongue. Tears prick my eyes as I struggle against the two voices simultaneously urging me on and pulling me back. Can I trust him? Is it possible I don't have to face this alone anymore? Don't be so ridiculous. Surely, he's toying with me, bored of his easy life so he's come to pry on my insecurities.

"Why aren't you eating your meals?" Wyatt suddenly changes tactic with what sounds like genuine concern, but I won't be so easily fooled. Not while 'Property of Perelli' has been tattooed across my flesh in invisible ink and Wyatt is still relying on the old man's praise to feel accepted.

"What's the point in delaying the inevitable?" I shrug out of his grip at long last, despite the protests of my inner hussy. That bitch needs to clamp it down, I'm trying to die in peace here. Taking the blanket with me, I edge across the ground and prop myself against the wall. Wyatt twists to grab a hidden item from behind his back before scooting over to me, placing a steaming travel mug in my hands. Holy mother of caffeine. My fingers skim his as I accept the mug, inhaling the intensely rich scent until it has filled my lungs.

"What's the point in suffering more than you have to?" Wyatt leans over me to speak directly into my ear, his stubble grazing my cheek. There's an unusual shift in his eyes, those orbs of green regarding me for a moment before pulling back. He remains still, sitting back on his ankles until I realize he is waiting. Resting the lid against my bottom lip, I blow gently before taking a sip. Creamy sweetness skates across my tongue, a secret shot of caramel gliding down my throat on a husky moan. My toes unfurl and my body loosens as I continue to drink until I've melted into a puddle of brief bliss. Simple pleasures and all that.

Wyatt's full attention is on me, his striking face taking on a solemn light. I attempt to smile for him, but my lips don't shift, my eyebrow twitching in confusion. My shoulders have slumped to the side, the coffee cup slipping through my immobile fingers. The door opens suddenly, the orange glow filtering in to show Wyatt's pitying gaze. Inside my mind, I'm thrashing and screaming every curse word I can at him, but I can barely get the 'ffff' past my lips. Black spots dance across my vision, my head lolling of its own accord.

He tricked me, again. And the worst part is I fell for it – again! My body is lifted back into the cradle of Wyatt's arms as he carries me from the cell, up the staircase and into the central house. Nixon's protests are cut off by the slamming of the cellar door, the entire underground section seemingly soundproof. Warmer yet fresher air tickles my nostrils as my vision blurs in and out. The second I have control of my arms again, I'm going to cause Wyatt so much pain, he'll wish he'd left me to rot.

Lying me onto a cushy sofa with more care than I thought he was capable of, Wyatt's hair flicks forward into my face as he presses a patronizing kiss on my cheek and speaks in a low tone so only I can hear. "For what it's worth, I am truly sorry for bringing you here."

Avery

One of the reasons I hate living out of bags is that I can never find anything I want, even though there's nowhere for my fluffy, grey socks to hide. Pulling out every item of clothing I have, I spill the duffle bags contents across the floor with no success. I bet Huxley's stolen them. Tugging his bag out from beneath the bed, I scoop out his sports kit and handfuls of white t-shirts.

"Ha!" I laugh to myself, my socks bundled up at the bottom. Replacing his weirdly neat stacks of folded clothes, I push the bag back into place and pull the socks on, covering the bottom on my purple leggings. Moving to stand, a crumpled piece of paper hanging from the side pocket of Huxley's bag catches my attention, the fancy script seeming odd for a man's tastes. Not able to resist, I sneak a quick peak and my heart plummets when I see my own name scrawled across the top.

My eyes race over the words twice, picking out key information before I drop back onto my heels and read it steadily. My limbs freeze up, an all-consuming ache growing so rapidly in my chest I forget how to breathe. I'm trapped between feeling elated I finally have a way to see Meg and furious that Huxley kept this from me. Questions race through my mind, none of which I can fathom the answers to alone.

Jumping to my feet, I storm into the hallway on a warpath to find him. He will feel my rage, see my pain, and look me in the eye while he explains to me how he could have this kind of decision on my behalf. I make it three steps until Dax steps out of the bathroom in just a towel and collides with me. His arms reach out to steady me, but I slap them away and then shove at his chest for good measure. Fuck him. Fuck them all for thinking I'm a meek, little girl that can't look after herself. They can shove their chauvinistic tendencies up their arses.

"Hey, wait," Dax grabs into my arm as I try to leave him far, far behind. "What's happened?" I whip back around with my fist raised, slamming it into his cheek without any hesitation.

"You happened!" I cry, attempting to swing again but he catches my wrists. Spinning and pushing me up against the wall, Dax pins me in place with the length of his body. His bronzed skin is damp from a recent shower, my fingers lingering a beat too long on his firm pecs. Growling at myself, I thrash and buck wildly, refusing to let him hold me back once again. He only moves in closer, every ridge of his abs pressing against me and his breath fanning my face.

"That's enough." I go slack and turn my head away so I can't fall victim to his piercing blue eyes and full lips.

"No." He replies simply. His erection is growing between us, only the press of our bodies holding the towel in place. "It'll never be enough until you take what you need from me. Break my hopes of ever having you, crush my heart to dust, ruin me for anyone else. I want your hatred and will take all of your punishment." My eyes alight with the challenge, the warring emotions churning within my chest aching for the outlet he's offering.

"I won't be able to hold back." He groans like that's the filthiest thing he's ever heard, biting down on his bottom lip.

"Then don't." The next second, my mouth is crushed against his and a moan spills between us. I'd forgotten how his lips are silky soft yet demanding, drawing my desire to the surface in an instant. Releasing my wrists, his hands trail a path of heat down my body and lift me by my ass. Winding my legs around his waist, I plunge my tongue into his mouth as he carries us out of the hallway with powerful strides. Our tongues mould together, stroking and caressing with an urgency to get closer.

My back is used to close a door, his thick erection pressing against my core demandingly. I whip away the limply hanging towel, the need to drown in his body driving my actions. Keeping me pinned in place with his hips, Dax breaks our kiss to pull my sports vest and bra over my head in one smooth move. My lips instantly find his again, licking and nibbling a path along his jaw and down his neck before biting hard into his collar bone. My nails score lines down his chest and abs until they find his cock, a hiss escaping him as I drag my nails up his rigid length.

Lifting me higher against the door, his lips wrap around one of my hardened nipples and I arch my back in response. Teasing the other between his fingers, he alternates between sucking and licking, ending on a painful clamp of his teeth which makes me yelp and then beg for him to do it again. I shamelessly rub my core against his chest as he repeats the process on my other breast, writhing with a building heat that threatens to burn me alive.

Spinning us around, he moves again and throws me back onto a springy mattress. My leggings and black thong are whipped off, his mouth closing over my clit before I've managed to catch my breath. I gasp, my wetness mixing with the rough pad of his tongue that licks a slow path up my centre. A flood of lava rushes to my core almost instantly, a groan escaping me as I try to hold it at bay. Each powerful suck and flick of his tongue keeps me hanging on the edge, fisting my hands in the cover and my eyes clenched shut. Two long digits plunge inside me and my walls clench around them tightly, the full force of my orgasm making me scream his name. My hands grasp his blonde Afro and hold him firmly in place while I ride out the waves of my climax, his tongue continuing to swirl around my pulsing bud mercilessly until I'm jerking and sprawled back into the mattress.

Giving me no reprieve, Dax looms over me within seconds to press his lips against mine, gentler this time. I lose myself in his touch, slipping my hand around his neck to pull him as close as possible. His masculine scent, the rough stubble lining his jaw, the body I ache to have wrapped around me every night. Our kiss is filled with the longing for impossible possibilities, jerking me back to reality. I can't have this with Dax or anyone, but what I can have is one last glimpse of happiness.

Breaking the intimacy between us, I push Dax onto his back and straddle his hips, sinking myself onto his solid length to avoid his questioning gaze. His body is mine in the moment, to use for my pleasure and forget about my impending date with the devil. Leaning forward on his chest and pinning his thighs beneath my feet, I begin to lift and ease myself back down leisurely. My inner walls stroke him, his ridges rubbing within me deliciously.

No matter how enticing his glistening lips look, I keep him at a literally arm's length, bouncing my hips to quicken the rise of my next orgasm. I need the release more than my next breath, a blissful few seconds of never-ending pleasure to grip onto when everything turns bleak. Sitting upright and fully impaled, I grind my hips back and forth, my head thrown back with my breathy moans filling the room. My hair is tickling the curve of my butt and no doubt, his balls, and thighs as I build up a rhythm, rocking in a fluid motion.

Suddenly, Dax lurches upright and his body crushes against mine. Pulling his Afro free of its restraint, he grasps my hair in his hands and winds it on top of my head, tying it in place with his band. I melt into his body, allowing myself a brief respite from fighting. His arms wind around my back, the raised bumps of my scars exposed to his touch from beneath the phoenix tattoo. Holding me tightly in place, he rocks and bucks beneath me, his dick pressing firmly against my G spot. I cross my ankles behind his back, gripping onto him as if he might disappear. My nails are imbedded in his tensed biceps, every jolt of his cock making me gasp and moan.

There's no need for a rushed pace, each roll of his hips reaching deep and filling me so completely. Latching onto his neck, I suck fiercely to leave a mark on him that will last long after I've gone. My breasts brush against his chest, everywhere I end he begins. Clasping my nape in one large hand and tilting my lower back forward with the other one, my walls begin to flutter around him. Tilting my chin up, he swallows my scream in his mouth as another climax slams into me, strangely more intense than the first. Dax follows me, his explosion pushing against mine and our groans mingling together. He kisses me deeply, pouring every ounce of raw passion into me until we have to break for air and slump into each other's arms.

"Why do I feel like that was the last time we'll be like this?" He whispers in my ear, his warmth permanently seeping into my skin as I say a silent goodbye. Placing a soft kiss on his cheek, I ease myself from him, picking up his damp towel from the floor to clean myself up and dress without a word. I feel his eyes tracking me the entire time, sitting patiently on the edge of the bed for me to answer his question. Placing my hand on the door handle, I sigh deeply, knowing after the way I've just used him, he deserves more than to live with 'what ifs' for the rest of his life.

"I've discovered where to find Perelli and I'm leaving to be with Meg. Don't follow me, I have to go alone. But do know if anyone could have been a perfect match for me, it would have been you. Maybe in another lifetime..." I risk a glance at his panicked eyes before darting into the hallway and back into my room, shoving on my oversized green hoodie and white Converse before grabbing Huxley's keys from the bedside table. I've made it halfway down the staircase when Dax's shouts reach me, yanking up his tracksuit bottoms as he chases after me. Grabbing a hold of my arm as I reach the bottom step, he whirls me back into his chest, but I twist and pull out of his grip.

"Avery, you can't go. They will kill you!"

"I know," I breathe. His eyebrows knit together in confusion, reaching for me once again which I dodge. "I've been upfront with you since the day we met. My life is a means to an end, a shit storm with a few rays of sunshine. Dying alongside my twin is the best way I could hope to go."

"I'm begging you not to do this. Stay with me, we'll find another way." I wish he was right, that there was any chance of saving Meg and having the future only he could provide me with. I reach up to cup his cheek and he leans into my touch, so much hope radiating through his features it destroys the last dim ember in my heart.

"I can't leave her to face this alone." Stepping back, I force myself out of the front door and unlock Huxley's Nissan, my resolve taking the impact of a sledgehammer with every step.

"It can't end this way. Tell me how to help, I'll do anything. I didn't save you for you to walk straight back into their clutches." I still with my hand on the driver's handle, rage taking place of any sympathy I just felt.

"You only saved me for your own selfish purposes!" I whip back around and level him with a scowl. "If you'd wanted to help, you would have handed me over, so Meg didn't take my share of suffering. I'd die a thousand times by her side rather than live a life she's not a part of. You knew that, and you kept me here, so I'd stay with you. You trapped me here and you are one who has been causing my suffering."

Dax's mouth drops open, his body going slack. Swallowing down the tears I refuse to let him see, I throw myself into the car and slam the door closed between us. Revving the engine, his palm rests on the closed window, muffled words leaving his lips I don't want to hear. "Avery please, I love- ". I push my foot to the floor on the accelerator and speed out of the driveway without looking back.

Wyatt

"Where has she been taken?" I demand the second my footsteps over the threshold to Ray's darkened office, trying not to sound as protective as I feel. He's made me stand around outside for well over an hour while he 'dealt with some business', an hour of pacing and fisting my hair in my hand since she's been gone. I'm glad I convinced him how much extra hassle she would be to move whilst awake, hoping this small reprieve will save her unnecessary force from the beefy guard that carried her out. My fingers are aching to clasp her face in my hands and make sure there isn't a single hair out of place on her hair or so help me, I'll be adding causal murderer to my resume.

"All in good time, sit down Wyatt. We have much to discuss." I shift foot to foot in the doorway, knowing I don't have a choice. Closing the mahogany door behind me, I sit in the armchair facing Ray's desk and rest my elbows on my thighs, eager to get this over with. Smoke fills my lungs and a choke lodges in my throat, the glowing embers from Ray's cigar just visible amongst the swirling cloud around him. There's a new machine in the room, silently monitoring his heartbeat through the electrode pads covering his bare chest.

"Do you want to tell me what happened with Mr Walters?" My eyes shift to the clock on the sideboard, my leg shaking impatiently which Ray mistakes for nerves. Sliding his engraved cigar box towards me, he reaches over to switch on the tabletop lamp so I can see the question in his quirked eyebrows.

"My men had no qualms with him being here and you've been spending a fair amount of time downstairs lately…." his voice trails off as if he's coaxing a confession from a five-year-old.

"He looked at me the wrong way," is all I can think to say without alerting him to the fact Meg managed escape on my watch. More for her sake than mine. A sinister grin grows across his wrinkled face.

"That's my boy." Leaning back in his leather chair, his faded tattoos catch my attention. A skyline of Sydney which has been made to mimic his heartbeat, from the opera house to harbour bridge straight across his wrinkled chest. I can't tell if Ray was a good father, his love for his lost daughter clear but he hardly seems the type to bounce a little girl on his knee and teach her to ride a bike.

Ignoring my probing look which clearly reads '*What the fuck am I doing here?*', Ray pulls his cell from the drawer to his right and checks a message, grunting as he types out a reply with the volume on. My teeth grind together with the tippetty tip tap of his thumbs hitting the screen. He's purposely prolonging this meeting out, testing my patience and obedience. Finally, he puts away his cell and focuses on me, crossing his arms across his front.

"I've had to make a difficult decision to proceed with the next stage of my plan. You've done a great job so far, but it's time for you to step away." *No.* "Meg has been moved to another secure location and trust me when I say this it will be for your own good. Don't worry though, there is another way to sate your anger. While I'm away taking care of the girls, I've decided to give you Nixon. Do whatever you like with him, we have a clean-up crew on standby." I open my mouth but no words come out. I should have been jumping at the chance to be relieved from babysitter duty and to have Nixon at my mercy, but for some unknown reason, neither of those options sounds appealing anymore.

"What makes you think you can find Avery all of a sudden?" I ask, an uncomfortable twisting in my gut which I can't explain.

"Ah, that's the best part. I've already found her and I'm certain she's on her way to Meg's location as we speak. Those troublesome twins have been the bane of my life since I discovered they existed and will finally meet their end by tomorrow night." His sneer fills me with dread, panic flaring to life inside me. I need to find a way to be allowed access to the girls. Ironically, I might be their only hope.

"I would like the opportunity to finish what I've started, see your revenge scheme through to the end." I remain calm, taking the logical approach if there is one when having a private meeting with a notorious crime boss.

"I don't think that is a good idea. You haven't seemed like yourself since she arrived." Slumping back into the velvet cushioning, I rest my chin on my clenched fist. Maybe it's true Meg has crawled beneath my skin and taken up residence in my head, but it could also be possible Ray doesn't know me as well as he thought. In fact, I barely know myself anymore. For years I've held onto the hate that's been devouring me, striving on the idea of a perfect family which clearly doesn't exist. Each day ending with a round of self-loathing before I close my eyes for the night. Feeling worthless, unwanted. Filling the void with ideas of punishing my parents which I never planned to actually bring to reality.

I miss how simple life came at Waversea, the things I cared about were my boys and my degree. I've never wanted to ride on my father's coattails, I had ambitious plans to carve my own path in the world with the guys who bolstered me through every set back. A few months ago, I would have thought nothing could come between us, least of all me. Fuck, how could I have messed everything up like this? There's no way to reverse the clock, bring Axel back to life and fix the bonds I've shattered. All

I have now is Rachel, and a sense of obligation to Meg.

But what this means for me, I have no idea. If I no longer have anger guiding my actions, does that mean the lightness she fills me with is permanent? Am I a sap who's falling for the pair of baby blues I'd never noticed before, or can this be a new start for me? Maybe if I could be good enough for her, that'll be enough. A dam breaks in my chest, feelings gushing through me as the thin rope I was grasping onto has snapped. I'm the monster who trapped her, but I'm also the one who's going to set her free.

"I've never been thinking more clearly. Let me finish this, I'll do whatever it takes," *to save her.*

Parking the sedan behind a towering building mostly made of glass, I lie my head back and tap my thumb on the wheel, despite how eager I am to race up to the penthouse suite Meg is apparently still unconscious in. Even after the convincing Ray took about letting me continue assisting in his scheme, I'm aware a Mini Cooper has been following me the entire way here. So much for blending in, the cherry red paintjob has held my attention ducking in and out between vehicles in my rearview mirror. I'd thought about speeding away but there's no use when Ray knows where I'm heading and I'm desperately trying to keep a cool façade in place.

It's only been a few hours but the need to see her again is burning me alive. My frantic heartbeat won't ease until I know she's safe, especially after what happened with Frederick. A shudder ceases me, the thought of his hands anywhere near her almost too much to handle if I hadn't made sure he won't hurt anyone else ever again. I should be worried with the ease I was able to end his life, but I couldn't find a shred of guilt if I tried. At least a second demonised mirage hasn't appeared alongside my mom in the backseat, only her floating outline pressed against the rear window.

Figuring that's long enough to not seem too keen, I exit the car and remove my backpack from the trunk before strolling into the hotel's lobby. Golden arches decorate the ceiling, all joining in the centre to hold the glittering chandelier. Black marble spreads beneath my feet to the match onyx surfaces and bannisters.

Following the signs, I ignore the gawping receptionist who is using the counter for extra breast support and push the golden button to call the elevator. A bell chime announces its arrival, a couple looking at me curiously as they exit hand in hand. As soon as they've stepped out of the way, my reflection in the mirrored wall reveals the reason for their stares; I look like shit. Stepping into the large space, I push for the top level and try to fix my constant state of bedhead.

Running my hands through its overgrown length, I smooth down the stubble lining my jaw with a frown. Jeez, this isn't a date, I'm simply attempting to convince the girl whose life is ruined because of me not to hate me completely. I won't let myself dream she could ever actually forgive me, but maybe I can fix the mistake I made and that will have to be enough.

The doors slide open behind me, the reflected image of her sleeping form on a corner sofa immediately drawing my eye. Stepping into the living area, no one else is in sight as I close the distance between us. Her hair has spilled across the cushions like melted chocolate left out in the sun, the faint freckles splayed across her nose I had forgotten about now visible in the well-lit room. I'm about to reach out to brush my hand across her cheek when a red flashing in the corner of the ceiling catches my attention. Reaching up to scratch my own head instead, I sneak a look around to see surveillance cameras are dotted around the whole penthouse. Fuck it.

Meg begins to stir, her eyebrows pinching and a groan escaping her lips. Blinking rapidly, her pale blue eyes take a moment to adjust to the sunlight pouring through the floor-to-ceiling windows and probably the drugs leaving her system, before landing on me. "You," she growls, her nostrils flaring. Pushing up onto wobbly legs, she composes herself quicker than I would have been able to and glowers right at me without a trace of fear. *Shit, that's hot.* No matter what is thrown her way, Meg keeps getting back up and proving the extent of her inner strength again and again.

Hiding the grin I'd like to give, I open my mouth to warn her we are being watched when her fist snaps out and catches my jaw. My head shifts to the side but not with as much force as I had expected from her when she suddenly uppercuts me. *There it is.* My head cracks backwards, the taste of blood filling my mouth. Taking full advantage of the hand she's just dealt me; I grip her upper arms and drag her through the penthouse.

Passing through an enormous bedroom featuring a circular double-king, I tug her kicking and screaming into the open en-suite. With a quick, fruitless hunt for cameras, I spin sharply and use her back to slam the door closed. My mouth is on hers in the next moment, the length of my body pining her helplessly in place. She bites down on my bottom lip hard and yanks on my hair, but her actions only make me grow harder against her abdomen. Every deep scratch and aggressive shove at my shoulders make me try harder, pushing my tongue into her mouth to fight with hers.

Finally, she stops resisting the heat I know we both feel and fists her hands in my t-shirt, now pulling me impossibly closer. Her body melts into mine, her lips moving in time with my hungry ones. I'm a starving man and only her taste with fulfil me. I lift her into my arms, her legs winding around me on instinct as I turn and walk us straight into the shower. Twisting the dial, a cool spray of water rains onto us while I push her back against the tiles and grind my now solid erection at her core. Moaning into my mouth, she reaches for the edge of my shirt and I force myself to pull back.

"Wait-" I pant, struggling to form a sentence when she's coiled around me like a boa. She can have it all, my withered soul, the blackened blood running through my veins and my last breath. "I need you to know- "

"I don't care," she responds, tugging my soaking shirt off and kissing a trail from my neck to my chest. I groan, savouring her touch. "Whatever you have to say, don't bother. Your words mean nothing to me now," she breathes against my skin. Nodding gently, I accept I can't make her understand with an explanation. I shouldn't have the right to belong to anyone, especially not the girl I helped to kidnap, but Meg has ensnared me with her resilience and shown me the world wasn't as bleak as I had been led to believe. Now it's my turn to show her who I can be, how we could be. With every kiss, lick, caress and thrust, by the end of tonight she'll feel my promise to save her since she's already done the same for me.

Dax

I pull out yet another drawer from the vanity, dumping its contents out onto the floor before moving on to the next. There must be a clue, I need to find her. Throwing her duffle bag onto the bed, I toss the clothes over my shoulder and shakes the bag vigorously until every loose hair tie and stupidly small bottle of lotion falls out. How can there be nothing?! I pick up the bedside table and throw it across the room with a roar, the wood splintering on impact with the opposite wall.

"What the fuck is going on in here?" Huxley bursts through the door.

"You," I hiss through my teeth. Rounding the bed, I grip Huxley around the neck and push him backwards until his back is arched over the railing. "You must know where she's gone."

"I don't know what you're talking about," Huxley chokes out, not even trying to overpower me. Releasing my hold on him, I stalk back into the room with my fists clenched.

"She's said she's knows where Meg is and left, this time for good." I clench my eyes shut as the words leave my lips, a fresh slice of pain cutting deeply every time I think of how she left me alone and speechless on the driveway. Huxley curses under his breath, rushing past me towards a makeshift bed on the floor and grabs his bag. Handing me a crumpled letter from the side pocket, he stalks over to the broken bedside table and sifts through the broken slats.

"Has she taken my fucking car again?!" he huffs, dangling himself out the window to search for the burnt orange vehicle he won't be able to find. Shuffling in the hallway announces the arrival of Garrett and Axel, looking around the trashed room curiously with their hands linked. I scan the letter, grabbing the only information I need – the name of the casino. Huxley fills in the others while I pace back and forth, scrubbing a hand over my face.

"And you just let her go?" Axel turns to me accusingly. His amber eyes are churning with anger, looking to his partner for backup but Garrett is unusually silent.

"It's what she wanted so yeah, I stood and watched her leave. But about twenty seconds later I realized I can't let her go and came to find a clue as to where she's gone. Which I have now, so if you'll get the fuck out of my way, I'm going to save the girl I love." I say the words out loud without thinking, attempting to shove through the pair blocking the exit.

"Oh yeah, and how are you going to do that?" Huxley calls over. "We're basketball players, not felons. You can't waltz in and say pretty please may I have my '*would-be girlfriend if she stopped hating me long enough to realise she feels the same way*' back." I snarl at him over my shoulder, more pissed off that he's right than by his sarcastic air quotes. There's no way I will be able to save Avery without back-up.

"Well stop stating the obvious and help me find something to take – a baseball bat, an axe, a hammer. I don't fucking care but I'm leaving in 5 minutes regardless." Ramming my shoulder into Garrett's to escape the negativity holding me in the room and moving onto something more productive. Luckily for me, there's a driveway full of cars from the weekend workers and a large fishbowl on the sideboard in the central lobby holding all of their keys. Part of some game they are planning on playing tonight but looks like someone's going to have to sit and watch.

Ascending on the bowl, I skim through looking for the fastest set of wheels in case I need to make a swift exit, preferably with Avery locked in the trunk if she refuses to come back willingly. Logos on keyrings sift through my fingers - Ferrari, Dodge Viper, Porsche, Jaguar. Settling on the Mercedes Benz, silently praying it belongs to the GT I saw earlier in yellow with black race stripes to match the custom alloys, I turn to the three arseholes I love like brothers standing behind me.

"Here," Axel steps forward with misery etched into his features to hand me a heavy camo backpack. Unzipping the top, I find several handguns and hordes of filled magazine clips. My eyes widen, the danger of the situation settling on me. I'm so not ready to deal with this, but if that's where Avery is, it's the only place I should be. Accepting it with a nod, Huxley passes me my grey timberlands and puffer jacket next, like I'm a high-class knight preparing to head into battle with some serious style. Garrett's hands are pushed into his hoodie pockets, regarding me seriously.

"I'm going with you," he exclaims, his hazel eyes not wavering from mine. Axel hangs his head in defeat, clearly unhappy with his decision. I spare a moment glancing between the two, but ultimately, it's not my place to interfere. I could use the help if I'm being honest, even if I know it will affect Axel to be left behind. Huxley steps closer to Axel on instinct, sensing his misery and places a hand on his shoulder on comfort. Aware that I need to get on the road, I quickly pull the two remaining into a one-armed hug and head for the front door.

Pressing the button on the keys, the GT's headlights flash and I smirk. Fuck yes, let my luck continue until I'm back in my bed with my blonde angel curled into my side, thoroughly satisfied and fully aware of the lengths I would go to for her. Sliding into the driver's seat, I throw the bag into the back seat and wait for Garrett to join me, tapping my thumb on the wheel impatiently.

"You know normal boyfriends don't run off to fight the mob right after professing their love to another, right?" A tear rolls down Axel's cheek, his attention completely focused on the man in front of him. Dropping their shields for a moment, I'm stunned at the level of love shining through their eyes. Garrett cups Axel's cheek, pulling him for a kiss with enough passion to make my heart squeeze. If those two stubborn asses can find love in each other, surely there's hope for me yet.

Garrett breaks their kiss, pressing his forehead on Axel's and exhaling deeply. "I've never been one to follow the rules, but I'm learning to follow my heart. I won't be able to rest as long as there is a threat this close to you. Someone entered your home Axel, without anyone even noticing. This world isn't good enough for you, the least I can do is shelter you from one small part of it."

"Fuck you Gare. Fuck you so hard."

"I'll give you the honours when I get back," Garrett grins, flashing Axel his dimples before releasing him and hopping into the car. Axel holds his hand until I gently pull away, the sound of his sobbing sounding as we leave the driveway. I see Huxley pull him into his embrace in the rear-view mirror just before I turn and leave them behind. Garrett's jaw matches the tension in his shoulders and I'm sure his eyes are glistening slightly as we sit in an awkward silence.

"Do you wanna talk about it?" I offer after a while, needing to break the friction amounting between us.

"Just drive."

The start of a new day is due to break any moment as we enter the state of Chicago, after Garrett and I took turns driving through the night. Not that we could have stopped even if we felt the need, not when Avery is driving herself directly into the danger, I've been trying to keep her away from. I've never felt anything close to love before, after my parent's prime example of why two people who aren't right for one another shouldn't be together. I was content to wait as long as it took until the right girl came along to stir those feelings I've never felt. And holy shit, she did not disappoint.

Avery landed in my life like an atomic bomb, destroying my existence as I knew it and leaving a fresh slate in its place. Now all I need is to save her life once again so I can start to rebuild a world she can be free in. All her fears will vanish when she realizes I won't to cage her, I will encourage her to fly. I'd give her every opportunity to flourish and find a reason to live, even if that meant I could only watch from the side lines.

I slow to stare through the passenger window as we pass The Harbour Bridge Casino, a neon sign displaying a logo to match its name. The lavish interior is visible through a set of gold-handled, glass doors with a set of security already in position outside. Continuing past, I take the next turning to round the tall stretch of glass to find a car park at the rear. My eyes immediately land on a burnt-orange Nissan and my heart double flips in my chest. I'm torn between being thankful Avery has arrived safely and terrified of the danger awaiting her inside. Swinging the Mercedes round to park beside Huxley's beloved car, Garrett's growl grabs my attention.

His hazel eyes are pinned on a black sedan across the lot, his shoulders bunching with the heavy rise and fall of his chest. In contrast to how Axel wears his gentle nature like a coat of armour, Garrett uses sarcasm and anger to shield his true emotions, but I know him better than most. As much as he will rightfully want to make Wyatt pay for the hurt he's caused, he also feels the loss of one of our own like I do. Our group with never be the same without Wyatt's comforting presence and easy-going smirk at the ready. The one that seemed to have the best handle over his demons turned out to be our downfall.

Reaching over to clasp Garrett's shoulder, we share a determined nod and exit the vehicle. I stretch my arms above my head, my back cracking into place. If I never have to drive again this year, it will be too soon. My dad has a private jet I could use whenever I like, but that would involve speaking to him and I'd rather walk the length of the country than do that. We've come to a mutual agreement to pretend the other doesn't exist, so long as he keeps transferring the generous allowance into my account each month as hush money. The stories I could tell would ruin his career and reputation overnight, and he's knows I'd do it too.

Rounding the Mercedes, I find Garrett has dropped to the floor between the cars to do some push ups, most likely to either rev up his adrenaline or to appear as butch as possible. Rolling my eyes, a flapping piece of paper tucked into the Nissan's windscreen wiper catches my attention. I frown, looking all around as a prickle running down my spine tells me we're being watched. A red Mini on the road beyond the car park bursts into action, speeding out of sight before I can get a look of the driver. Removing the paper, I unfold it to find a handwritten message inside.

Convince him to let you play for your life,
he can't resist a game with high stakes.

"Garrett, get up," I command, flashing the note for him to read. We share a concerned look and turn as one to race into the casino. Worry claws at my heart as we burst through the doors, the knowledge that so much is at stake almost more than I can bear. Whoever left this note clearly meant for Avery to see it, and if she hasn't, I dread to think what's happening right now.

Meg

Warm arms circle me, rhythmic breathing skating across my nape. How can something so wrong feel so damn right? I shouldn't crave Wyatt the way I do, but last night he barrelled through my defences and left me bare. There wasn't a place he didn't touch, physically and otherwise. Every inch of my skin tingles with the memory of his touch, especially the tender flesh between my legs. His tongue devoured me like a savage, wringing an onslaught of emotion from me as my toes curled and walls clamped around his fingers. And that was before he took me, the full length of his shaft imbedded in me whilst he held my eye contact. No pretending I was someone else or shamefully thrusting in the dark, his emerald green eyes gave me their full concentration as if he wouldn't have wanted anyone else right then.

The sun creeping into a pink and orange sky doesn't bring the regret I'd expected to feel, instead a strange contentment has me sinking deeper into his hold whilst staring out of the window. I can almost imagine this is how life could be, if mine wasn't due to end in the near future. I don't know why I was brought here or what will happen next, but for one moment I'm glad I was given the chance to feel worshipped and adored. Maybe this was like my last meal before my death sentence is delivered, which would mean Wyatt's basically been pimped out to me but I'm too sated to complain.

His fingers twitch against my stomach before trailing up

my torso, between my breasts and stopping on my chin. Twisting my head, he leans over to kiss me passionately. I'd expected to be tossed out of the bed as soon as he woke, but his lips begged me to stay. Slanting across mine with longing mingled within their soft caress, his hands turning me into the curve of his body. His cock juts between us, his morning glory living up to its name and pressing into my hip. I groan against his mouth, allowing his tongue to slip in to coax mine out. Our limbs tangle, unable to get close enough.

Lifting my leg in the crook of his arm, he slides into my wetness in one easy movement with a moan like he needed that much as much as I did. Languid strokes of his dick grazing my G-spot, gently kneading my breasts without releasing my mouth long enough to breathe properly. I'm torn between needing the escape from the reality he's offering and wanting him to lay me to ruin. To cherish and fuck me simultaneously like it's my last day on earth.

Rolling me onto my back, Wyatt looms over me. His broad shoulders and thickly muscled arms block the rest of the world out of view, only me and him existing for now. I run my fingernails down the length of his spine, his firm ass clenching with each steady thrust. A choke rises in my throat, thoughts of this being the last time I am wanted churning in my mind. Reaching up to grab a handful of his brown hair, I yank his head aside and hiss into his ear. "Faster." I demand, desperate to break the intimacy.

"No," he replies simply. Gripping my wrists, he lifts them either side of my head and watches me intently. His hair flicks forward but he doesn't break his gaze, watching me moan and squirm beneath him. I try to kiss his enticingly close lips, but he deflects me with a grin, refusing to be distracted. A flutter in my lower abdomen builds to an intensity that has me gasping, my limbs prickling in anticipation. I pointlessly wriggle to break free from his stare, my building orgasm making me bite back a groan.

"Look at me," his voice says softly. I shake my head, clenching my eyes closed instead. My thighs lock around his waist, trying to slow his relentless rhythm so I can hold onto this blissful feeling of impending release for a little while longer. "See how much you affect me," he steals a quick kiss which has me staring into his handsome face. His stubble is becoming more of a permanent feature, making his square jaw and green eyes more prominent. Strain pulls at his features a moment before I feel him erupt inside me, his climax triggering mine like a bulldozer ploughing through my centre.

Refusing to look away, we hold each other's gaze as we groan in unison. Releasing my wrists, I immediately latch onto his body and ride the waves giving me a new lease of life with each roll of my core. My walls clamp around him with an impossibly tight squeeze, milking his every drop as my nails pierce his chest. Sweat lines our bodies as we pant together, goose bumps covering my flesh.

"Why didn't I see you sooner?" he breathes, resting his forehead against mine as a door further within the suite bursts open. The sound of thumping boots race towards the bedroom, Wyatt jolting to pull some boxers on while I have no choice but to hold the cover tightly around my body. A small army of men appear in the doorway, guns strapped to their backs as they all lunge for Wyatt and restrain him between them.

My eyes fly between them frantically, Wyatt's shouts filling the entire penthouse as Ray Perelli steps into the room. A cruel smile is rooted into his wrinkled lips as he regards me, a shiver of dread telling me we've played directly into his hand.

"Sleeping with the enemy, son? I don't know whether to be proud or disappointed in you. Either way, you've broken your promise to me." Clicking his bony fingers, the guards instantly drag Wyatt away as if he were as light as a feather, his animated struggles meaning nothing as he's ripped from my sight. I pull the sheet around me tighter, my heart being torn from my chest and carried away with the guy I just completely and unashamedly fell for.

A woman emerges next, her shoulder-length brown hair swaying with each step she takes towards me. Knee-high boots are laced above a dark pair of jeans, her top half covered by a charcoal grey coat with a tie at the waist. In her hands is a lengthy clothing bag, which she places beside me on the bed without any trace of an expression. I now notice Ray is dressed in a full suit, despite the early hour.

"Get dressed and join me for breakfast." Perelli has turned by the time the last word leaves his lips, his command non-negotiable. The woman remains standing by my bedside, her eyebrow arching in a challenge to fight her. Huffing, I grab the bag and stride into the bathroom, the sheet firmly in place as I go. Hooking it on the back of the door once closed, I slump into a heap on the tiled floor and rest my head in my hands. I can sense this is the final stretch of Perelli's revenge plot, but it isn't me I'm worried for right now. What will they do to Wyatt and why did his last glance back at me seem so filled with regret? Regret for the things we should have realised and for the feelings we should have put into words.

I pick myself up off the floor, figuring I won't be given long to myself and hop into the shower. My hand glides between my legs, the throbbing still present as I force myself to clean Wyatt's mess away. Watching his seed swirl down the drain, I press my fingers to my lips and hold a sob at bay. It's not like we picked the best moment to find each other, there could never have been a happily ever after for us but at least we had last night. The most perfect night which will stay with me until I take my last breath.

Drying off, I wrap the towel around my head and unzip the clothing bag. A black halter neck dress stares back at me, silver gems forming a repetitive geometric pattern all around. Below the criss-cross neckline, there's a gaping hole which will show off plenty of cleavage as well as having an open back. Well there's no point moaning or refusing, so I slip the dress over my head and pull it down to the slender hem at my knees. A pair of black heels are hooked onto the hanger which I also don, brushing my hair through my fingers and leaving to air dry.

Emerging from the bathroom, the woman is waiting in the same position I left her with her arms crossed. Having removed her coat, a shiny police badge sits on her hip which I eye curiously but she doesn't seem to notice. Sighing loudly, she crosses the room to plant me on a stool before a vanity and mumbles about 'grooming spoilt brats not being a part of her job description'. I chew on the inside of my cheek while she dries and styles my hair into loose curls and then turns her attention to my face, the roughness of her power application making me snarl.

Finally, fully dolled up, I'm permitted to leave what I'm sure is the worst part of torture I'll face today and find Perelli eating at a dining table by the unused kitchenette. An empty plate sits before him, his nose buried in a newspaper as I take the opposite seat and pick at the breakfast laid out for me. Half a pain au chocolat and a yogurt later, I clear my throat to grab his attention.

"What am I doing here?" Perelli looks around as if he's only just noticed where he is, my eyes rolling impatiently. "Why am I out of the dungeon? This wasn't in the plan I overheard you tell Wyatt." My gut twists as I say his name, silently hoping he won't be punished too much. I'm a dead woman walking anyway, he can lay all the blame on me and my irresistible body if that makes it easier on him.

"Have you ever wondered why a killer whale flings a baby seal around with its tails before gorging on it?" The glint in his eye shows how intelligent he thinks he is, but I'm not easily impressed. Essentially, he's brought me here to toy with me, have a little fun before snuffing out my light. Except in his metaphor, he's pegged himself as the predator and me as the meek pray. Hah.

"Mmmm, yet despite being the biggest creatures on the planet, the whale lazily chooses to feed on krill scavenging bottom-feeders. Is that why you pry on offspring of your enemies, because you're too lazy to find the real deal?" His smile drops as he refuses to answer and throws his newspaper down, using the table to push himself upright. Once standing as straight as he can manage, he holds out his arm to me which I simply quirk a brow at. Pulling his cell from his pocket, he taps the touch screen before turning the screen to face me. A live stream of Wyatt is displayed, blood dripping down his bare torso but I can't see his injuries as his head in hanging forward limply. *Fuck.* My heart squeezes and my hands twist around the arms of the chair, on the verge of sweeping out this malicious old man's legs with it.

"Play along and he won't be hurt anymore." Pocketing the cell, Perelli offers me his arm again which I stand to accept without complaint. The crooked cop joins the room with her phone pressed to her ear just in time to step into the elevator we've entered, generic music carrying us all the way to the bottom floor. The hotel lobby is as grand as the penthouse, no expense spared on the miniscule details only those with more money than sense would pick up on. The cop mutters her apologies and veers off the second the doors open, leaving Ray and I to cross the black marble floor, and push through a set of glass doors and step into the bustling casino beyond.

Despite being barely morning, people are dressed finely to wander the stretches of slot machines and huddle around roulette tables. My heels push against a spongy carpet, the repetitive logo of Harbour Bridge's outline spanning in front of me. Lights flashing and fumes of visitor's smoking inside start to stir a headache within me, the peaceful solitude of my cell more appealing right now. Ray's grasp is surprisingly tight for his age, tugging me through the crowds when I attempt to see where the sudden uproar of cheers has come from.

Guards keep their distance, their black outfits blinking between the machines as we travel through the centre aisle towards a set of opaque double doors at the other end. This section of the casino is weirdly muted, only the tinks and clanks of machine levers being pulled, or buttons being tapped. No one speaks, merely hunched forward and then leaning back on a huff in quick succession.

The ceiling is littered with shiny domes across its hand painted expanse, cameras hidden within so I can't see which way they are facing. Two bald men security uniforms stand between us and the doors Ray has led me to, instantly parting to open the doors for their employer. Inside is dark, a low hum of mumbling reaching out to draw me in. Something tells me not to enter but I don't have any other choice since I'm not the one who will suffer for my actions from here on out. Either Perelli is more cunning than I thought, or he got lucky, but the only way to keep me in line is to threaten someone I care about – which now includes Wyatt evidently.

The guard leans over as we pass through to whisper to his boss although I can hear every word. "You have a guest." A cruel smile lifts Perelli's lips, his pace upping as I'm pulled into the dimly lit lounge. Blue LED bulbs lining the ceiling and floor match the light emanating from behind a bar at the back, waitresses dressed in lingerie gliding through filled booths to serve a full house of greying gentlemen. All their eyes are glued on a slender woman artfully spinning around a pole at the front, black hearts covering her nipples being the extent of her clothing.

I know where we are headed before Perelli begins to walk me to the booth in the far corner, the curved suede seat raised to have a clear view over the whole lounge. A net curtain has been half pulled across the front, the outline of a figure sitting inside the booth just visible. Crooked Cop veers away, heading for the bar with purposeful strides while Perelli pulls me up the wide steps and draws back the curtain. My eyes land on the other half of me, the one I've missed so dearly but would rather have never seen again than know she was in danger too. *Oh Aves, what the fuck are you doing here?*

Avery

"Meg!" I try to jump up from my seat, but my hands are cuffed behind me, the chain resting through a metal loop poking out between the padding. Unlike the rest of the seating in the lounge, there is no table before me, only a bare circle of carpet and various hoops attached to the curtain rail for bondage equipment to be fastened to. I shudder to think of how many women have sold their bodies to a monster like Perelli, strung up like puppets for his own amusement but I suppose everyone has their price. Meg shoves out of Perelli's fragile arm to rush to me, throwing herself around my body in a painfully tight grip. I rest my head on her shoulder, my heart finally cementing back in place after all this time. I don't care that my death is in sight, one last hug from my twin and best friend all I need to endure whatever Perelli is about to bring my way.

"You shouldn't have come," she whispers into my ear, sitting beside me but not letting go.

"Nothing would have kept me away." We both look to a smirking Perelli, completely at his mercy which is laughable since he is incapable of any. Two guards' step in either side of him with malice in their expressions, a promise of inescapable pain heading our way. I glance around, figuring our current arrangement is too public for an execution right here, but given who runs this establishment I wouldn't put it past everyone present to give Perelli a solid alibi. Mellow music plays in the background while hordes of older men gawp at the beautiful woman on stage, no one speaking or wolf-whistling like you'd expect, as if her curves have them under a spell.

"I've waited so long for this- "His words are interrupted by a holler from nearer to the stage.

"Boooooo! Where's the men? Ray Perelli may be one old ball sack, but surely he's heard of gender equality!" A collective breath is sucked in across the whole room, the woman on stage halting with wide eyes and slowly backing up like a bomb is about to explode. Perelli's hands clench in time with his jaw, spinning slowly on the heels of his dress shoes. His guards are gone in an instant, hunting down the interruption as a stampede of men drive from their seats and run for the exit. Two silhouettes remain seated at the front, not bothering an escape attempt as if they wanted to be caught.

The pair are dragged from their seats roughly, the guards not so accidently throwing them into tables on their way back to their master. With each thud of a table to the stomach or chair leg to the shin, a manic laughter I seem to recognise fills the air more and more. Soon, there is a tall guy with floppy hair forced to knee before Perelli, his hazel eyes searching for me and then winking in the blue lighting. The other arrives a second later, this one much more cooperative with a suspiciously similar Afro to the one I left far behind in Atlanta and my heart.

"You've got to be kidding me," I mutter, shaking my head. I can't even pretend to be surprised, knowing at least Dax wouldn't have let me walk away while he still felt there was a chance for us. At least if he had, his heart would have been mostly intact to be given to another. The idea makes me irrationally jealous, but his happiness is more important to me than my own.

"I know who you are, and had expected some sort of rescue attempt but this seems a little lacking, don't you think?" Perelli is looming over Garrett, who is grinning like the Cheshire Cat while I focus my questioning stare on Dax. His stunning blue eyes flick to me apologetically before puffing his chest out and taking control of Perelli's attention.

"Do you or do you not consider yourself a fair man?" He asks boldly, quoting the wording from the note he must have found. Perelli's head swings to the side, his posture growing rigid from the accusation. "You've had a target on the twin's heads since they were conceived. I think it's time you gave them the chance to win back their freedom."

"And what do you have in mind?" Perelli bites back. Dax doesn't falter in his confidence, a new forceful side of him coming to light. I share a concerned look like Meg, who is clutching onto my arm like we might start to merge into conjoined twins if she holds on tight enough.

"A game in your casino of your choosing. I will play for Avery's life and Garrett will pay for Meg's."

"Erm, no. I don't think so." I pipe up, not letting a man swoop in to save my ass when I'm perfectly capable of saving myself. "We will play for ourselves and the game will be blackjack." Perelli glances over his shoulder at me, the smirk back in place and a new light dancing in his eyes.

"Deal."

Meg rubs my wrists as we walk until the sensation returns enough for me to move my fingers. I hadn't realised how awkward my restrained position had been until I was released from the cuffs, my shoulders screaming with stiffness as I'd first tried to move. Perelli's phone is glued to his ear as he leads us through the busy casino with one of his goons up front, our two failed rescuers and another set of guards following behind while lights flash at us from all directions.

Except for the musical tunes filtering through the rows of slot machines, the casino is oddly quiet, cautious glances being thrown our way. This is a haven for the serious gamblers who have some serious cash to blow. I notice the security by the main door peering through the glass curiously, probably wondering why I'm being given a tour by the owner after two guards had rushed out upon seeing me and dragged me inside.

I lean into Meg, eager to be as close as possible until the inevitable end. I'm not an idiot, I know Perelli won't let us go free or will find a way to cheat but this charade is solely for Dax's benefit. He clearly needed to burst in and be my faithful knight but letting him play a crooked gangster for my life would only have made his mourning for me that much harder. Hopefully, this way, he'll be able to grieve knowing he tried his best and it was my stubbornness that caught up to me in the end.

Pushing through a set of double doors, we pass through a hotel lobby and all squeeze into a normally spacious elevator. Dax's fingers find mine in the crowd, so I grip onto his firmly, giving him the last bit of comfort he needs. I don't let the image of how life could have been between us enter my mind, banishing it before the longing starts.

The doors slide open to reveal a long corridor, black carpet with silver logos lining the floor to match the casino. The closed doors either side are gleaming white, black flourishes surrounding fancy numbers as we approach the one at the far end. The four of us huddle together in the doorway like penguins desperate for reassurance in the face of a raging storm. My eyes flick around yet another lavish space, not that I expected any less. Every inch of the casino is dripping with money and the hotel is no different.

A green felt table sits before a wall of glass facing an incredible view of Chicago, people as small as ants going about their business below. The day is that perfect mix of sunny yet fresh, a gentle breeze flowing through various open top windows which makes me long for a picnic in the park. Four brown leather chairs have been placed around the table with a deck of cards still in the cellophane placed in the centre already prepared for our arrival.

The tension in the room is thick enough to choke on and there's so many things we need to say but no one moves or speaks until Perelli has shuffled with the use of his cane and takes a seat across the table. Dax's fingers are yanked away from mine as guards shove the pair over to a cream corner sofa across the room and I instantly miss his touch. No turning back now, I stride over to drop into the chair opposite the old man, ready to see what fate has in store for me. Meg lands next to me in the next second, a guard roughly pushing her down while Perelli unwraps the cards and begins to shuffle.

"Who's the other chair for?" I ask to fill the awkward silence. Perelli nods to a guard who has taken position by a door through the living area, who promptly enters the room and returns a moment later with a slumped figure held up in his meaty hands. Holy shit.

Wyatt is barely recognisable except for his hair flicking forward into his swollen eyes. Blood coats his cheeks, a bend to his mid-section and limp in his left leg speaking of further hidden injuries. And fuck I know I should want to laugh and cheer, but my heart squeezes at the sight. Meg's gasp grabs my attention, her hand clamping over her mouth and tears rising in her pale blues. I watch curiously, figuring she'd be rooting for his suffering more than any of us. Wyatt is led to Meg's side and willingly slumps in the seat, groaning from the movement. She reaches over to grasp his hand, rubbing her thumb over his split knuckles where he clearly tried to fight back.

"You two-faced motherf-" Garrett's words are cut short and his attempt to dive from the sofa is thwarted by a direct punch to the jaw, courtesy of the guard watching the two of them like a hawk. There is way too much testosterone in this room for my liking and my foot taps impatiently.

"Come on then, let's get this over with." I urge. Perelli chuckles, still absentmindedly shuffling the deck in his bony fingers.

"You amuse me little Avery. It's been a long time since a female has shown more balls than one pledged as my own. But I prefer my chances three to one. All three of you can play for the chance to relieve your father of his crime against me. One game. If you beat me as the house, you will walk out that door and never see me again. But if you lose, you are to come willingly." I nod in agreement, holding his eye as he begins to deal out the cards and a silence falls over the room.

An ace is placed in front of Wyatt, who can barely open his eyes to see, a nine for Meg and ten of spades for me. Perelli places another ace in front of himself with a smirk. Shit. Everyone holds their breath as the jack of diamonds is placed before Wyatt and releases him from our father's debt. He instantly leans into Meg, uttering apologies, and reassuring words I force myself to block out. Eavesdropping has never been my style, but his words sound too private for even the nosiest of people to pry on.

The four of hearts is dealt for Meg next, and a seven to me. I keep my poker face solid, not betraying the rising panic for Meg's hand. I know she isn't a fan of blackjack, but we've practiced enough during our time at the safe house for her to make a rational decision. Perelli finally lays a face-down card next to his ace and links his fingers together beneath his chin.

"I'll stick," I say first, looking over to Meg with raised eyebrows. Come on, you've got this. There's still hope.

"Hit me," she breathes, a quiver in her small voice that has Wyatt pulling her into his lap. I've definitely missed something here but she's not resisting so I leave it for now. Picking the top card from the deck, the shining silver bridge logo stamped across that too, Perelli slowly leans forward and turns it at the last moment to reveal the ten of spades. Bust.

A sob bubbles from Meg's lips, Wyatt crushing her into his body and cradling her gently. Perelli's wicked smile has my teeth grinding together, the urge to leap across the table and strangle the bastard overwhelming. But men as powerful as him always have a second in command, briefed and ready to step into his vacant spot and continue his work. Flipping his last card over, the three of clubs' glares at me as all the breath leaves my body. I'm safe. I open my mouth to protest, or even beg and grovel for another round if that's what it takes for only me to be on the chopping block, when Wyatt beats me to it.

"I'll take Meg's place." I stare at him, stunned, and confused by his words. A cut on his lip has reopened, blood streaming down his chin and onto Meg's chestnut hair and she cries into his shoulder. Surely, she should be seeking comfort from me? The one who's fought tooth and nail to find her, the one who came to be with her and half her suffering. Not Wyatt, who kidnapped her in the first place and doesn't have a thoughtful bone in his body - right? Perelli starts to shake his head but Wyatt gently eases Meg back into her seat and rises with a grunt.

"You know ending my life would prove more satisfying to you. A traitor you can torture and make suffer for as long as it takes before my heart gives out. Why would you take a helpless gazelle when you could mount a lion's head above your mantle place?" A tense moment passes, the cogs turning in Perelli's mind visible through his cold eyes.

"So be it." Using the table to push himself upright, two guards rush to Perelli's sides while one unnecessarily grasps Wyatt's arm, despite the fact he's not resisting. Meg lurches upright, clinging onto his body tight enough to make him wince. Kissing the top of her head, he bends to whisper in her ear as Perelli rounds the table and this time I can't help but listen to what he has to say.

"Live life for the both of us, Sweetness."

I hurry to hold her back as Wyatt twists free of her grip and leaves with Perelli. The second the guard watching the boys turns to leave too, Garrett attacks. Jumping on his back, he tries to catch the guard in an arm lock but the hefty guard peels him off like a jacket and slams him into a wooden coffee table. The furniture splinters and cracks under Garrett's weight, not that it keeps him down. Dax surprisingly steps forward and delivers a clean punch to the guard's face, knocking him back a few steps while Garrett sweeps him legs out from beneath him.

Meg writhes and claws at my arms as I struggle to restrain her, screaming Wyatt's name as he reaches the elevator at the other end of the corridor and turns back to look at her. Placing his hand over his heart, the doors draw closed and she collapses to the floor crying harder than I've ever seen her cry before.

The scuffle to my right ceases with the guard getting the upper hand and thumping Garrett's skull with a solid fist, striding from the room with taut shoulders while Dax rushes over to Garrett's unconscious form. My head is spinning from trying to process everything that happened and my heart torn in multiple directions but clearly my twin is my priority. She's the reason I came and she's safe from harm, although I don't feel as relieved about that now she's hunched over and washing the carpet with her tears. Dropping to my knees, I stroke her back and bend forward to push her hair behind her ear.

"What the fuck was all that about?" Her tear-streaked face turns to me, more emotion than I've ever seen etched in the pale depths of her irises. She struggles to catch a full breath, choking on her own sobs as her cracked voice washes over me.

"I love him." The truth of her words washes over me, a determination rising to the surface. I'd once thought love wasn't real, but more of a fantasy people buy into to live content lives side by side. A way for those who are uncomfortable with their own company and have a deep-rooted fear of being eaten by their twenty-two cats to feel complete. But not now I can feel through our twin bond the sincerity of her emotion. Meg's eyes are pleading me to help, the endless flow of tears confirming my suspicion – if Wyatt dies tonight, so will Meg's spirit. Life for her will be empty and monotone, no colour worth seeing or flower worth smelling.

Sneaking a glance over to the boys, I see Dax is still trying to wake a blissfully sleeping Garrett behind the pile of shattered wood that was until recently a rather sturdy coffee table. Shoving the heels from her feet and gripping Meg's under arm, I mouth for her to move and we quickly dash forward in crouched positions. I stop quickly to remove the key from the back of the door, pulling it shut and rushing to lock it on the other side. Dax's fists pound on the other side in a second, yelling for me to return this instant but he must know that won't be happening. Even if I was obedient enough to follow instructions, he still doesn't seem to understand cutting ties with me earlier rather than later will be in his best interest.

We race through the corridor, my heart pounding in my chest as Meg reaches the elevator first, jabbing her finger on the button repeatedly until the doors finally open. The sound of wood crashing jerks me around, Dax's furious expression now visible through a fist shaped hole. Unable to resist, even though I really shouldn't poke the beast I've never seen in him before, I blow him a flirty kiss as the doors slide closed and block me from his view.

I've figured out why The Shadowed Souls are drawn to me. They think I need saving. I've often thought men are more affected by fairy tales than the ladies, boosting their noble intentions and giving them a false sense of purpose to always be the saviour, even when the damsel is more than capable of saving herself. Would prefer to, in fact.

Bursting into the lobby, we race across the marble and spill into the car park beyond. Halfway running towards the Nissan, I stop and feel around in my pockets. Fuck! I was frisked upon entering the seedy lounge, too caught up in searching for my twin to realize those pig-headed guards must have taken Huxley's keys. Meg whirls around, panic in her eyes while her dress flaps wildly in the strengthening wind. I don't know what to do, my brain going completely blank as I hunt for an answer.

A red Mini speeds along the central row among the parked cars, skidding to a halt between Meg and I. A brunette woman in the driver's seat reaches back to pop open her rear and swings her brown eyes back to me.

"Get in, I'll take you to him." I don't move, looking to Meg over the Mini and then back to the middle-aged woman. The long hair falling to her waist stands out against her pale skin, freckles covering her entire face in that unusually pretty way.

"Who are you?" I ask when all other words fail me.

"I'm Sydney Perelli, and I know exactly where they are headed."

Sydney

"Happy birthday to you, happy birthday to you..." mom's sweet voice wakes me from a wonderful dream, my lips curving into a smile before opening my eyes. "Happy birthday to Sydney, happy birthday to you." She places a kiss on my forehead as I roll onto my back, cracking my eyelids to see her wide smile. Noticing the tray in her hands, I sit up and shuffle over to let her sit down on my mattress.

"Mom, I'm ten now. I'm getting too old for you sing me awake," I giggle, taking the plate of eggs and bacon forming a smiley face from her hands. She is the best.

"I don't care if you're a hundred and ten, you'll always be my baby and I'll sing to you all I want." Her brown eyes have crinkled in the corners with her huge grin. "Eat up and get ready sweetie, your father has a surprise planned for you." He does? He doesn't normally pay me much attention other than to ensure I always have the latest gadget or fashion trends. We're the only family in the community to have our own computer at home. I'm a reflection on his worth, so if I'm not dripping with money then he looks bad. Sounds great, but with all the guards and visitors we have, it means I can never just lounge around in my pyjamas.

My family isn't like the others I see at the school gates. I don't get invited round houses for play dates or to join the kids that go to the park every Friday afternoon. No one talks to my mom either, they huddle together and whisper and sometimes point. Even the teacher treats me differently, she always picks me first or lets me go to lunch before everyone else but sometimes when she thinks I'm not looking, she huffs and rolls her eyes as if she doesn't really like me.

My mom pulls a bag out from under my bed and hands it to me. I forget about my breakfast, reaching inside to pull out a pair of denim dungarees. No way! These are the fashion right now; everyone will think I'm so cool! I jump up to hug her, feeling all giggly and excited inside.

"Let's get you dressed; you don't want to keep your dad waiting." I see the tightness of her lips, but I bet that's because my surprise is a huge party and she's not used to having so many people around. I've never had a birthday party, but I've been secretly hoping this year I'll get one. I'll walk outside and there will be a bouncy castle and a magician and a petting zoo and a whole table of cake and ice cream. But best of all, all the kids in my class will be there waiting to play with me. Not like when we are in lesson and they avoid sitting near me as if they are scared.

Mom pushes me into the bathroom to wash and then braids my hair while I pull on the dungarees and snap the metal links together over my white t-shirt. When I'm finished, Mom takes my face in her hands and kisses me on the forehead, her smile seeming sad and her eyes glistening a little. After strapping on my sneakers, I skip from my room and down the huge staircase.

We moved into our house when I was in second grade, after Daddy had it built especially. I've always thought it was too big though, since he is away for work a lot so it's just me and mom unless you count the guards. There's been a lot of new ones lately and they don't bother with me, but a couple have been around since I was born and they are like strangely quiet uncles who fill the empty gap where the rest of my family should be.

I hear voices in the kitchen so I head that way, looking for balloons or decorations as I go but there isn't any. Yet. Rounding the corner, I see Charlie, Gunner and Arti sitting around the middle island. Charlie smiles widely, his dark hair brushed to the side so I can see his blue eyes. I've always liked Charlie, even though he's ten years old than me and wears too much jewellery for a man. He's studying to be a lawyer and goes to some fancy university in the week, so I'm surprised to see him here. Obviously, he had to see me for my birthday.

Arti reaches out to pat me on the head like a giddy puppy and passes me a small box wrapped in pink foil with a bow double the size of the gift. I hurry to open it, finding a pink bubble watch inside. Its chunky strap is not as heavy as it looks, a gold hand ticking with each second beneath the glass face. I laugh as I put it on, knowing this is Arti's way of saying stop asking for the time. I know he can't answer since his nickname is short for 'inarticulate', not that I know what that means but it's probably something to do with the jagged scar across his throat. But still, sometimes I get so lonely and even his irritated frown is better than being ignored completely. Besides, his watch is so flashy he should be happy to show it off.

"Come on Kiddo, your dad's already waiting." I bob up and down while the men pick up their bags and lead me outside, two caddy's parked side by side waiting for us. I hop in with Charlie, his hair blowing in the wind as we tear across the huge lawn behind the house. We have eighty-two acres of unneeded land, so much daddy had to buy these caddies to get around. I spot a few gardeners dotted around, mowing the grass near the house for my party no doubt.

We drive towards the woodland area towards the back of our grounds, a clear line of trees standing together like soldiers waiting for an order. I'm not usually allowed to go into the woods, but sometimes when daddy is away, Mom and I will sneak over to hunt for pinecones to paint or hang homemade suet balls for the squirrels and birds.

Charlie parks and offers me in hand before walking with the other two behind, following a trail of dirt amongst the fallen leaves and tiny plants growing all around. Acorns crunch beneath my shoes and the pine-filled air travels into my nose. I love the woods, the spots of sunlight poking through the shade and sounds of animals rushing around. I'm about to ask Charlie how much further it is when a whinny sounds through the trees, birds scattering from their branches. No. Way.

I run, slipping past Charlie's arms as they try to catch me and enter a huge clearing when a beautiful white horse stands before me. There's a patch of black over her left eye and covering her nose, her hair flying wildly as she bucks against a rope tying her to a fallen log. Daddy steps out from behind her, his thick black hair pushed back and his suit looking out of place amongst the trees. "Happy birthday sweetheart."

Stepping towards the magnificent creature slowly, I stretch out a hand and wait for her to push her nose against my palm. Warmth and softness nuzzle against my fingers, a rumbling noise sounding in her chest. My heart is ready to burst but I contain my squeals, not wanting to spook her. Finally, I have a friend to keep me company! Daddy moves to stand behind me, his hand on my shoulder gently pulling me back a few steps. Her black eyes search for me instantly, her front trotters lifting in panic, but Daddy's grip tightens so I can't rush back to her.

"For your birthday this year, I'm gifting you a life lesson money can't buy," he speaks quietly into my ear. Turning me, I see Arti lifting a pistol from his bag and passing it to my dad. "Beasts come in all shapes and sizes, but the cruellest of them all will be the most beautiful. The ones that crawl beneath your skin and steal your trust, the ones who make you vulnerable. You need to know you are always the strongest one in the room, everyone else is inferior when you hold the power to end them." He takes the gun Arti is offering, spinning it around his pointer finger and gives it to me. "Now, kill the horse."

Ice freezes my bones and makes it hard to breathe, the forest tilting around me. The black metal in my hand is so heavy and all I want to do is drop it and run. I can't kill the beautiful mare behind me.

"Sydney, do it. Now." I glance back, the horse's black eyes filled with the same panic I feel. It doesn't matter if she were a horse, a cat or a beetle, I can't kill any creature because I understand what it's like to feel worthless. For bad men to think they have the power to

say who lives or dies. We talk about children's rights at school, and Mrs Dawson told me I have a right to grow up in a family environment full of happiness, love and understanding. The horse lifts as far from the ground as she can, fighting against the rope to get away. Her whinny's fill the forest, pain so clear in the sound I begin to whimper too.

"You'll thank me for this one day my dear, love is weakness." My eyebrows pinch together. Love is weakness? But Daddy always says he is not a weak man, a fair one but never weak. My chest starts to pound, the guards and Daddy shouting at me while the horse screams in fear. My ears hurt from the loudness of it all, the ground blurring beneath my feet as I find a glimpse of bravery to grab onto. In the next second, I've raised the gun and pulled the trigger.

Everything goes silent. The birds stop tweeting, even the horse knows not to move. Daddy's eyes are furious, staring down the gun I have pointed at his head, the safety catch firmly in place.

"Oh, no I didn't…I'm so sorry Daddy," I rush to drop the metal onto the ground and start to back up. At first he doesn't move, standing still except for the heavy lift and fall of his chest. Suddenly he jumps forward and grabs me around the waist, dragging me through the forest while I kick and scream how sorry I am. He keeps a tight hold on me as he sits in the caddy, Charlie quickly jumping behind the wheel to drive us back to the house.

A gunshot echoes from the forest and I know in that instant, my new snowy friend is dead. Tears fall down my cheeks, all my fight leaving me as I wait for my punishment. Even when we stop, I don't struggle as Daddy carries me through the house, just hanging limply while the weight in my heart pulls me down. Daddy takes me to the main staircase and then turns sharply to yank open a door hidden around the back. A door I've never been allowed into before.

The air is cold, my dungarees not keeping me warm enough to not shiver. And it's dark, pitch black with no lighting. Next thing I know, I'm thrown onto the hard floor which scrapes my forearms and knees and a door is slammed behind me. Jumping up, even though my legs seize with pain and I can feel the warmth of blood trickling towards my socks, I run to bang my fists on the door as I start to cry again.

"Daddy! I'm sorry, I didn't mean to! Please let me out! Mom? Mommy, please help me!"

"Wait, aren't you supposed to be dead?" I lean through the open car window to get a better look at the driver. It's difficult to tell is there's a family resemblance since my point of reference is a decrepit old man, but she does have the same oval shaped face and small bump to the bridge of her nose. She rolls her eyes at me, revving the engine impatiently.

"We'll talk on the way, get in!" I jump into the passenger seat and Avery hops into the back, the car speeding off before we've managed to close the doors fully. I fasten the seat belt across me securely, the strap cutting into my exposed cleavage and I curse under my breath. Damn Perelli for dressing me up like a doll and making me jump through his hoops whilst dangling Wyatt's safety in front of me. Look where we've ended up now, racing through the streets of Chicago in a Mini with a dead woman behind the wheel and the one I've fallen for slipping away from me. Sydney slams her foot down in time to stop at a changing red light, a boy slipping out of his mother's hand to skip across the road.

"Time to spill." Avery sits forward between the seats and I chastise her for not wearing a seat belt. She grumbles, clicking it into place and sticks her tongue out at me. "Okay now, why are we paying the price if you're alive?"

"I've been in witness protection," she huffs as if that explains everything, too focused on winding through a confusing network of roads. I share a look with Avery in the rear-view mirror and we hold our questions until Sydney takes the turning for the freeway. The second she pulls into a free lane of straight, open road, we both order her to give us every detail possible.

"I'm sorry you all got dragged into this, but you know what my father is like. You won't believe the things he did to me as a child, what he made me do. When I turned eighteen, he announced he would be searching for a husband on my behalf to continue his legacy. I thought he may have forgotten since a whole year went by but then one day, a sleezy man three times my age arrived at the door, his suit slicker than his thoroughly oiled, thinning hair. So, I fled."

A yellow Mercedes pulls up beside us, honking its horn loudly and swerving to grab our attention. In the driver's seat, a seriously pissed looking Dax is screaming through the window and waving his fist at Avery in the backseat, who is pouting and batting her eyelashes at him. I can't help the snigger that leaves me until my eyes land on a dozy Garrett beside him. He's holding the back of his head, blood colouring his fingers as his eyes close and jolt back open a few times. I frown, wondering how many people are going to suffer before this is finished. It's not like I asked them to come but still feel guilty my need to have Wyatt back is putting others in danger.

"Ignore them, please continue." Avery waves her hand as the Mercedes falls back and pulls into the lane to trail us.

"Hang on Sid," I put my hand up as she opens her mouth, twisting in my seat to glare at my twin. "How long have you been in love with Dax for?" Avery half chokes and splutters but I narrow my eyes on her, mentally telling her to cut the bullshit. She sighs and looks away, a rosy pink colour rising to her cheeks. I know Avery better than she knows herself but even she must be aware of the way she's overly deflecting him. Her seemingly innocent flirting is more than she's ever given anyone else, not wanting to give the wrong impression which means he's managed to crawl beneath her skin.

"Maybe since the campfire. Who knows anymore? But it doesn't matter, I'm not loveable." She sighs dramatically, her hands slapping against her thighs. Avery is one of the toughest nuts to crack, but once someone nudges through a crevice into her heart, she can't shove them back out and close the door like she wishes she could.

"Well I love you, so clearly that's incorrect."

"You either love a psychopath or have some serious Stockholm syndrome going on so I don't trust your judgement right now." My eyebrows knit together, wanting to jump to Wyatt's defence but knowing there's no point. He has to mend the relationships he's torn to shreds, provided we manage to save him in time to do so.

"You don't know him like I do," I mutter, facing forward. "We've heard most of the story from Nixon but please continue," I gesture to Sydney who has been silently looking between us.

"So yeah, I ran away and found Nixon. He wasn't the successful man I've seen on the news back then, but he and Cathy were so down to earth and accepting. It was naïve of me to think I could escape my father so easily, but it was going so well until it wasn't. I don't remember the pain, but I remember hearing the gunshot and then the lights fading out around Nixon's silhouette. Next thing I know, I'm jolted awake by a defibrillator with a paramedic flashing a light in my eyes. Then the pain began." Sydney indicates to exit the freeway and veers onto a ramp with the guys following right behind.

"I gave a fake name at the hospital until the police arrived, but my father has so many cops working for him I had to be careful with who I could trust. Clearly, I chose well, I've been living under an alias for twenty years now."

"But how did you find out about us?" Avery asks.

"By mistake really. I snuck into Cathy's funeral, needing

to pay my respects and guess who I saw hunched over the buffet table, filling their arms with canapes and champagne bottles? I knew Cathy before she became famous enough to have her hair and make-up professionally done each morning, and you two are clones of her. After that, I started to keep a watchful eye just in case. My father doesn't let go of a grudge, trust me."

We sit quietly for a while, Avery and I absorbing the overload of information. This changes everything. Maybe if Perelli sees his daughter alive and well, he'll let Wyatt go. But I already know that won't work and probably put Sydney in the danger she's be hiding from all this time. I've been staring at the passing landscapes on a narrower road for so long, I don't realise there's a black sedan directly in front until Sydney leans across to remove a baseball cap from the glove box. Pulling it low over her eyes, she veers onto the wrong side of the road to pull alongside it.

Suddenly my view has changed to an image of Wyatt slumped back in the back seat, deflated, and resigned. His emerald green eyes flick towards me, widening as much as the swelling allows and sitting upright. The immediate surprise in his expression shifts to one of horror, signalling for me to go away with his hand. I shake my head slowly, not caring about anything else right now than being with the one I love in any circumstances.

My heart is going to explode if I don't get the chance to tell him, and soul is going to shatter if he doesn't say it back. Perelli leans forward next to him, his shrewd eyes pinning me as a target as he shouts orders to his driver. The sedan swerves into the side of us, testing our resolve and hoping we fall back but there's no chance. After the horrors I've faced in Perelli's dungeon, a little nudge isn't going to scare me, and it seems the woman beside me feels the same. Sydney pushes back, our two vehicles grinding against each other on the single traffic intended tarmac. Grassy banks stretch either side of us with fenced fields of wheat further beyond, a scenic route our revving engines are ruining.

The sedan pulls aside before ramming back into us, the scrape of metal on metal piercing my ears. Wyatt is pressed against his window with fear imprinted in his beautiful eyes, mouthing for me to leave him. If it weren't for the two panes of glass between us, I'd be able to reach out and cup his cheek while telling him that's never going to happen. Instead, I lift my hand to rest over his, so close yet so far.

A deafening horn sounding from in front breaks the moment as a large truck is heading directly for us. The screams which instantly leave all of us add to the volume of noise, Sydney twisting the wheel sideways on instinct. The truck ploughs towards us, catching the back end of the Mini as we fail to get out of the way in time and sends us spiralling off the road. My stomach rolls in time with my head, the world around me spinning until I squeeze my eyes shut. I'm going to throw up and then die in my own vomit.

Crashing to a halt, I crack an eyelid to find we've luckily landed upright again, the vehicle rocking on the tyres before sagging to a halt. My heart is thrumming in time with my shuddering arms, my hands gripped tightly enough around my belt to make my knuckles turn white. I go to turn and shout 'Ha! I told you so!' to Avery when a figure appears at my window, making me scream instead. Garrett struggles to get the door open, tugging roughly on the handle before it flies outwards with a screech.

I remove my belt and bundle into his arms, just needing a hug while my bones continue to quake. Garrett bends to cradle my body in his arms and carries me a safe distance from the destroyed Mini. Once I've been placed on the grass, I watch him sprint back to assist Sydney until Avery catches my attention. Or to be more specific, Avery's mouth devouring Dax's. He grips her like she's his lifeline, like the world will crack and swallow him whole if Avery isn't anchoring him.

Garrett walks up to me, tossing the Mercedes keys over to a determined-looking Sydney by his side. "Ready to end this Megamoo?" he asks cockily, back to his usual self. I roll my eyes and accept his hand up, turning to the haphazardly parked Mercedes with black racing stripes lining the bonnet. Avery's voice yells over for us to wait up as my hand lands on the handle, a sigh leaving my lips.

"This is my fight. Take your victory while you can," I bob my eyebrows towards Dax and force a small smile that doesn't portray any of the jealously I'm feeling. I hate to leave her behind, but the simple fact is her happily-ever-after has his arm around her shoulders and is inhaling the scent of her hair. If anyone deserves to benefit from the fucked-up situation Nixon's mistake has landed us in, it's her. It's my turn to struggle and I can only hope I will be rewarded in the way she has.

Sydney throws a cell phone across the space dividing us, telling the pair to call a recovery truck but Avery's eyes don't leave mine. The tilt to her eyebrows and puppy dog eyes which normally work on me are begging me to stay, but there's no way I can do that. Blowing her a kiss, I quickly jump into the back seat behind Garrett and close the door between us. Once again, I've fallen for the bad boy, so all that's left to do now is to save his ass and never let him go again.

Wyatt

My heart spirals and crashes as I watch the red Mini do the same through the rear window. We speed away before I'm able to see the car fall still, unsure if my sweet Meg is safe, injured or worse. Until now I've been compliant, sitting calmly in the back seat like the good boy I've spent years perfecting. Good for nothing maybe. But I have been acutely aware any resistance from me could still fall back on the brunette that's stolen my heart. Not even the sharp slap Ray delivered to me in the elevator was enough to make me push back. Ray thrives on power and control, but now uncertainty is pulling me in all directions.

She'd been right there. On the other side of the glass, her blue eyes declaring everything we hadn't had time to share. What if we'd met sooner and under different circumstances? Would I have paid any attention to the girl with resilience made of steel, her quick-wit and unbreakable will? I already know the answer is no. I would have glanced over her because I was too lazy to put in the work, too selfish to give her what she needed from me in return. But everything has changed. She's the light in my darkness, the sugar to my bitterness. My Sweetness.

Every mile along the tarmac road drags away another piece of my heart, the weight of my soul reflected in the thickly grey clouds fast approaching. I recognise this last stretch of road as we near Ray's hidden estate, the edges of a forest enveloping us. Branches knit together in an arch overhead, blocking out any hint of light as we fly towards an estate looming in the distance.

The modern mix of grey brick and exposed wood I had thought as my one true home now seeming too unfamiliar without the headstrong brunette stashed beneath.

I can't bear it anymore. What if I die with only what if's filling my mind? The whole point of my sacrifice being null and void because she's already waiting for me on the other side. Which is better than what I imagine is waiting for me in hell, but that defeats the point. She should finally be free. Free to live and love, to have a career doing whatever she wants, to have a family that will fulfil her and die an elderly, wise woman. Adrenaline fills my veins, the pain of my injuries momentarily forgotten as I throw my elbow into Ray's face. A sickening crunch sounds from his nose, a bellow leaving his throat which has his driver swerving in panic.

Ray's cane snaps out in a flash, his reaction instantaneous to lash me across the chest. His skeletal hand grips my arm with more force than I'd expected, ignoring the gushing of blood from his nose while his eyes are fixed on me with fury swirling in their darkened depths. On the next attempt to whack me with it, I make a grab for his cane and push all my weight behind shoving it against his throat. A gunshot pierces the air and a bullet hole appears in the seat an inch from my face. The car swerves and screeches as the driver spins around to try to take another shot at me.

I shove Ray away, lurching across the seat for the handle. He's on me in a second, literally heaving his body weight onto my legs. My fingers graze the handle, my legs kicking wildly and connecting with various parts of his body. A shout comes from the front seat but I'm too distracted to hear it, gripping the handle and heaving my shoulder against the door until I fall forward. My forehead meets the asphalt first, the rest of me following as I roll continuously until I flop onto my back. Every inch of my skin is screaming as cuts and grazes flare to life, my head spinning and previous bruises throbbing. But I'm alive.

The ringing in my ears gives way to a high-pitched screech of tyres a moment before metal grinding and glass shattering fills the air. I force to sit myself up, seeing the utter carnage of the sedan imbedded into the side of the mansion. The fountain in the centre of the driveway has been destroyed, pieces of concrete flung in all directions and water spewing from the ground. I notice Ray and his driver's figures through the smashed back window scrambling for the far side of the vehicle since their doors are now a part of the mansion's outer structure, and that's when I see the oil leaking from beneath.

My legs skid under me, my body slow to react to the voice blaring in my head. *Get the fuck up and move!* Bent in half, I hobble as fast as I can away from the house, remembering Ray's grand plan involving gas cylinders fixed into the underground vents. The vents that will leak into the dungeon where Nixon is being held, not to mention – *No.* I turn back, Rachel's name on my tongue as the car explodes first, the two figures going up in flames just before the entire house blows.

I'm thrown what feels like miles back, my body sailing through in air in slow motion and a scream leaving me I can't hold in. My arms float above me freely, a moment of zero gravity ending abruptly as I collide with the unforgiving ground. All the air in my lungs whooshes out and agony seizes me tightly. I can't tell where the intensity of the rising blast ends, and the heat of my broken bones begin. Cracking my eyelids, the flames roar towards the sky, goading the rain to fall and wash away the horrors which once took place within its ruins.

I lie still, unable to move even if I wasn't content lying here to watch the display. Each breath hurts so much, I don't know if I'll manage to take the next until it happens, but for a moment I can rest easy. I'm on borrowed time to enjoy the knowledge there's one less monster in the world. A shadow lingers on the edge of my vision, a twitch to one corner of my lips forming a slanted smile. *There you are mom. Don't worry, I'm on my way to you.* She edges closer, her open arms reaching out to carry me over the threshold to the afterlife until it's not the green gems for eyes I was expecting that hover over me.

Brown hair falls around me like a curtain, tears stinging as they drip into the open cuts covering my face. Her lips press against mine in the sweetest kiss, the one I thought I'd be longing for all eternity. A choked sob burns its way along my throat, my immobile arms protesting to crush her into me. Careful not to press any of her weight down, Meg rests her head on my chest and listens to the thump inside my ribcage. The heart that is only still beating for her.

We remain cuddled on the ground until my limbs begin to regain feeling, my toes wiggling and fingers flicking. At long last, I'm able to lift my arms enough to wind them around her body and place a kiss in her hair. Voices sound in the background but I block them out, not ready to face the onslaught of grief waiting for me. A few random drops of rain land on various parts of my exposed skin to signal the coming downpour, my flesh pleading for the cool reprieve. The heavens open to release a wave of water, washing away the evil that claimed this patch of land.

Meg lifts her head, her pale eyes regarding me before rising completely. A figure I used to call brother steps in beside her, bending down to lift me despite the snarl on his face. "I still hate you," he mumbles, carrying me with long strides and easing me across a leathery back seat. Leaning over me, he then lifts my head and shoulders with more care than I deserve, his hazel eyes glowering as Meg slides beneath me and her beautiful face comes back into view. I open my mouth a few times, words failing me, but one thought comes to mind, a name I can no longer ignore.

"Rachel." Meg strokes my cheek as I manage to shift onto my side slightly, facing away from her as I begin to cry. My tears soak the material covering her thighs, her fingers gently stroking my hair and I slowly curl up my legs in full fetal mode.

"I'm so sorry Wyatt," she leans over to breathe into my ear and places a kiss to my swollen temple. I lean back into her warmth, clinging onto the comfort only Meg can provide me. Despite the sinking ache in my chest, I have an underlying feeling I will be okay. Rachel reached a part of me I'd stopped trying to fix and gave me the one thing I'd been searching for all of these years - to feel wanted. Her sincere intentions and kind hugs, the automatic smiles and motherly nature.

She saved and fixed me without even trying, and that's the beauty of it. I realise now I've been wasting all my energy being angry, making myself the outsider when all I needed was to let someone in to see the best parts of me. Which is exactly why I'm going to cling onto Meg and show her the future we will have. Life has given me a second chance and I'm sure as shit not going to waste this one. I'll do whatever it takes to prove myself, to give her a life free from heartache and suffering like she deserves. I'll be her everything like she is mine.

"I never- "I shift onto my back, swallowing down a lump my throat. "I never thought I'd find someone like you, so I didn't bother looking. And when I found you, I gave you a hundred reasons to push me away. But you see me like no one else can and I'll love you until my breath for that." Her eyes glisten in contrast to the smile lighting up her face.

"I love you Wyatt. The devilish, the deceitful and the dangerous, I want it all." My grin is stupidly wide, my heart expanding in my chest and threatening to burst. I don't know how I've become lucky enough for this angel to love all of the damaged parts of me, but I do know with her by my side, I will be better.

I try to sit upwards, needing Meg to help me despite the world of pain attacking my body, but not even the fires of hell could keep me from getting closer to her. Shuffling into her side, I lean my head on her shoulder as she traces ticklishly light patterns up and down my forearm. Beyond the windscreen, a woman is standing alone in the downpour of rain facing the destruction that was, until very recently, Perelli's mansion. Her dark hair is drenched, her size and shape so similar to Rachel's I almost thought it was her, but Rachel's hair is shorter and hips slightly wider.

I grip Meg's hand for reassurance, needing her to ground me as grief swirls around my chest. Tilting my chin in her fingers, she presses her lips against mine so softly, but my mind is reeling nonetheless. Someone who has lost so much shouldn't feel this blessed, but she gives me a reason. A reason to move forward and start a life worth living. Through the depths of agony and darkness, our love will reignite the dying embers of my heart and burn away all traces of the man I was until I am worthy of her. My rescuer, my salvation, my Meg.

Epilogue - Avery

Dax uses his powerful calves to leap with all the grace of a pouncing cheetah, gliding through the air to net the ball in the basket. A moment of silence ripples through the packed stadium just before the claxon blares and declares the Waversea Weavers the winners. Axel and I shoot up from the wooden bench on the edge of the court together, screaming and hugging as we jump around excitedly. I know how much he wanted to play alongside his brothers, but doctor's orders were to take this semester off. Luckily for him, this was the last game before the holidays and his team have smashed it on his behalf.

Hunting for the blonde Afro amongst the crowd of people rushing towards their victors, I find him grinning at me and run into his arms. His lips find mine in an instant and his large hands lift me easily, warmth coiling in my centre as adrenaline shifts into something much more potent. The skirt of my cheer outfit lifts for a touch of coolness to caress my bare thighs, the roaring of cheering drowning out to the thump in my chest.

"Alright break it up you two, unless you are prepared to have a few other members join your sex fest." I choke on a laugh, breaking our kiss to bob my eyebrows at Garrett mischievously. His dimples pop out on a wide grin, although we know it's all in jest. He and Axel haven't been with anyone except each other for the past four months and Dax is strictly selfish in that department. Huxley strides through the swarm of beautiful girls vying for his attention to pull the four of us into a bone-crushingly tight bear hug, whist I'm still hoisted in the centre. I may have lost both of my parents this year, but I gained a family I could only have dreamt of.

A chant begins across the court, the cheer squad shaking their black and yellow pom poms high in to air to lead the basketball team, and hordes of fans through the open doors. I wriggle free, my feet touching the floor so I can run to join them at the front, but Dax's hand grasping mine pulls me back.

"Don't you dare change out of this before I get my winning lap dance," he whispers into my ear and I giggle with a schoolgirl. Well, I guess that's because I am one. Today marks the last day of my first full semester studying musical theatre at Waversea, and already I've grown so much more than I could have through home schooling. Dax insisted I didn't move into their frat house on campus but instead share a dorm with students in my class. It was barely a week before the girl across the hall invited me to cheerleading try-outs and I made the team that afternoon. Just another way Dax has proven himself to be my ideal man, his thoughtfulness for me to have a real college experience without him breathing down my neck.

My name being called through the crowd has me looking around but it's Huxley who spots her first, turning me by the shoulders and pointing to the top of the indoor bleachers. She made it! I push my way through the guys with the brute strength of a quarterback, and jog towards my twin who is sprinting down the steps.

"Careful!" I shout to her, holding my hands out to protect her swelling belly if she were to fall. She swats my hands away and pulls me in for a hug. It's been way too long since I've had my Meg-fix. Pulling back, she regards the brown hair I've let grow out and cut into a shoulder-length bob with a smirk.

"Stop trying to bubble wrap me, I could still take you on," she laughs.

"Now that I'd like to see," Garrett walks up behind us

with the others, each pulling her in for a hug and kissing her cheek before my eyes fall to her mid-section again. I still can't believe I'm going to be an auntie! Everyone else has exited the stadium now, quiet falling as we all share glances and avoid the obvious until I can't take it anymore.

"How is he?" Meg's pale eyes flick away for a moment, a sad smile forming on her lips.

"Wyatt's doing well. There was a lot for him to sort through in taking over Nixon's companies, and he's completing his degree online. My mom says he's making great progress in their counselling sessions, but what he really needs are his brothers back." Her eyes flick to Garrett's the same time all of ours do, knowing its mainly him that's holding us back. Even Axel has admitted he's prepared to work on rebuilding their friendship, but Garrett is as stubborn as a strong, independent woman who refuses to wash the dishes two days in a row. I often wonder who wears the pants in their relationship.

"Look, I know it won't happen overnight but maybe it's worth a shot trying?" I pitch in on Meg's behalf. I haven't come close to forgiving Wyatt myself yet, but he's steadily proving himself by making my twin happier than she's ever been, so I can make some effort too. "Don't you think baby Harbour would want to know his Uncle Gary?" I snigger.

"Remind me not to ask you for help picking baby names," Meg rolls her eyes. "Why don't you all join us for Christmas? Susie is desperate to have some guests to fawn over, and I have a mansion I need help decorating. Or would you rather I was climbing ladders and lifting heavy boxes of baubles around myself?" Meg puts on a perfect display, battering her eyelashes with a full-on pout and rubbing her rounded belly at Garrett. He grinds his jaw and crosses his arms, but I don't miss the glint of amusement in his eyes before he looks away.

"As long as I'm never *ever* called Uncle fucking Gary, I'll come. But no promises on the forgiving and forgetting front."

Meg and I squeal together, excitement over a proper family Christmas setting in. Axel slides his arm around Garrett's shoulders and starts to lead him away while asking why he hates that nickname so much.

"I'm not some fat, bald hillbilly! I'm gorgeous Garrett," he whines. Axel chuckles and pulls him in for a kiss, the sight of them making me smile and seek out my own companion. Dax's arms wind around me on instinct, his mouth finding my neck. Meg leans into my other side, her fingers linking with mine and mouths 'all set for tonight?'. I nod slowly, a smirk pulling at my lips. Tonight, is more than just the guys mega end of term party.

I haven't been able to bring myself to say those three little words to Dax yet, even though he's earned them ten thousand times over. And the best/worst part is how understanding he is, accepting a simple kiss in return when he tells me it every day. I want to be fair to him, knowing those words need to be filled with every ounce of devotion, but so much has happened, and I needed to find myself first. To be the best version of myself before I give him my heart. It's the least he deserves.

"I'll catch you at the party, there's some twinning that needs to be had." I twist my head to kiss Dax before slipping out of his hold, throwing a wink Huxley's way and grabbing my backpack. Guiding Meg through the back doors to the car park, I stride towards the burnt-orange Nissan Huxley has gifted me with a huge smile. He gave up with me borrowing it without asking and bought the midnight blue version sitting in the next bay along.

Huxley's relaxed back into college life well, hints of the man I first met becoming more frequent, although he still doesn't speak without reason to. Switching his degree to psychology has done wonders, his thesis to be based on men's mental health, and not to mention he'll be here the same length of time as me now.

"Saw your big routine during half-time. You were incredible! This is cute too," Meg reaches out to pick a hair from my black vest with yellow lettering and trim. I spin side to side for the matching skirt to dance around my thighs with a smile. I'd never imagined I could be a part of a team, to have a group of people looking out for me and boosting me to the top of a literal pyramid. I'd originally been sceptical of venturing out without Meg, but we have to live our own lives, chase our own happiness.

"You could have come down to sit with us, you know. They don't blame you for anything." Meg sighs for a moment and then forces it away with an exaggerated smile, sliding into the car without spilling how torn up over the guys rift she clearly is. Luckily for her, I'm on the case and by Christmas day, the gang will be together again like old times, plus a pair of brunette twins and baby on the way.

"Are you sure you're alright to party with us tonight?" I drop into the driver's seat with a frown.

"If you ask me that one more time, I'll go all Sydney on your ass and disappear."

"Still no word, huh?" Meg shakes her head with a twist to her lips. Hopefully wherever she is, she has found the freedom she spent years dreaming of. Twisting the key in the ignition, I rev the engine and leave my worries behind in the car park as I drive us in the direction of Waversea to prepare for tonight.

"Open your eyes," I say, sitting on Dax's bed with a wrapped box in my hands. The white paper is decorated with golden basketballs and a gold bow, because I'm fancy like that. Dax's piercing blue eyes narrow on me suspiciously, his fingers grazing mine as he slowly accepts the gift.

"What's this for?" His thigh is pressed against mine in black slacks paired with a powder blue shirt. The open buttons revealing most of his chest and his biceps straining inside the material makes my mouth go dry.

"You'll see," I bite my lip to focus, putting my libido in the naughty corner. He takes forever peeling the tape back to preserve the paper and I nearly jump across to tear it off myself. Pulling the box inside free, he doesn't react whilst gazing at the image on the outside which has my stomach fluttering and toes tapping simultaneously.

"You got me a polaroid camera? Why?"

"It's not a camera," I grip his face in my hands and pull his focus onto me. "It's a promise. You've been so patient and understanding, given me the room to grow and explore. But I don't want that anymore. I want to be with you, to fill our rooms with photos of our happiest moments and start our life together. It won't always be sunshine and rainbows because, well I'm me, but I promise to give you all I have. With everything I am and will ever be, I love you Dax."

His mouth is on mine the second the words have left my lips, the burn of desire and love scoring a line through my body. I melt against him, weak on his taste and relying on his strength. My walls are down, my soul is bare, my heart syncing to the steady rhythm of his. His lips quiver slightly, pressing against mine firmly before pulling back. He removes the camera from its packaging, lifting it in front of us and presses a kiss to my cheek as the flash blinks brightly.

The next second, a glossy paper is in my hand for shaking until our image becomes clear. Dax's Afro takes up half of the picture, his bronzed skin a stark contrast to mine but that's not what strikes me first. My eyes are the boldest blue I've ever seen, brimming with joy to match my beaming smile. I didn't believe love like this could exist, and even if it did, I never would have thought I could manage to find it. This man has quickly become my lifeline, knowing what I need before I do and providing me with a life I didn't think I deserved.

"Come on, we'd better show our faces from at least an hour or Garrett will never stop moaning about it. Then I'll be ripping your clothes off and have you screaming my name." His low, husky voice has my core clenching and I briefly wonder if Garrett's bitching would be worth staying in here all night. However, I'm fairly certain he would come looking for us and not hesitate to drag us downstairs butt naked.

Walking from the room hand in hand, the music begins to thump downstairs and a throng of people burst through the door. Each one has a beer bottle or red cup in their hand, heading straight for the now furniture-free living area to dance. A couple try to slip past us on the stairs until I plant myself in their way with a glare that says 'not in this house' that has them scuttling away.

Not seeing anyone I recognise; we head outside to find a small campfire has been erected in the front yard. Meg and Huxley are talking easily on a picnic blanket with their backs to us, an empty blanket to their right and Garrett and Axel cuddling opposite. On the far side, two guys are hunched over their knees with their backs to one another. I eye the pair curiously, wondering why they have matching busted lips or would wear full black to a party, not to mention one with a beanie hat pulled down to his ears.

"Who are they?" I whisper to Dax as we move towards the spare blanket. Garrett jolts upright upon seeing us, checking his invisible watch with a sigh as Dax drags me down into his lap.

"Meet Rhys and Clayton," Garrett answers for me. "They've just become members of the basketball team starting next semester. I found them fighting in the locker rooms and thought I'd invite them over for a little story time."

"And like I said, fuck you and your stories. You don't know anything about me," Beanie hat rages, clenching his fists and lifting his shoulders back as if he thinks he could take on Garrett, who is chuckling at his outburst.

"Trust me, I know your type. I've been you. And you're going to need to hear what I have to say if you plan on surviving long enough to pay off mommy's debts." Beanie's mouth falls open, his eyebrows creasing, but Garrett doesn't seem surprised. "Yeah, I know a guy who works in admissions and read your files. So, I know you're both the perfect fit."

"The perfect fit for what?" I ask across the dancing flames of the fire.

"To continue The Shadowed Souls, of course."

Thanks!

Wow! I hope that was as much as an emotional rollercoaster for you reading as it was for me writing. This marks the end of my first full trilogy and I'm thrilled with how it turned out!

Be sure to follow me on Facebook in 'Cole's Reading Moles' and on instagram @abigail_cole_author for announcements, giveaways, reveals and more! Hope to see you there!

Acknowledgement

I would like to express the biggest thank you to all of the wonderful ladies who have helped me on this journey! Each one has given me invaluble help to make these novels the best they can be and I'll always be grateful for their support. To Teresea and Kirsty for proof reading, and Gemma, Danielle and Denise for being my ever-so faithful beta readers all the way through.

I would also like to make a special mention to Bed and Books for her incredible help, promoting, creating teasers, finding bookstagrammers, keeping me on track ;). You have done so much more than I could have hoped for!

To all the bloggers and bookstagrammers, thank you so much for your reviews. I hope this book was everything you hoped it would be. All of you are helping to bring my dream of becoming an author to reality.

Printed in Poland
by Amazon Fulfillment
Poland Sp. z o.o., Wrocław

62592754R00150